THE
NORTON
CASE

Jackson Bass

Duckboat Books
P.O. Box 1017
Hayward, WI 54843

ISBN: 978-0-9841499-1-9
       0-9841499-1-0

Library of Congress Control Number: 2010930527

To Arden and Ellen Atherton, who led the way.

Author's Note and Acknowledgements

This novel is a work of fiction. Any resemblance to persons living or dead is purely coincidence. That said, most of the geographical features are real, including the world's largest bay laurel tree, the California cliffs, and the Wisconsin woods. Al Capone did have a hideout near Couderay, Wisconsin, and the village of Post really was drowned beneath the waters of the Chippewa Flowage, though I have altered the time line somewhat to fit the story. The map of the village and original lakes is the work of John Dettloff of Hayward, Wisconsin, who kindly granted permission for its use. A fuller version of his map appears in the interesting book *Where the River Is Wide: Pahquahwong and the Chippewa Flowage*, Rasmussen, Charlie Otto. Published by Great Lakes Indian Fish & Wildlife Commission Press, Odanah, WI, 1998, 2000, ISBN 0-9665820-0-4.

Even though the characters in this book are fictional, as are their actions, there *is* an Ojibwe society called the Medewiwin, a more benign organization than its fictionalized image herein. From among various possible spellings, I have chosen "Ojibwe" because that's the spelling used by the Lac Courte Oreilles Ojibwe. I realize there might be some controversy over the term "Indian," which I have selected instead of "American Indian" or "Native American." If so, I apologize, but I had to choose one of the alternatives. The Ojibwe have steadfastly held on to their rights, taking on all comers, including the U.S. government. The Millard Fillmore story is true, as are the tribe's later successes, including building a community college and library.

The Soo Line story is fiction, but the railroad line itself is real. Indeed, my grandfather drove engine number 4006, one of the 4-8-2 N-20 steam engines.

The GPS coordinates given in the book *are* on the Chippewa Flowage, but only approximately over the sunken village. In other words, "don't try this at home."

I gratefully acknowledge the wonderful singer and songwriter, Ian Tyson, who granted permission to use his lyrics from the song "The Renegade."

The past is not dead. In fact, it's not even the past.

—William Faulkner

1

Mid-September. North Wisconsin woods.

Leland E. Denton, Esq., fled through thicketed undergrowth, dodging pine and birch trees. Rain lashed. Lightning painted iridescent murals upon lattice-worked branches. Thunder refracted off tree trunks, its harsh echoes snuffing Denton's thoughts as he stumbled through the night. One fist held a black automatic pistol and shoved away sharp-tipped branches that reached for his eyes. He tripped and skidded into a rain-swollen creek, its ice water sucking warmth from his veins.

The odor of dead vegetation stung his nostrils. Sharp rocks cut his hands and knees as he scrambled up the far bank. He struggled to his feet, trying to ignore burning muscles and a ragged cut across his stomach. He knelt in wetness, his hand exploring the wound. Blood flowed black in the dark. Rain and thunder now concealed earlier sounds of pursuit. But he sensed they were still there, still trying to kill him. Who were they?

He sprang to his feet and ran, heaving lungs aching. If only he could pause. But he had to push on through the gauntlet of low branches, tree trunks, and saplings. Despite the cold, his exertions produced sweat that mingled with rain, stinging his eyes.

He didn't see the thick stand of broken timber until he slammed into it. The impact knocked him down. He lay compressed into a wet matting of dead leaves. Primal instincts took control, and he burrowed into the twisted pile of wood until he reached shelter. There he stayed, fingers splayed across his belly wound, forcing down an impulse to retch. Thunder rolled. Lightning created Halloween monsters in the laced branches of his refuge.

He closed his eyes, summoning his black belt tae kwan do training, using it to overcome the primal dread of raging nights. He slowed his breathing, willing his thumping heart to calm. What he had witnessed numbed him. *A tomahawk? Indians?*

A new noise intruded—a harsh snorting that cut into storm-sound. Something big moved into the sheltering timber, shaking nearby branches. Cold water splashed his face. Denton, now in control of himself, shifted away from the trickle and pressed the light feature of his Timex Ironman watch. Almost ten p.m. *And now a fuckin' bear.* He kept quiet as the bear made itself comfortable on the far side of the stand of timber. *Jesus, a bear. Men in buckskin. The tomahawk. That huge knife.* The idea of the knife forced his hand up under his clothing to his stomach. He probed the long gash. *Not that deep. Not bleeding much now.*

Another "wuff-wuffing" snort claimed his attention. He unzipped his Gor-Tex jacket, grateful it was warm and waterproof. He wiped his 9 mm Browning Hi-Power on his flannel shirt, dropped out the clip, and with blind fingers checked his loads. *Nine shots left. I shot four times. What did I hit?*

He shoved in the clip, cocked the hammer, and switched on the safety. Would a 9 mm hollow-point kill a bear—or just piss it off? Still, the gun, his lucky gun at that, comforted him. *Better keep it dry.* He put the gun on safety, slid it into his belt, and zipped his jacket. He lay back, willing himself into the soft, leaf-covered soil. *Relax. It's gonna be a long night. You'll fight the bear in the morning.*

He meditated. He sat, crossing his throbbing legs, his knees on the relatively dry soil of his lair, the product of a bygone storm that had knocked down the trees now sheltering him. He made fists and placed them palm down on his knees. *Breathe in. Breathe out. Slowly. Don't focus. Surrender to your mind. Let it focus itself on you.*

He let himself merge into his breathing, allowing his mind to drift. The whirlpool of violent images continued to play within him. *Breathe... in... breathe... out.*

Turbulent fears broke up, dissolving like mist in a morning river's sunshine. He contemplated molecules of air flowing in and out of his essence. He unified with the steel of his inner self. An hour passed as he saw nothing, felt nothing, thought nothing. Then he allowed his newly calmed awareness to return into the violent night.

He stretched out his legs and lay back, inuring himself to the harsh weather. Now he was merely uncomfortable. Nothing was trying to kill him... for the moment, anyway. Tomorrow morning would be another matter, though, and he needed rest to prepare for the coming ordeal. He lay quiet, longing for sleep.

But it was not to be. Instead, memories of seven months ago swirled, banishing sleep and re-creating the sunny day he and Sandy Jones had sailed his 34-foot sailboat, *Bruja Loca*, out of San Diego Harbor and laid her into the west wind blowing at a steady fifteen knots. He had turned on the autopilot, an Autohelm ST 4000, and punched the button that told it to steer their predetermined southerly course.

Denton popped the cork of a bottle of champagne, a 2002 Louis Roederer Cristal. He and Sandy sipped their wine as the wind in the rigging sang its addictive music. They said nothing, letting their smiling eyes caress one another's happiness. Gleeful hands raised long-stemmed, boat-safe plastic glasses.

Denton said, "To us, baby. And to our freedom. May the spirits of the wind bless our cruise to the South Pacific."

"Amen," Sandy replied, her cornflower blue eyes shining, her long blond hair streaming. "And here's to our peerless vessel, *Bruja Loca*. May she sail safe and true."

Two weeks later, they picked up the trade winds a few hundred miles south of Cabo San Lucas. Denton altered course for the Marquesas Islands, a part of French Polynesia. Sandy turned on the stereo and they sang along with Crosby, Stills, Nash and Young, their minds on the Southern Cross, trade winds, and the South Pacific. It was the fulfillment of Denton's dreams, this escape from sleepless nights and sinister dreams.

Denton hand-steered *Bruja Loca* and stopped singing. He didn't want to interfere with the beauty of Sandy's clear soprano. Her voice came from the purity within her, mingling sweetly with subtle pings and clanks from the rigging, with sea slaps against the hull. Emotions flowed within Denton; a warm sense that caressed his lungs, feathering softness into his heart. He steered with gentle hands, feeling *Bruja Loca* ride the building seas, allowing her to surf down the faces of the larger waves.

Now, in the cold Wisconsin night Denton remembered his happiness, recalled how he'd believed he'd finally accomplished his dream. He and Sandy were crossing the ocean, seeking green islands and soft beaches. A thirty-day sail. Then they'd be there. Free.

2

Mid-June. Secluded atoll, South Pacific.

Bruja Loca swung on her anchor in the secluded cove of a small, unnamed island somewhere within a day's sail of Rarotonga, deep in the South Pacific. The sun shone down through the water, casting shifting, sub-surface sunbeams. Sandy Jones swam alone and naked; diving, pirouetting, a sleek form gliding within translucent light.

Denton and Mutt, his thoroughbred Brussels Griffon, sat on deck watching Sandy as she glided to the boarding ladder. Reaching out a hand, she allowed Denton to pull her, dripping, up out of the water.

She embraced Denton, her wet body straining into him. "Let's go below."

Later, Denton came back on deck carrying a drink. He sat in the corner of the cockpit, took a sip, and scanned the horizon. A far-off dot moved toward him. It grew closer and closer until Denton discerned an outrigger canoe paddled by two South Sea Islanders carrying a big man who waved a truncated left arm.

A loud bellow carried across the still water. "Boss, boss! It's the fucking Norton case!"

Denton's mind reeled. How could Afa Tavita have found him? He knew the one-armed Samoan ex-wrestler, now an investigator for his law firm, was smart. But this was... bewildering.

Soon the dark wood of the canoe's outrigger bumped gently against *Bruja Loca's* white fiberglass hull. Tavita's huge bulk convulsed with laughter as he confronted Denton's open-mouthed surprise.

"Shit, Tavita, what are you doing here?"

"Charlotte sent me. It's the Norton case. Someone is killing them off."

Denton visualized his assistant/paralegal, Charlotte Logan, a retired Marine sergeant major. He imagined her blue eyes peering through half-rimmed glasses as she ran nimble fingers through his credit card bills. She would have seen the latest charges he'd made in Rarotonga when he resupplied. He might as well have drawn an X on a map. *I should have kept sailing, not stopped here. Shouldn't have spent these two weeks so close to Rarotonga.*

But how was he to know Charlotte would send Tavita all this way? *Well, I'm not going back.* Escaping the messy litigation of the Norton case had been a prime motivation for Denton's flight. His stomach churned at the idea of re-immersing himself in complex details, endless arguments and counter arguments. All that was meaningless against the prospect of the endless eternity awaiting, of the death that had almost claimed him as he searched for "hard numbers" in the Security Life matter he'd just concluded.

He also had been exhausted by the paranoid bickering, the virulent hate between the two warring groups of cousins battling over Asa and Sarah Norton's multi-million-dollar estate. Denton had labored hard for his clients, who supported the will, but it was time for them to find another lawyer. *Hell, I'm barely recovered from the gunshots I took in the Security Life case.*

But now there was Tavita, his almost-three-hundred-pound body weighing down the handcrafted canoe so that its gunnels were barely above water. Tavita bobbed up and down with the motion of the canoe, his soft brown eyes staring at Denton while the two South Sea Islanders sculled their paddles to keep the canoe in place as Tavita's good hand clung to *Bruja Loca*.

Denton crossed his arms, thinking, *If that wasn't an outrigger, they'd flounder.* He looked into Tavita's pleading eyes, shook his head, and said, "Go away, Tavita."

"Boss, Charlotte said to come back. You have to take care of this. It's your duty."

"I've quit. I don't have any duties."

"Charlotte told me you'd say that, boss. She told me to answer 'that's not true.' She said you took a lawyer's oath. She's asking you to come home."

Sandy Jones eased behind Denton, slipping her arms around him, pressing her breasts against his back, her lips caressing his ear. "Let him come aboard, Lee."

Sandy's caress worked its usual magic. "Okay. Come aboard."

Tavita stood on the edge of the canoe, his stump on *Bruja Loca's* deck, his big fist grasping Denton's. Even the canoe's outrigger couldn't prevent water from flowing into it. "Watch out, Tavita. You'll sink the damn canoe."

Tavita managed to scramble aboard with the canoe still afloat. The paddlers bailed frantically with coconut shell scoops. Tavita passed them a wad of bills. "Thanks, you may return."

Turning to Denton and Sandy, he laughed and said, "I'm starving."

Denton grinned. "As usual."

Sandy made a ham and cheddar sandwich that Tavita ate one-handed. Denton watched him chewing, enjoying the man's exuberance even as his own mind whirled alternatives in a kaleidoscope of resistance. Denton watched the Islanders paddling the canoe toward the far horizon as Tavita swallowed.

Denton opened his mouth to yell for them to come back, but his thoughts filled with visions of Charlotte peering over her granny glasses, wearing some bright-colored voluminous dress suitable for reaching high filing cabinets. He imagined her blue eyes squinting at him, her stern lips repeating the words, "Come home. You have a duty."

The fucking Norton case. It never ends. Denton thought of Queeg, the carved wooden idol with hair of hanky blond twine. Queeg, his lucky charm, now standing on a cabin shelf below, its base secured to the shelf with silly putty. Once again Queeg's protective powers had let him down. Or had they? Who knew the fate that pursued him? Really, how could Tavita have found him if it wasn't meant to be? *There's duty. And there's fate. Duty you can flee, but fate's got you by the balls.*

"Fate," Denton murmured.

"What was that, boss?" asked Tavita between mouthfuls of sandwich, smiling as he used his hand to reach for the cold bottle of Royal Kale Gold beer Sandy had given him.

"Nothin'."

"Mmm, this is good beer. I see it's from Tonga. A bottle of Vailima from Samoa would be better."

"Goddamn it, Tavita, why did you have to come?"

Tavita's brown eyes grew sad beneath drooping eyebrows, his smooth tan face adopting the incongruous whipped puppy look Denton had seen before. Tavita cradled his maimed left arm across his massive chest, his eyes downcast. It was too much. Denton raised his eyes to puffy clouds drifting in a high blue sky, spread his arms, and laughed.

Tavita smiled, his handsome face beaming. "Char said: 'Don't make me come down there.'"

Denton's "Arggggg!" roared out over the lagoon's placid surface.

3

Late August. San Diego.

The outer door of Denton's law office slammed behind him. Former Marine Sergeant Major Charlotte Logan's blue eyes widened as he approached her desk.

"All right, I'm back. I hope you're happy."

Charlotte removed her gold reading glasses, her hand slow and deliberate. "No, I'm not happy. Not when you act like this." Tears sprang into her eyes.

He snorted and stomped into his private office, where he dropped into the seat of his expensive, big-backed leather chair. He stood back up, took off his suit coat and hung it on the hook sprouting from the back of his door. *Christ, it feels like a straitjacket.*

His eyes scanned the office. Charlotte had kept it shipshape. The books were neatly arranged on their shelves, their spines aligned like the toes of Marine boots at attention. The polished walnut of his empty desktop smelled of pine cleaner. The clear expanse of his usually cluttered desk mocked him. *Welcome back, sucker.* He pulled his good luck charm Queeg from his duffel bag and placed it on the normal spot at the front corner of the gleaming desk.

Denton sighed. Queeg stood with ready fists, his hanky blond twine hair forming a lion's mane around his ugly devil face. A small, crouching god. An infidel's plea for mercy in a hostile world. *Good luck charms are bullshit. Especially this one.* "Thanks for all the good luck, Queeg," Denton muttered as he considered shoving Queeg into the trash can beside his desk. But what if Queeg had aided him in unknown ways? *What if shit-canning him creates bad vibes?*

Thinking about all the permutations of good and bad luck made him weary. *Damned if you do, damned if you don't.* He shifted into the comfort of his leather seat, then pivoted the chair so he could look at San Diego Bay. A gray aircraft carrier worked its way from the harbor into the sunlit Pacific. He wished he was out there too.

During the long sail back to San Diego, he was frustrated with the prospect of again being submerged by the rigors of the Norton case. It wasn't fair. He'd followed his stars only to be dragged back by elusive notions of duty. By the time he'd entered his office suite, he was angry.

But now his anger faded. He regretted the thoughtless words to Charlotte. He'd come across angrier than he really was. He knew he had to apologize. He rubbed his palms against the uncomfortable blue pinstriped cloth of his suit trousers. He swiveled back towards his empty doorway and stared at it like a convict contemplating the door of his cell.

He stood, slipping a hand down to adjust his cramped testicles. *I'm busting my own balls. And this fuckin' tie has to go.*

Stubborn pride shouldn't come between him and Charlotte Logan, who managed his law office with a sure hand and who was only doing her duty as she saw it. He sucked a deep breath and let it seep out. He squared his shoulders and marched out his door.

Charlotte sat at her desk. He noticed her light blue, practical dress. It looked new, bought for his homecoming, one more effort to transition from Marine to civilian. She held a wadded white handkerchief in one fist and a single sheet of paper in the other. The hand that held the paper trembled.

"I'm sorry, Char."

She peered at him over her glasses. Her eyes were wet.

Denton admitted, "I know you were only handling the mission."

She lifted her chin, once more the efficient Marine sergeant major. Denton glanced at the photos on the wall behind her of generals and colonels pinning medals on her uniform.

Her voice was low and quaking. "It's not my fault Nortons are getting killed. Not my fault the judge called a special hearing. Do you think it was easy to get Hem down here from L.A. to fill in for you?"

Good ole Hem, thought Denton, envisioning his good friend and fellow attorney G. Hemmington Johnson. Blond and six foot four, two hundred thirty-five pound Hem was a partner in a large national law firm and had better things to do than fill in for Denton. Especially with the Norton case.

Denton stared down at the black Church's wingtips cramping his toes. The costly footwear had once seemed appropriate, but now he wished for his worn boat shoes. He composed himself, then looked into Charlotte's angry eyes. "No. I realize you had an emergency. I'm sorry."

"Well. Do you know what this letter in my hand is? It's my…"

The outer office door opened, gliding easily upon its brass hinges. They both watched as Clyde Norton, the eldest of Denton's surviving Norton clients, entered the office. Clyde wore a black suit, a white shirt, and a tie with a muted dark pattern. His black eyes were dull, his face pinched with sorrow.

"Good morning Clyde," Denton said, thinking the man looked all of his eighty-one or eighty-two.

Charlotte tossed a "Hello, Mr. Norton" over her shoulder as she turned to the credenza behind her, opened a drawer, and searched its depths. Apparently, she needed a pencil, because when she turned back, her eyes were dry and she held a well-used pencil stub in her hand.

11

She projected a smile. "Coffee?"

Both Clyde and Denton said "Yes," then Denton ushered Clyde into the conference room. "I'll be right back, Clyde," Denton said and returned to his office to put on his coat and re-adjust his tie.

When he returned to the conference room that dominated the long outer wall of the reception area, Clyde sat at the head of the table, as was his custom. Denton thought, *Always in control, aren't you, Clyde?* Before sitting down, Denton opened a drawer of the mahogany credenza standing against the wall. He took out a blue plastic ballpoint and yellow legal pad.

Denton chose a chair near Clyde, facing away from the outside window. He didn't want the glare of the window interfering with his concentration. "Clyde, do you understand what's going on?"

Clyde's black eyes turned serious below gray bushy eyebrows and a broad forehead. He spread his thin hands, trembling fingers splayed. "That's a good tan, Lee. I'm sure you remember it wasn't just a coincidence I picked you to represent us. Your Uncle Bill Higgins is a distant cousin. Heck, we ran together as kids. I remembered he had a nephew here in California that was a lawyer. He said good things about you, and I didn't want to hire a total stranger."

As Clyde's eyes flashed disapproval, Denton thought of his Uncle Bill, his mother's brother and a childhood idol. *Uncle Bill's probably pissed off, too.*

"But the others will be here soon. I wanted to see you alone. We were hurt that you left us in the lurch."

Denton stifled the first reply that rose to his lips. "I'm sorry, Clyde. But it was something I had to do."

"Yeah? Well, I'm glad you're back to your job."

Denton nodded. "I'm sorry for your losses. Tell me what's happened."

"As you know, my nephew Jim, who lived in the San Francisco Bay area, was killed in a car accident. He drove off a cliff on State Road 92 in the mountains between Hillsborough and Half

Moon Bay. He was just thirty-four. He was on his way to his sail-boat. A few days later my nephew William drowned when he fell off his boat in a lake up in Wisconsin. He'd been scuba diving. He was only thirty-nine."

Tavita had already briefed Denton about these deaths back at the lagoon when he'd talked Denton into returning. Jim Norton had been Denton's client, but William Norton was on the opposite side of the litigation. The idea of someone killing clients on *both* sides of the lawsuit was bizarre. Denton had tried to puzzle it out during the long weeks of sailing home. But the deaths weren't nec-essarily lawsuit related. The feud among the Norton clan had begun long before the lawsuit started. The reasons were lost in time's con-fusion. Somebody didn't invite someone to a party. That someone showed up anyway. Halfway through the festivities, women were slapping each other. Men threw punches. Physical combat even-tually gave way to the ongoing bitter lawsuit.

And now, there were deaths. Could there be a connection be-tween Denton's client, Jim Norton, killed by driving off a California cliff, and William Norton, an opposing party, who'd drowned fif-teen hundred miles away? Anything was possible, but coincidences happened—these deaths didn't have to be connected.

Denton sensed the heat of Clyde's hollow eyes, watching his thoughts. Denton felt the need to make a note, but the loosely held ballpoint slipped from his fingers and clattered discordantly on the glass top of the wooden table.

Clyde's eyes followed the blue ballpoint, then flicked back to Denton. "There's more."

Denton watched Clyde struggle to control his emotions. "My cousin, Sylvia Norton Smith, was killed early this morning in her home in Stone Lake, Wisconsin. It seems a burglar stabbed her forty-seven times. She was seventy-nine and on oxygen for severe emphysema. Her caretaker found her."

Gears in Denton's mind slipped as he processed the news. The unbidden memory of a Cuban woman's screaming red mouth took control. His mind saw again the blood spurting from the hole his 9 mm bullet had blasted into her chest. Denton squeezed the thoughts into the dark mental vault where he kept them confined. He had seldom dreamed of her while in the South Pacific, but last night she'd returned, her pale face and bright red lips again vivid in his recurrent nightmare.

Clyde's thin lips barely moved when he said, "And I think you know that my cousin Peter Norton died of a heart attack last month."

Denton nodded.

Clyde's eyes stayed on Denton as if he were trying to decode Denton's thoughts, then the dour man said, "Yeah, I know what you're thinking, and I agree Peter probably died from natural causes. Still, he was seventy-seven—our family usually makes it into our mid to late eighties." Clyde rubbed his time-worn hands and smiled at Denton. "My hands always ache after I drive in traffic. I grip the steering wheel too hard. Anyway, I suspect someone's killing the other Nortons—someone with an interest in what happens to the will. Someone who wants to eliminate heirs."

It's like an Agatha Christie story, Denton had thought. *But that's too weird, there must be...*

The opening conference room door interrupted Denton's memories. Clyde's son, Asa II, and Clyde's daughter, Joan, entered, followed by Clyde's niece, Mary. All were well-dressed in stylish, well-tailored dark clothes. They made somber greeting sounds as they filed to the table, taking seats in a row across from Denton. A handsome, long-haired man wearing a checkered sports coat over blue jeans and hand-tooled boots trailed behind Mary.

Asa II said, "Sorry, traffic was horrible. As usual."

Clyde replied, "No problem."

Denton gazed at Mary, lovely as always. At thirty, she still looked like the graduate student she'd been when they'd first met. *What was it she got her master's in? Anthropology?* Her blond hair was smoothly curled, framing her oval face. Her clear, hazel eyes were bright below her wide forehead, now partially covered with a black veil drooping from a small black hat. She dabbed her eyes with a white handkerchief. From beneath long eyelashes, her eyes searched Denton's. Three-year-old memories of dancing with her at the Top of the Mark in San Francisco coursed through Denton's mind.

Denton nodded and smiled. Mary suddenly remembered the gray-eyed man who sat next to her, staring at Denton. She gestured a slim white hand and said, "Lee, this is Gustav Cutler. He's, ah, my boyfriend."

Denton's eyes absorbed Gustav's shining brown hair, his smooth-skinned, regular features. He felt a twinge of jealousy. "Well, well, nice to meet you, Gaston."

"It's Gustav."

"Yeah, Gustav," Denton responded, thinking, *Why bring her boyfriend along?* The guy looked okay, but he projected the egotistical shallowness so common among the youthful and handsome. His gray eyes remained hostile.

Denton shifted his gaze to Clyde's shy daughter Joan, whose black eyes and dark brown hair revealed the Indian genes of her great-grandmother, Sarah Deerfoot Norton. Joan, who was about the same age as Mary, also held a white handkerchief that she applied to the corners of her almond-shaped eyes.

Denton's attention was drawn to Asa, Joan's older brother, who was adjusting his shirt cuffs, revealing gold links that glinted in sunlight streaming through the outer window. Asa's dark eyes seemed frightened.

Asa nodded to Denton and said, "Mr. Denton, we just don't know what's going on. All this bad luck. What happens to the lawsuit?"

"Yeah, bad luck," replied Denton, thinking of a lucky penny he'd picked up on the sidewalk in front of his downtown San Diego office building that morning. He'd whispered the mantra, "Find a penny, pick it up; all day long you'll have good luck," as he stooped for it. He knew most people wouldn't stoop to pick up a quarter, let alone a penny. But he'd had to protect his luck. Sitting at the conference table, his fingers strayed to the outside of his trouser pocket. He rubbed the lucky penny through the fine cloth that now entrapped his legs.

"But bad luck has a way of changing," he added. "As to the lawsuit, your cousins' lawyer has filed a motion to render judgment in their favor. It's based on the idea that the deaths of some of the parties now terminates the suit. The motion is partly based on a complicated law called the Rule Against Perpetuities. It doesn't stand much of a chance, but I've got to treat it seriously. I'll argue against it in court next week."

The Nortons exchanged nervous glances, Joan reaching for Clyde's hand and Asa using a gold-tipped Mont Blanc pen to make a note on a small index card. Mary began to cry, small sniffles at first, but these turned to long shuddering sobs. She stuttered out, "My father just died, and now Jim is gone, too. I don't know how I'll cope."

Gustav patted the back of her hand, his gaze on Denton.

Clyde stood and put his arm around Mary. "There, there, dear. Come stay with us for a while. We'll take care of you."

Mary's red-rimmed eyes beamed gratitude at Clyde, fluttered to Denton, then looked down at the white hanky clutched in her fist. She said, "Thanks, Uncle Clyde. I'll come over for a few days. I'd like to be with family. I just wonder if Dad really had a heart attack, and if Jim's death was really an accident. Those *Johns* wouldn't stop at anything."

Denton's Norton clients referred to their opponents, John Norton Jr. and John Norton III, as "the Johns." They hated the Johns for playing dirty, trying to grab the entire inheritance by destroying the will.

Denton's cheap ballpoint smeared blue ink as he jotted a note to investigate whether Peter Norton's heart attack was real. There were ways to fake heart attacks. The smeared ink was irritating. Denton glanced at Asa's pen and wished for his own Mont Blanc, lost during his cruise to the South Pacific. *Gotta get a new one.* He scribbled until the ballpoint again flowed.

Denton answered, "That could be true, Mary, but don't forget, your cousin William Norton recently drowned. He was on the opposite side of this lawsuit. Besides, he was in Wisconsin, over a thousand miles from here. And so was your Aunt Sylvia, who, just this morning, was found dead—stabbed to death."

"Aunt Sylvia!" chorused the two women and immediately burst into tears.

Clyde Norton's sorrowful eyes and shrugging shoulder signaled he'd not had a chance to give the latest bad news to Mary and Joan.

Helpless, Denton watched Clyde and Asa comfort the women. Denton took a deep breath. *So much death… could such deaths be accidents? What if they weren't?* That would mean someone was killing heirs on both sides of the equation to enhance their own inheritance. But who would have that kind of mind?

Denton watched Clyde, who with John Junior now comprised the elder generation. They were the two surviving grandchildren of Asa and Sarah Norton. Clyde was watching Mary. What was the emotion in Clyde's deep-set eyes? It didn't seem like love.

And why was that asshole Gustav giving Denton the evil eye?

4

Mid-September. North Wisconsin woods.

Gruff snorts from the other side of the brush pile interrupted Denton's reverie of the Norton meeting a month before. The sharp noises of snapping twigs broke the rainy continuum. Denton's hand twitched to his pistol. But the bear became quiet. A rock pressed against Denton's aching shoulder. Leaves crackled as he shifted his body. *Shit. I hope the bear didn't hear that.* He listened, but heard nothing. *I'll aim for its eyes.*

Denton shifted his shoulders, seeking comfort on the uneven ground. He felt a sharp pain in his thigh and shoved a hand underneath, grasping the pointed branch and pushing it away.

After nesting into the pile of timber, he'd fallen into exhausted sleep. But now the storm was abating, and the blue of impeding dawn shown through the latticework of his hiding place. He worked his stiff body, making his cuts sting. Fresh memories of painted Indians crowded away thoughts of his last Norton meeting, of Mary's face and her boyfriend's glare. The personal violence could only mean one thing: *It's true. Someone is killing the Nortons. And now they want to kill me. But why?*

He pondered motivation. What provokes one person to kill another? Sure, hot tempers flash and people die. But that's not the same as cold-blooded, premeditated murder. *And… well, sometimes you can kill someone by accident. Like the Cuban woman.* But now wasn't the time to think of her. *Think about the Nortons. Arrange the facts. Use logic to connect dots.*

His thoughts wouldn't gel. They swirled like dirty smoke, choking away logic. At least he'd had the foresight to dress for the north woods. He wore waterproof boots with thick wool socks, tough blue denim pants tucked into the boot tops, and two layers of shirts beneath a yellow Gore-Tex jacket. He also carried a razor-sharp folding knife and his Browning Hi-Power. He put a hand on the 9 mm pistol. His special California concealed weapons permit was invalid in Wisconsin, but he'd carried the gun anyway.

He'd had a feeling, a foreboding. The concept made Denton chuckle, despite his predicament, because it evoked images of his friend and client, California Insurance Commissioner Jason Montgomery Stubbs, known to his friends as Stubby. Stubby used to say, "Forearmed is forewarned." *Good thing I got forearmed.*

A trickle of water found its way through the maze of vegetation, splattering Denton's cheek. He shifted away, moving gingerly to avoid arousing the bear. *What a situation!* He wished he could see the bear. *I'll shoot the rest of the magazine into the son-of-a-bitch!*

No. No, he wouldn't. He'd learned long ago that his temper could turn violent. Violence overcame good judgment. So what if he was wet and cold? He was alive. In the light of morning, he'd be calm. He'd deal with the situation. He gathered pine branches around him, welcoming the warmth of thick, slim leaves.

Denton began to doze, but questions filled his mind. Images of Clyde, Asa II, and Joan claimed his thoughts. They all had dark eyes. Eyes inherited from Sarah Deerfoot, a full-blooded Ojibwe. And now, Indians had tried to kill him. Of the entire Norton clan, only Clyde's immediate family had been untouched by the recent disasters. The Johns had lost Sylvia and William. Mary had lost her father Peter and her brother Jim. Was there a connection between Clyde's group and the attack?

Despite his concerns, Denton thought of Mary, summoning fond memories. Dancing with her had been an ethereal experience, as if the very essence of dancing had taken over their supple bodies. One thing had led to another. And the other had led to the end. Now she was with gray-eyed Gustav, who liked to stare at people he barely knew, people who just might kick his boney ass. Denton's mind drifted back to his conversation with Charlotte immediately after the Norton meeting.

5

Late August. San Diego.

When his meeting with the Nortons had ended, Denton loitered at Charlotte's desk. Their wary eyes locked until Denton's gaze strayed to the sheet of white paper Charlotte had shown him earlier. Charlotte glanced at the paper, now lying on her desk, then back to Denton. Her pink lacquered fingertips picked it up. She held it so the overhead lights shone on it, letting Denton think about its contents. She waited four or five beats.

Denton tensed, worrying about what was coming.

Charlotte grinned and ceremoniously tore it up, strip by strip. She dropped the shreds into her brown plastic trash can.

Relief coursed through Denton, but he covered it up, saying, "Well, Char, I think you'd better bring me up to date."

"Okay, boss, we better go into the conference room. I'll bring the files."

Denton went to the conference room with its panoramic view of San Diego Bay, now shining beneath clear skies, soaking up the sun, offering shelter to those coming home from the sea. He unbuttoned his chafing shirt collar and loosened his tie. Long months of casual, if any, clothing had had their effect. The business suit was confining, a symbol of his entrapment. He shucked the jacket and took a chair on the window side of the smooth mahogany table, putting his back to the bay and its mocking promise of infinite getaways.

Charlotte entered, her light blue dress growing pale in the sunlight shining through the window. "Okay, boss. Here's a folder with all the court filings since you left. The main document is the formal…" She paused, lifting the document closer to her eyes. "Ah, let me read it to you: Suggestion of Death of Parties and Motion to Render Judgment in favor of the John Norton group."

Denton took a breath and let it out. "The Johns. I haven't missed them a bit. By the way, remind me to get a decent pen." Denton walked to the credenza and located another plastic ballpoint. He sat, pulled open a manila file, and flipped through its contents. Photos of the several Nortons fell out and littered the tabletop, sudden claims upon his life, his peace of mind. Denton arranged the photos face up, recalling how five years earlier he'd gotten these photos to help him memorize who was who. He called them the "mug shots."

He again reflected on the close resemblance between Clyde, his brother Peter, and their cousin John, Jr. Even Sylvia Norton Smith bore a family resemblance. All that generation was dark-eyed and dour, but hot blood flowed through their veins, and the animosity between the two sides of the lawsuit was palpable. Hot blood usually led to sudden crimes of passion, but these were all socially gifted people. People used to dissembling, camouflaging emotions.

Charlotte's concerned voice interrupted his thoughts. "Boss, you've got two days to file an answer to the Motion to Render Judgment."

"Yeah." Denton slowly gathered the photos, thinking of his own childhood and summers in Wisconsin with his cousins. These people had been kids together, too. They must have played happily at family gatherings, eating together, loving their grandparents. But those were the days of childhood's innocence, before money had entered their lives. Now they squabbled over their grandparents' money. Some were dying. *Why does love stop? How does it change to hate? How...*

Charlotte's more strident voice claimed his attention. "Boss. Hem didn't want to file a response until you got back. He already got two delays for you." She handed Denton another file. "But here's a response Hem drafted to help you out."

Denton snapped out of his reverie. "Okay... That's good. I'll get on it."

"The judge said no more delays. The hearing is in five days. There's something in their motion about the Rule Against Perpetuities."

"Yeah, I know."

Charlotte left. Denton's hand strayed to the stack of Norton photos. He pushed them around with a fingertip, a thin deck of tarot cards.

6

Denton put the Norton "mug shots" away and turned his attention to the stack of manila folders crammed with legal documents. He located his sketch of the Norton family tree and circled the names of the recently dead. He pondered the finality of their absence.

His new ballpoint was made of clear plastic with red ink. It was already smearing his yellow legal pad. He stared at the red splotches, quelling the rising memories vying for control.

Was it significant that only Clyde's immediate family had escaped a death? Mary had lost a father and a brother. John Norton Jr. had lost a sister and a son. The family line on the far right of the chart had ended with George Norton Schneider, who had disappeared long ago.

Charlotte entered with a chicken salad sandwich and diet Coke, wordlessly placed them on the wooden table, and left. After Denton's months at sea, the white paper napkin and toothpicked triangular halves of the sandwich seemed elegant. Denton bit idly into the sandwich and sipped his drink. The sun felt good on his neck, and he glanced behind himself to look at the bay. A sleek schooner, all sails hoisted, slipped past Point Loma into the freedom of the Pacific. He forced his attention back to his messy legal pad. His right index finger was stained red from the ink.

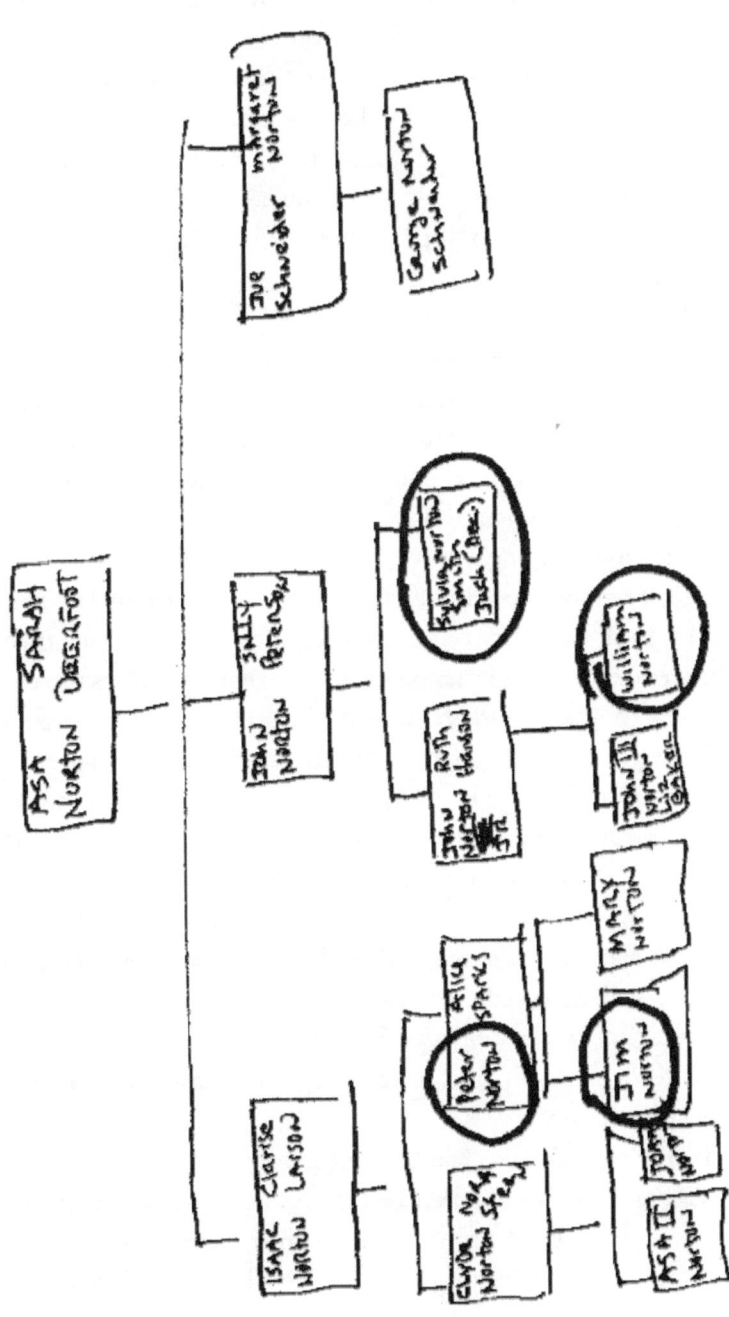

Asa and Sarah Norton's will had left their property to each other. The document provided that on the death of the survivor, the estate went into trust for their then living children or the deceased children's heirs. But only the direct descendants could inherit; wives and husbands were excluded. Sarah, much younger than Asa, had survived him by sixty years, the last twenty of which were spent living with her son, John Junior, on his dairy farm near Hayward, Wisconsin.

The will provided that Asa and Sarah's children did not get the full estate. Instead, the then six million dollars went into a trust from which the children split the annual investment income, but the principle remained in trust for the grandchildren. In turn, the grandchildren also received only the income. This formula repeated itself on down the generations.

Denton had thought it was an overly complicated way to deal with the estate, but Asa and Sarah had become wealthy late in life, when iron ore was discovered on three hundred acres they owned in the Penokee-Gogebic range of northeastern Wisconsin. At the beginning of the twentieth century, Wisconsin had become the fourth largest producer of iron ore in the United States, and the Penokee-Gogebic range had produced millions of tons of the stuff, making Asa and Sarah rich. But Asa and Sarah retained their modest ways and designed their will to impose similar modesty on their descendants. Each year the trust, run by a bank, provided ample income to allow their heirs to live well, but not lavishly. Careful investments had increased the trust fund to ten million.

Certainly, living well wasn't enough for the "Johns." They wanted to live lavishly and were trying to set aside the trust and seize all the money.

By the time Denton had become involved in the Norton litigation, Asa and Sarah's children had died and the trust had come to their grandchildren. Denton wrote out their names: Clyde Norton, Peter Norton, John Norton Junior, and Sylvia Norton Smith.

Denton couldn't get used to calling this group the *grandkids*. Not with them all in their seventies or eighties. Clyde sure was right about the family being long lived. And not only that—the men had emulated their grandfather Asa by having children relatively late in life.

Denton checked the notes he'd made on the never-ending litigation. *Yep. Clyde had kids in his forties. So did Peter. John III was born when John Jr. was thirty-eight, but William came along when he was forty-five.*

Denton's fingers drummed a non-rhythm on his notepad. *Could be some of the grandkiddies are getting antsy for their share of the dough.*

But Peter Norton had died, vesting his share of the trust fund in grandchildren Jim Norton and Mary Norton. Jim's death gave everything to Mary. Sylvia had no heirs, and her death gave her share to Clyde and John Norton, Jr., who were now the only surviving grandchildren. They were on opposing sides of the litigation.

Denton closed his eyes and sat back in his chair, thinking it through, searching for a pattern to the deaths. The two men were like the last players in a long poker game, facing one another across the table for all the chips.

But Clyde and John Jr. weren't alone at the table. With her father and brother dead, Mary now sat with her uncles. She'd been elevated above her cousins. What was more, the deaths of her brother Jim and cousin William had thinned the ranks of the great-grandchildren.

Denton opened his eyes, noticing the red ink stains on his finger. *Who would stab an old lady forty-seven times? Was Peter's death really a heart attack?*

Denton took a bite of sandwich and a swig of Coke. The glass was beaded with condensation, and he wiped his wet hand on his pants leg. *Where's that note from Sarah Norton?* He searched through files until he found his copy. The handwriting was thin and shaky, but its message was simple:

I hereby revoke the ... and ... Norton Trust all to my grandson John Norton, Jr.

This was the lynchpin of the lengthy Norton litigation: a document revoking the trust, supposedly signed by Sarah Norton just before her death.

Denton recalled how Clyde Norton had first contacted him. Clyde's cousin John Norton, Jr., had filed suit to set aside the Norton Family Trust on the theory that Sarah Norton had revoked the trust and left the entire estate to John Norton Sr. John Sr. being dead, the estate would go to John Jr. and his sister Sylvia. And now Sylvia was dead of stab wounds.

Clyde had explained, "The suit was filed as a diversity of citizenship action in San Diego federal district court. You know how that works: suits by citizens of one state against citizens of other states can be filed in federal court. All my side of the litigation lives in California. Your Uncle Bill and I were good friends. Still are. We talk every now and then on the phone, and I called him up when all this trouble started. He knew most of the Nortons when we were kids. He suggested I ask you to handle the case."

Denton had understood Clyde's reasoning. Denton's mother's family had lived in the Hayward, Wisconsin area. He'd spent many summer vacations up in those dense woods, camping, fishing, and running around with his cousins. It made sense that Clyde would seek out a homeboy to defend him. Well, an ex-homeboy.

John Norton Jr., the leader of the group suing Clyde's group, claimed the original will was unfair because his father was the only child to care for Sarah Norton during her declining years. None of the other children had helped. He claimed the Sarah Norton note was effectively a will that revoked the trust and left the entire estate to John Sr.

As Denton processed all this, the conference room phone rang. Denton's friend and fellow attorney G. Hemmington Smith was on the line.

"Lee, you ole bastard. Welcome back to civilization."

"Thanks. You call this civilization?"

"Well, at least you can get a good bottle of wine."

Denton laughed, happy to be talking to Hem. "Good to hear your voice. How are lovely Allison and the golden twins?"

"Fine, fine. The twins are in second grade now. In the gifted children class."

"Of course. I wouldn't expect anything less of them. Good thing you married a lady with brains."

"Yeah, yeah. Well, you need to get on up here to L.A. for dinner. Do you need any more help on that crazy Norton case?"

"Not right now. Thanks for covering for me, Hem."

When Hem rang off, Denton let his fond memories of their friendship seep through him. But the good memories led to memories of when they'd first met, when they'd been in the Army Reserve and took part in the invasion of Grenada—where Denton had killed two people. One was a Cuban woman, an "advisor" to the Coard faction that engaged in the bloody coup that took over the government. Denton and Hem had gone in with a Navy SEAL unit to destroy the Grenadian radio station. They'd flown at dawn in a Blackhawk Helicopter and captured the two Cubans as they seized the radio station. A gunfight had broken out, and the Cuban man had gotten Hem's pistol when a bullet hit Hem's helmet, knocking him unconscious. Denton had shot the man. Then the woman grabbed the gun and aimed it at Denton.

The memories still haunted Denton, and he often dreamed of the woman's eyes as she pointed the gun. At the last second Hem had knocked her gun away, but Denton's finger was already pulling the trigger that blew a 9 mm hollow-point hole through her chest.

Denton pushed away bloody images of the Cuban woman's lipstick-crimsoned mouth screaming and the blood spurting from the hole between her breasts. He pressed his trembling right hand against his leg, trying to stop it, pushing his mind back to the Norton case.

Now the Norton case was also full of death. John Jr.'s son William had recently drowned in the boating accident. That left John Norton III the only remaining heir in that line after John Jr. Could the Johns possibly be greedy enough to kill William, one of their immediate family? It seemed impossible. Still, with Sylvia Norton Smith brutally murdered, John Norton Jr. would inherit the entire estate if he won his lawsuit. Eventually, John III would inherit it all from his dad.

Denton's clients had included both Clyde and Peter Norton, but now Peter was dead of a heart attack, and his son Jim had died in a car wreck. That left sweet, lovely Mary, who had danced so lightly in Denton's arms, her slim body pressed tight against him.

Personal relationships could get so complex.

Denton re-did the math. The Isaac Norton descendants had lost two: Peter and Peter's son, Jim. The John Norton Senior descendants had also lost two—Sylvia and William. It was hard to see a pattern, but Denton tried to puzzle it out.

If John Jr. died, his son John III would get the entire estate. On the other hand, if John Jr. *and* John III died, all the money would go to Clyde.

Working it another way, if Clyde died, his children, Asa II and Joan, would get their share. *Hell, if Clyde, Asa, and Joan die, Mary gets it all, the whole banana.*

Christ! Denton closed his eyes. His thoughts filled with the memory of Mary's radiant eyes staring into his as they danced. *No way.* He couldn't see Mary as a killer. *But that asshole Gustav would fit the profile.*

Denton stood and stretched. *It's like one of those connect the dot pictures. Nothing's clear until you connect enough dots.* But connecting more dots would involve more deaths.

7

That evening Denton left his office and entered his building's parking garage, the clip-clop of his shoes echoing against the concrete. He recalled the times James Gridley had appeared there, surging out of the dark. The first time, Gridley had shot Denton in the stomach and left him for dead. The second time, Gridley, newly released from prison for shooting Denton, had been seeking atonement. Shaking off memories of Gridley, Denton climbed into his ten-year-old white 735i BMW and headed towards Highway 5 for the drive home.

A set of headlights stayed in his rearview mirror. *Am I being followed?* The idea sent chills through Denton, who remembered the last time he'd been followed. Then he'd had to shoot his way out of an ambush by two hired killers.

Denton sped up, then slowed down. Each time the tailing car stayed with him. Denton reached for his brown leather briefcase sitting on the passenger seat, his lucky briefcase that held his lucky Browning Hi-Power within a concealed weapon pouch. He withdrew the pistol, which was cocked and ready. *Condition One.* All he had to do was thumb off the safety and pull the trigger.

This time, I'm not running. He exited the Five at Ardath Road and pulled to the roadside at the bottom of the off-ramp. He slid quickly out of the car, gun in hand, and took shelter behind the passenger side. The tailing vehicle was a red Ford F-150, and it moved cautiously down the ramp towards Denton. He thumbed off the gun's safety and leveled it across the roof of his BMW, aiming at the approaching threat. Two big men inside stared at Denton. The driver hit the gas, took a left and roared off into the night, leaving Denton standing behind his car, his gun mocking his caution.

Better prepared than dead, Denton thought as he put the gun on safe and re-entered his car. Denton felt silly as he drove home. *I just got back and I'm already twitchy.*

Sandy Jones hugged him when he walked in the door, pressing herself against him, her hand caressing the back of his neck. Her loving warmth aroused him.

"Lee. Is that a pistol in your pocket?"

He laughed at the old joke, deciding not to mention the real pistol he was carrying in his briefcase. Best not to alarm her needlessly. He'd jumped to conclusions about that pickup truck with the two ugly guys in it.

Denton's little dog, Mutt, had greeted him along with Sandy. Mutt was busily engaged in his favorite trick—chewing on Denton's shoelaces, pulling them undone, emitting tiny growls. Denton stooped and tousled Mutt's shaggy head. "Hello, Mutt, how was your first day back home?"

Mutt emitted a non-committal snort as Denton picked him up and carried the little dog into the den, where Sandy poured Denton a generous Jack Daniel's on the rocks.

Denton tasted his drink and set Mutt on the floor, tossing his red ball across the room. Mutt eagerly fetched it back, fighting Denton for possession. After a while, Mutt tired of the game and concentrated on a chew-toy.

Sandy poured herself a slim-stemmed glass of chardonnay and said, "Let's go outside and watch the moon and stars. My special linguini with clam sauce will be done in thirty minutes."

They sat on the porch swing, their thighs pressed against one another, sipping their drinks while star and moonlight shone silver upon the undulating Pacific.

"Nice," said Sandy, "but not like our lagoon."

"Yeah, babe. Too true. I should have this case worked out in a couple of months. Then we could take off again."

Sandy's eyes glittered in the moonlight. "Lee, I like being back home, but you're a wandering spirit. If you could ride the wind, flow around the world with the clouds, that's where you'd be."

Denton pondered the thought, sipped his Jack Daniel's, and looked for the resident red tail hawk that lived in the high branches of the big eucalyptus tree beside his deck. There it was, its obsidian eyes staring down on Denton, without passion, without interest.

8

Five days later, Denton passed through the bronze and glass entrance of the Edward J. Schwartz United States Courthouse at 940 Front Street, San Diego. The reddish five-story building was an apt tribute to the long-sitting chief judge in whose court Denton had frequently appeared.

Denton worked his way through the security screening process and found his way to the first-floor courtroom of Judge Maynard Sands, now the eldest, but not the *chief* judge—a circumstance that embittered Judge Sands, who had already been crotchety.

Opposing counsel Albert C. Mecklenburg and his two junior associates were already in the courtroom, arranging their papers on the counsel table. Despite his charcoal gray pinstriped suit and light pink tie, Mecklenburg's fading blond hair pegged him for the aging surfer he was. Mecklenburg spotted Denton. "Hello, Leland. Nice to see you. You didn't need to come back for this. It should be over pretty quickly. Then you can take off again. Where was it? Lusitania?"

Mecklenburg's two assistants laughed at the joke. One was young and pretty, a lithe, dark-haired woman wearing a tailored green business suit. The other was a skinny, middle-aged man with a Donald Trump comb-over. They withered under Denton's scowl and went back to stacking files, forming a temple-like mound on the polished wood of the counsel table.

"Yeah, Dick, all those folders make it look like it'll be quick."

Mecklenburg winked. "Gotta put on the show, Leland. Gotta put on the show."

The court stenographer and the clerk entered. The clerk barked, "All rise," and the lawyers stood at attention while the black-robed judge carried a huge paper-filled file up the few steps to his bench.

"Good morning, counsel."

The lawyers harmonized, "Good morning, Your Honor."

Denton had only a thin file containing his brief on the motion and a few notes for argument. He eyed Judge Sands, gauging his mood. He seemed calm.

Mecklenburg, as counsel for the moving party, would go first. Denton resumed his seat, laying his notes on the table in front of him. Someone had carved the word "justice" on the edge of the table. The letters seemed to glow in the lights of the wood-paneled room.

Judge Sands' reedy voice rang out, "Mr. Mecklenburg."

Mecklenburg stood. "Yes, Your Honor."

Judge Sands shook his gray head and peered over his tortoise-shell glasses. "I'm not dismissing this case just because some of the heirs have died. That often happens in a will contest. That's the whole point of having a will."

"But Your Honor, there is no will. Sarah Norton revoked it with her holographic codicil."

"You mean the handwritten note you claim she signed and that Mr. Denton's clients say she didn't sign, and that even if she did sign, was the product of undue influence?"

"Well, I wouldn't put it that way, Your Honor."

"I'm sure not, and in the end I may agree with you. But in the meantime, those contentions are the core of this lawsuit, and they raise questions of fact that prevent my granting summary judgment. Mr. Denton's clients are entitled to a full trial on the merits."

Mecklenburg spoke, "Your Honor, we have also moved for dismissal under the Rule Against Perpetuities. Even if the will had not been revoked, its terms are such that the Norton estate may not vest within a life in existence, plus twenty-one years. That invalidates the will, *ab initio*."

Judge Sands frowned, paging through Mecklenburg's brief. "Mr. Denton, what's your response to that?"

Denton stood straight, holding his brief in one hand and punctuating his words with the other. "The will was written in Wisconsin. Therefore Wisconsin law controls."

Judge Sands replied, "Okay, what's Wisconsin law on the point?"

Denton held up his brief. "We discuss it on page five of our brief, Your Honor. Under Wisconsin law the will remains valid because the People's Bank, the trustee under the will, has an unlimited power to sell the trust assets. That means the estate *could vest* within the required period. The case we cite, *In Re the Estate of Johansson,* is the controlling precedent. Wisconsin has its own unique enactment of the Rule Against Perpetuities."

Mecklenburg rose to respond, but Judge Sands interrupted, "Hold on, Mr. Mecklenburg. I'll take the motion under advisement while I read the Wisconsin statute and the Johansson case. You may submit any other case law you want me to consider. Send copies to Mr. Denton."

Mecklenburg's shoulders sagged. "Yes, Your Honor."

Denton said, "Thank you, Judge Sands. I request a sixty-day recess to investigate the circumstances of the recent deaths of the Norton heirs. Under Wisconsin law, an heir responsible for another heir's death cannot inherit. I may need to amend our answer if any of Mr. Mecklenburg's clients are implicated."

Mecklenburg came to life. "The same goes for me, Your Honor. I'll investigate too."

"Granted. I'll enter an order that you two will prepare a report to the court of your findings, and we'll go from there."

As the courtroom cleared, Denton noticed Clyde Norton had arrived during the argument. Clyde shook Denton's hand. "Good work, Lee." He handed Denton a thick packet.

"What's this?"

"This is a document written by my dad, Isaac Norton. It's the story of my cousin George Norton Schneider's disappearance. I don't know if it means anything, but I think you should read it."

"George Norton Schneider? Is that the one who disappeared in... well, a long time ago?"

"Yeah. It didn't seem relevant. He was my Aunt Margaret and Uncle Joe's only son. George disappeared back in 1944. I just want to be sure you've seen everything that even remotely relates to our family."

Denton scanned the packet of yellowing paper that bore the logo of the Soo Line Railroad. It was titled, "Statement of Isaac Norton Regarding the October 4, 1944 Incident Concerning George Norton Schneider."

Clyde's fingertip flicked at the document. "That's the statement my dad gave to the railroad detectives when they investigated my cousin George's disappearance. As I say, it might have some bearing. I don't know."

Denton thanked Clyde, put the document inside his briefcase, and left the federal courthouse to walk to his office. After a block, he sensed he was being followed. He paused at a handy storefront and looked at his back trail. There he was—a tall, skinny guy in blue jeans and a loose Hawaiian shirt with red flowers. As Denton watched, the man put a hand to his long brown hair and stopped to study the women's clothes in a nearby store window.

Oh, good cover, pal, thought Denton as he resumed his walk. Skinny followed. Denton let the traffic light at the next corner turn red and stood on the curb, waiting for the man to catch up.

"Are you tailing me?" Denton asked.

Skinny's voice was a surprising deep bass. "Whaddaya mean?"

"Just what I said. You following me?"

"Fuck off," Skinny said, his brown eyes angry as he turned away, retracing his path. Denton noticed a bulge at the small of his back. The loose shirt covered a weapon, probably a gun.

Denton's thoughts whirled as he watched the man walk away. *Just what I need—a new stalker.* Barely a year had passed since Denton had shot it out with thugs who tried to kill him. Visions surfaced— red mist in the rain, dead bodies in California sand, a woman's life ebbing against white hospital sheets. Denton suppressed thoughts of the past. *Gotta make a plan. Be on my guard.*

9

After the incident with Skinny, Denton sat behind his desk, considering the implications. No question the man was following him. No doubt, someone had hired him. But who? And why? It certainly could be someone involved in the Norton case; one of the Nortons, or even his opposing counsel, Mecklenburg. But it could be totally unrelated to the Norton case. *I'll just have to wait and see. Stay on the alert, and keep my gun handy.*

Denton reached into his briefcase for the Isaac Norton statement Clyde had given him. He spread out its several pages. The ancient typewriter ink had faded, but was still legible. Soon he was engrossed in the story.

Statement of Isaac Norton Regarding the Disappearance of George Norton Schneider on October 4, 1944

I, Isaac Norton, being first duly sworn upon my oath, do depose and aver as follows:

As of October 4, 1944 I was employed as a chief locomotive engineer for the Soo Line Railroad. I was assigned to N-20 locomotive number 4006, one of the first 4-8-2 engines deli-vered to the Soo Line. The engine was called a 4-8-2 because it had two front tracking wheels, eight big driv-ing wheels, and the four trailing wheels. It weighed 344,500 pounds. I provide these details to explain why I was absorbed in the tasks of driving this huge engine.

As I left the depot in Chicago, I saw my nephew George Norton Schneider board the train as it pulled out of Chicago. George was my sister Marga-ret's son and I had helped him obtain his job as brakeman for the Soo Line. He always did an excellent job and was always a reliable employee. But that night I knew George was not assigned to the run. I didn't know why he boarded the train, which was a fif-teen-car passenger train. When I saw George board the train, I noticed he was carrying a pillow-sized package under his arm.

The night was dark and it was snow-ing. I had to concentrate on my job. At 6:30 p.m. I had to wipe snowflakes from my goggles as I peered along the railroad track to find the big oak tree I used to mark the place where I needed to push on more steam for the climb up Devil's Crest.

I could barely see the mark through the swirling snow, but I managed to spot it and poured on the steam. As I topped the crest, I had to baby the throttle because, as the front of the train began the descent, I still had most of the train still climbing up the incline. In 1935, Pete Murphy plunged two hundred feet off the side at that exact point, taking fifty ore cars down into the gorge and killing himself and six others. I give these details to explain why I had no time to inquire into George's presence on the train.

At 4:21 a.m. I pulled Number 4006 up to the water tower in Couderay, Wisconsin and took a short rest while the crew filled the tender's 24,500-gallon tank with water. I remember rubbing my sore shoulder when I saw a fancy black Packard touring car parked beside the small depot, its motor idling as the sharp smell of exhaust drifted into my engine compartment.

In the dim light filtering from a small depot window, I saw the driver of the Packard wearing a thick overcoat and a dark fedora pulled low over his brow, hiding most of his fleshy face. Another warmly dressed figure sat in the back seat. I caught sight of the passenger's face as he took a drag of a long cigar. In the red glow I saw his scarred cheek and thick eyebrows, but he also wore his hat-brim low.

The two looked like gangsters. I was wondering what they were doing there when my nephew George Norton appeared out of the night, stepping up to the black Packard and tapping on the back window.

The passenger rolled down the window and George shoved the pillow-sized package through the open space. The passenger placed it on the seat and passed a fat roll of bills out the window into George's hand. I couldn't believe my eyes.

I saw the passenger's thumb then gesture towards the front seat. George walked around to the passenger side and opened the front car door. Just then, the scar-faced passenger looked directly at me. I'll never forget his hard black eyes. I've seen them in my memories ever after. I believe this man to have been the gangster Alphonse Gabriel Capone. I had read he'd been released from prison. It was common knowledge in the area that Mr. Capone had a large estate near Couderay, Wisconsin. It was also well known Mr. Capone's brother, Raffaele James Capone, known as "Ralph," owned property, including an automobile garage, in Mercer, Wisconsin, not far from Couderay.

```
The driver of the car may have been
Ralph Capone.
    I've never seen or heard from
George Norton Schneider again. I have
no knowledge of his whereabouts. I do
not know what was in the package.
    Sworn to and subscribed before me
this 10th Day of December 1944.
```

The signatures of the notary public and Isaac were old and faded, but the weakened ink carried powerful authenticity. Denton ran his finger over the impression of the notary seal over the pale signatures. He thought of long dead witnesses, their verity spanning the decades. *Jeezus, the Capone mob?* Denton thought. *Why did Clyde give this to me? What's the connection?*

As a teenager, Denton had read all about Al Capone and knew that by 1929, the FBI was focused on the Chicago gangs and on Al Capone in particular. In 1931 the federal government indicted him for tax evasion. He got an eleven-year sentence. Capone ended up in Alcatraz, where the syphilis he'd contracted years earlier began to scramble his brains. He got out of prison in 1939 and went to Florida, where he continued to degenerate. There he ranted about foreigners, communists, and enemies he thought were trying to kill him. The end came in 1947 from a stroke. It wasn't clear what Capone had done between 1939 and his death, however. *He could have been doing a lot of things. The guy had a lot of enemies, sure, but he had a lot of cronies, too.*

Syphilis. A nasty disease. They'd had penicillin then, but didn't yet know it could cure syphilis. When things went bad for Al Capone, they went bad all the way. *That's how luck works.*

10

Mid-September. North Wisconsin woods.

Now, as he lay in the rain-wet stand of brush, Denton considered the George Norton Schneider question again. What was the
Capone connection, if any? What was Clyde trying to communi-
cate?

And who would be trying to kill Denton? The same person
that had hired Skinny to tail him back in San Diego? And this recent attack? Were those real Indians? Was there some bizarre connection to the 1944 disappearance of George Norton Schneider? If
alive, George stood to inherit a lot of money, especially now that
his cousins Peter and Sylvia were dead. But the guy had vanished
long ago.

A muffled series of growls interrupted Denton's thoughts,
turning them back to his companion in the wood pile. He examined his Hi-Power, making sure it was dry and free of debris. All
he had to do was take off the safety, then start shooting. *These Hornady XTP hollow points ought to do some damage.*

Denton recalled selecting the XTPs at a gun shop in San
Diego. Sandy was with him. She'd teared up when she saw the
deadly hollow maws of the bullets. When they got home, she'd said,

"These bullets remind me of how that man shot you. You could have died."

Her hand moved to his chest. Her fingers found the scars. He knew she could feel the hard ridges through his shirt. He'd often fingered them along with his other bullet scars. How many times could this happen? If he kept at it, someday a bullet would kill him. Perhaps someone else's XTP that mushroomed when it hit, tearing out bone and flesh, leaving a gaping exit wound.

He's kissed Sandy, smiled confidently, and said, "Yeah, but that's the reason I need to protect myself again."

"I wish you'd quit this case, Lee. You've had enough of this."

His memories of Sandy dissipated when the bear moved again, its bulk breaking twigs, reminding Denton where he was. He wished he'd stayed in San Diego with Sandy. He'd be lying next to her right now, snuggled up tight, his hand on her smooth skin.

He shifted his weight, shaking the branches above his head. A gush of water splashed his face, a frigid dose of reality. He checked his watch. Five a.m. Almost dawn. Thank God it hadn't gotten too cold.

Denton's thoughts turned to his warm, well-equipped office. He remembered that, after his court hearing with Judge Sands, he'd met with Charlotte and Tavita in the conference room. The three of them had clustered around one end of the long table with a pile of legal files, trying to find dots to connect to other dots.

11

Late August. San Diego.

Now that he'd returned and was getting back into the swing of things, Denton found himself happy to be working with Charlotte and Tavita again. They'd been through a lot together, including a gunfight that had left both Denton and Tavita wounded. A battle that had ended when Charlotte's .45 bullet sent the bad guy to hell.

Denton grinned. "Well, here we are again. I suppose I should refresh our recollections of the Norton will." He thumbed through a file, pulling out a photocopy of the will Asa and Sarah Norton had executed in 1934. It was eight pages long.

"The couple left all their property in trust for their children, Margaret, Isaac, and John, share and share alike. The heirs could use the income for living, medical, and reasonable entertainment expenses. But when each died, the property passed in trust to their children under the same terms."

Charlotte smoothed her dress across her knees and made a note on her green steno pad. "So when John, for example, died, his share of the income went half and half to his kids?" She looked at a file. "That would be to John Jr. and Sylvia?"

"Yes, they'd split John's share if they were both still living. With Sylvia dead, her share goes to John Jr. because she has no heirs."

Charlotte and Tavita made notes. Tavita scratched his truncated left arm. "That's nice for John Jr. But what if Sylvia had a will leaving her share to somebody else?"

Denton thought it over. "Smart question. Her lawyer, Albert Mecklenburg, didn't mention a will. But make a note. We'll check that out."

Charlotte summed it up. "So if a parent dies, the kids split the dead parent's share of the trust income. Like Mary and Jim Norton split their father Peter's share. Or they would have if Jim Norton hadn't driven his car off that cliff."

Tavita nodded. "Yeh, how about that? Mary gets all that money now that her dad and brother are pushing up daisies." Denton gazed at Tavita long enough to make Tavita add, "I'm just sayin'."

Denton felt irritation from Tavita's insinuation, but suppressed it. He dropped his glare and said, "Yeah. It's possible."

Tavita rubbed his stump as if he had phantom pains. "And if something happens to Clyde, then his kids will get his share."

"Right. In the meantime, John Jr.'s been trying to set aside the entire will based on this handwritten note." Denton flashed a copy of the note supposedly written by Sarah just before her death leaving "all to John."

Charlotte nodded. "So maybe John wants to hedge his bets about the lawsuit. If the Clyde clan is killed, John gets everything whether he wins the suit or not."

Denton put his papers away. "Unless there's another heir somewhere. In the meantime, we have to investigate these Norton deaths while Judge Sands sorts out the Rule Against Perpetuities issue, which I think we'll win. I think it's best if I look into Peter and Jim Norton's deaths here in California. Tavita, I'd like you to go up to Wisconsin to look into Sylvia and William Norton's deaths."

Tavita smiled. "Sounds like an important job, boss. Thanks."

"Well, you've got your PI license now, and Charlotte says you can handle this. It's best if she stays here to run the office. I think things will be less complicated in Wisconsin than here in California, but you could use someone local to help. My Uncle Bill lives on Sissabagama Lake, not far from Hayward."

Charlotte's blue eyes grew wide, tracking this fresh insight. "An Uncle Bill? In Wisconsin? You never mentioned him before."

"Ah, yeah. My mom's brother, Bill Higgins. He's a bit of a character. They call him Bobcat Bill because of the way he could stalk game without making a sound. When he was young, he'd slide through the woods, quiet as a bobcat. Mom always said he could get as mean as a bobcat too, but he was always nice to me. I haven't seen him in years."

Denton's voice trailed off as he thought about youthful times with Uncle Bill. He recalled the summer his father had died in an airplane crash and how he'd spent two months with Uncle Bill, who was on a sixty-day recuperative leave from wounds he'd suffered in a military operation he wouldn't talk much about. He'd fought two days with a bullet in his arm before the medics hauled him off in a stretcher. He'd gotten pissed off when the medics hauled him off the "field of honor," as he put it. Uncle Bill had taught Denton to fish, to stalk deer, and to drink beer.

"Boss?"

"Yeah. I hung out with him some when I was a kid. Christ, he must be pushing eighty. I'll call and let him know you'll be coming. At a minimum, he'll provide local knowledge. You don't want to go blundering around up there if you don't know the way things work."

12

As Charlotte and Tavita left his office, Denton paged through his address book and found Uncle Bill's number. A still-familiar gruff voice answered.

"Hey, it's Lee."

"Lee? Lee who?"

"Denton. Leland Denton. Your favorite nephew."

"Leland... oh, Amy's boy. How ya doin'?"

"Fine, Uncle Bill, just fine."

"You still a little fat kid?"

Denton cringed, knowing Uncle Bill was referring to the summer they'd first met. At twelve, Denton was short and plump, a condition that an adolescent spurt of growth had cured. "No, Uncle Bill, I'm now six-two, one hundred ninety-five pounds. I work out all the time. How about you? I'm guessing you're old and drooling, with the mental capacity of a gnat."

Uncle Bill's laugh cascaded through the phone connection. "I deserved that. Hell, I knew you'd grown up good. Amy used to send me pictures. I got one of you in your U.S. Army rig somewhere around here."

Thoughts of his Army uniform evoked red memories, thoughts Denton shoved away.

"Uncle Bill. I've a favor to ask."

"Clyde Norton told me how you left him in the lurch, Lee. I been meanin' to talk to you. I guess you know that's not the way to handle things."

Denton's stomach fluttered. "Yeah, but it's a long story, Uncle Bill. I've got my own side."

"Yeah, I'm sure you do. Well, what the hell. You're back in the saddle now, right?"

"Yessir."

"Okay, I guess that *does* make you my favorite nephew. Only one, too."

Denton laughed and outlined the circumstances, explaining about the Norton deaths and about Tavita's upcoming trip.

"A Samoan? What the hell's a Samoan?"

"Come on, Uncle Bill, no kidding. It would be a big help if you could just show him around the territory. Show him where the police and sheriff's offices are. Places to eat. Just a few hours would be enough."

"Aw, sure. Send him on up here to the lake. I've got lots of room. He can bunk in with me for a few days. I could use another hand around the house."

"That's what he's got."

"What?"

"One hand. It's a long story, Uncle Bill. I just wanted to let you know so you wouldn't... well, say anything."

"Yeah, like I would. Anyway, it's fine. Send him up. Tell him to bring rain gear and warm clothes."

"Thanks, and I will." Denton hung up. He buzzed Charlotte and asked her to send in Tavita, whom he knew would be hovering around her desk.

"Okay, Tavita. Uncle Bill says you can stay with him for a few days and..." Noticing Tavita's doubtful expression, Denton added, "Look, he volunteered. I just asked him to take a few hours to show you around. He'll be useful. He spent twenty-five years in the Marines. He landed at Inchon with General McArthur. Got a Purple Heart and a Silver Star. Retired as a full colonel. I'm sure he doesn't get around all that much these days. Hell, he's probably lonely."

The sour expression still clung to Tavita's face. "Well, okay. I just hope the place doesn't stink of old folks' liniments and stuff."

13

Mid-September. Madison, Wisconsin.

Wisconsin Attorney General Richard Elkin was home in his den, paging through a scrapbook lying on the gleaming surface of his mahogany and cherrywood desk. He wore khaki chinos below a gray angora sweater. His bare feet were encased in soft calfskin loafers with long tassels. The shining desktop reflected his image: steady eyes in an oval face under well-combed blond hair. He appreciated his own good looks a moment, then reached for his cut crystal glass of rare scotch. It was so nice to be rich and handsome. He sipped the expensive liquid, letting its smoky taste linger on his tongue. Life was good… or it had been.

Now he had problems. The quality scotch caressed his palate. Manicured fingers sorted through old newspaper headlines. "Capone Gang Runs Amok." "Capone Hideout Discovered Near Hayward, Wisconsin." "Capone Arrested. Will Be Tried for Tax Evasion." "Capone Diagnosed With Syphilis." "Capone at Alcatraz." "Capone's Two Sons." "Capone's Son Changes Name."

Elkin's pale hand trembled as he set down the glass. He picked up an old photo of Al Capone. The gangster's plump lips were curled in a cruel smile, a big cigar jutting at an angle from his mouth, a white fedora on his head. Elkin felt the alcohol's warmth spread within him. But his thoughts turned to the anonymous note he'd received a few months earlier.

Attorney General Richard Elkin. I have important information concerning your mother. I have a birth certificate and other documents that prove she was the illegitimate daughter of Al Capone. I realize this is very sensitive information because it might indicate your sister's mental institutionalization is connected with Mr. Capone's syphilis. Further, the press might suggest the disease affects you. I prefer to remain anonymous, but will turn these documents over to you if you will contact me as indicated.

The note had arrived in a white envelope postmarked Stone Lake, Wisconsin, just after he'd announced his candidacy for governor. *This is blackmail,* he'd thought. *This guy's out for a big payoff.* He stared at the 715 area code and phone number the blackmailer had provided. It was the area code for Hayward, Stone Lake, and a dozen other places in Sawyer County.

His first thought was *What bullshit.* Confident the blackmailer was lying, Elkin turned on his computer and logged online. Capone had gone to prison in the early 1930s. Elkin's mother Mildred was born around 1929 or 1930.

He had been drinking his expensive scotch then, too, and he'd taken a big slug and smiled as the liquor enhanced his confidence. He'd disprove the asshole's bullshit in five minutes flat.

But that wasn't how it worked. Instead, his confidence melted away as he did a Google search. Capone had been released on parole in 1939. He didn't die until 1947. *And, Christ, he'd had a son, possibly two. And the son was affected by Capone's syph!* It was called "inherited" or "congenital" syphilis. *Fuck!*

Elkin had rocked back in his desk chair, banging a knee on the computer keyboard tray. He'd yelled in frustration, thrown his glass across the room. His wife, Sally, had rushed into the room.

"Dear, dear. What happened?"

"Nothing. I banged my knee, dropped my glass."

Sally had eyed the glass lying in the corner, its contents soaking the carpet. "Okay, dear. I'll get a sponge."

Then, his mind had twirled with confusion as he watched Sally clean up his mess. But now he had to focus on this blackmailer. He had to clean up *this* mess before it spilled out into the news.

As the sitting state attorney general, he had ready access to numerous investigators. Still, he had to be careful. He wanted his investigators to find the man or woman without discovering the Capone thing. *Shit! If this gets out…* He could imagine the headlines: "Elkin Capone's Grandson!" "Elkin's Sister Brain-Damaged by Syph!" *No way. No fucking way.*

The note was handwritten on the top half of a letter-sized sheet of white paper. There were no watermarks, but Elkin knew the type of paper could provide clues. He'd cut the note in half and used the bottom part for a different demand note, one he wrote himself and printed out with his left hand. The new note threatened to kill his institutionalized sister if he didn't pay one million dollars. He would give the fake blackmail demand to his chief investigator, Allen Sanger, who would send a dozen investigators streaming out of Madison, Wisconsin, looking for the blackmailer. Allen Sanger was thorough. Even better, he had the balls to take any necessary action.

Elkin looked at his own face dominating the front page of that day's *Wisconsin State Journal.* At forty-nine, he still looked young. His blond hair, Nordic blue eyes, and smooth features made him a handsome candidate. His powerful jawline gave him the look of a genuine crime buster, a look the juries had adored back when he was a felony prosecutor. Wisconsin hadn't had the death penalty since 1853, but he'd sent dozens of men and six women to prison for life.

He stood and flexed his back muscles, glad that he stayed in shape, keeping his weight at two hundred. A little heavy for a guy six feet tall, but not bad.

He read the headline again: "Elkin Leads Polls by 12%." He would win the governorship in a romp. If he could keep the Capone connection quiet, that is.

He'd long known Capone had a refuge in northern Wisconsin, just a few miles out of the small village of Couderay. Nowadays, the Capone place was a tourist attraction called "The Hideout." It boasted a private lake, full restaurant, and guided tours. Elkin had grown up in Hayward, not far from Capone's place, now a restaurant and tourist site called The Hideout. He'd learned early on that, as a teenager, his grandmother, Lottie, had been a maid at the Capone place. But there had never been any hint of a Capone sexual connection. Family lore said Lottie had married Ivan Skonsky, a local farmer who was twelve years older than she was. They had a little girl named Mildred, who was born shortly after the marriage. Mildred was Elkin's mom. In 1960, she'd married a man named Jack Elkin, and Richard was born almost a year later. His sister Maud was born three years after that. Jack Elkin had died when Richard was six, and his mother had passed away five years ago after several years of Alzheimer's. *If it really was Alzheimer's. And what about Maud?*

His sister Maud had been institutionalized for years, diagnosed with schizophrenia. Cold chills rippled at his neck and down his back. *Shit! What if it's true?* The idea of syphilis disgusted him. The notion that the disease was lurking inside him, dormant but waiting for its time, was unbearable.

He stared at the tawny liquid in its delicately etched glass. He bought it by the case from a small island off Scotland. The glass reflected the photo of Al Capone's face, warping and distorting it, turning Capone into an ugly gargoyle. Elkin drank down the scotch and poured himself another three fingers. He stared out his window into the night, his fingers rapping on the old news article.

14

Late August. San Diego.

Denton squirmed in gray slacks and a navy blazer as he flew from San Diego to San Francisco to investigate Jim Norton's death. He'd loosened his blue and red striped tie as soon as he was seated, but still felt claustrophobic in his clothes. He stared out the airplane window, squinting in the early morning sun as the plane flew its low approach over the back of San Francisco Bay. He eyed Foster City and the park at Coyote Point, where he had sometimes jogged when he'd stayed at hotels near the airport.

He felt an urge to jog through the 670 acres of Coyote Point. Now a tree-filled park, in the 1940s it was home to a merchant marine academy. Now the only evidence of the academy was a bronze memorial on a stone hill overlooking the bay and a small marina. Denton had lingered there on a sunlit morning in the shade of old trees. He'd visualized young men standing in the same spot, spending a few moments of farewell before boarding their ships to run the U-boat gauntlet. Many were still at sea, among the six thousand merchant marine sailors who never returned.

But today, Denton had business in the Santa Cruz Mountains, where twenty-seven-year-old Jim Norton's BMW 328i had plunged off a cliff. He wanted to observe the scene of the accident to form his own judgment about how it might have occurred. Because the accident had happened while Jim was on the way to his sailboat in Half Moon Bay, Denton also planned to go to the boat and check it out. After looking over Jim's boat, *Mariposa*, Denton would drive back to San Francisco to meet with the doctor who had performed Jim's autopsy. Then Denton would meet with Jim's father's doctor. Maybe the doctor had an opinion whether Peter Norton really had had a heart attack.

When the plane landed at SFO, Denton hurried to pick up his rental car, a sleek silver Buick Lucerne that purred as he sped south on Highway 101. At State Road 92 he took a right and drove over the dam between Upper and Lower Crystal Spring Reservoirs, slim artificial lakes lying in the rift of the San Andreas Fault. On earlier trips to San Francisco, Denton had jogged the ten-mile trail that snaked along the eastern side of the lakes. As he'd run through a shaded gully, he came upon a placard declaring he was in the presence of the world's largest bay laurel tree. He'd jogged in place, looking at the tree, smelling the tannic aroma of fallen leaves. The biggest in the entire world. What was the term? *Superlative?* The biggest, the most, the rarest of its kind. Yet it stood lonely in gloomy light overshadowed by another superlative: the San Andres Fault that would eventually snap, plunging the laurel and much of San Francisco into eternity. Nothing is permanent; not the biggest, not the best, not the most.

Denton maneuvered the Buick along SR 92 as it wound through the Santa Cruz Mountains towards Half Moon Bay. Soon he came to the hairpin switchback where Jim Norton's car had flown off the cliff, landing several hundred feet down in Pilarcitos Creek.

Denton parked the car as close as he could against the brush-covered cliff opposite the drop. He exited the car and edged over to the chasm. Vertigo immediately seized him, and he had to sit down. *Fuck!* He closed his eyes, riding out the dizziness. *Goddamn this weakness.* His thoughts filled with memories of a desperate flight

through the cliffs and canyons at Torrey Pines State Park north of San Diego. *Just over a year ago.* Vertigo had hit him then, too. The disability could have allowed the thugs to catch him. Or he could have tumbled off the cliff. But he'd fought through it, the same way he was doing now. *I had to kill a guy then.*

A rising wind carried the smell of sage and fine sand. The dizziness passed. He stood and forced himself to look down the brush-laden cliff at the small stream below. Denton shivered as he envisioned Jim Norton crushed and bleeding in that cold water. The medical reports Charlotte had compiled suggested the young man might have languished in the wreck several hours before dying of exposure and blood loss. *A hard and lonesome death.*

A blue Miata buzzed past, its slipstream pushing Denton toward the drop-off. Denton caught a vague image of the driver's face, then the cloud of fine dust chasing the Miata fell upon Denton like malicious fog. Vertigo snatched at him, and Denton reared away from the cliff edge.

Damn! Why do heights affect me like this? He sneezed as he sidled back to the cliff and forced himself to again gaze at Jim Norton's death scene. Denton scribbled notes in the small steno book he'd brought along and drew a diagram of the area. As he finished the drawing, the pen ran out of ink. *Great.* He threw the pen over the edge and watched it bounce along the rocky slope until it disappeared into a swath of sage. He didn't expect pens to last forever, but it would be nice to have one last a whole day.

He contemplated the scene. It would have been easy for a driver to lose concentration for a moment and drive off this sharp turn. Anybody could do it.

But what if it wasn't accidental? How would a murderer have set it up? Denton doubted the movie cliché where killers cut brake fluid lines. Besides, Jim had driven a long way before he got to the turn. Damaged brakes would have revealed themselves by then. Probably.

He spotted a yellow Hummer coming around the sharp turn. Two burly men sat in the front seat. The vehicle came directly at him. He jumped aside and crouched at the very edge of the drop-off as the Hummer whizzed past, covering him in dust, shoving him toward the abyss. He turned his face from the dust cloud and spread his legs to maintain his balance. Small pieces of gravel stung the back of his neck. *Shit! I need to get off this place.*

He hurried to his rental car, tossed his steno book onto the passenger seat, and drove down the winding highway toward Half Moon Bay. As he carefully steered around the curves, trying not to look over the drop-offs, he realized the driver of the blue Miata had seemed familiar. He was youthful and smooth-featured, with long brown hair.

A rabbit dashed across the road. Denton swerved to avoid it, wheels churning gravel at the side of the road. *Fuckin' rabbit. Next time, you're road kill.*

Denton scanned his memory of the blue Miata and its driver, but he couldn't summon a clear picture. Still, the driver was reminiscent of that guy Gustav. Mary's boyfriend. But the image wasn't clear.

What *was* clear in his mind was the rabbit's desperate flight, its crazed eyes fixed on Denton's car. One millisecond slower and it would be a furry blob on the side of the road, the elusive spark of life within extinguished as if it had never been. *Just like drowned sailors. Or murdered heirs.* He smothered his thoughts, concentrating on the road and its abrupt turns, avoiding the chasms.

As he entered the small town of Half Moon Bay, he pulled to the side of the road and checked ink-smeared notes in his steno pad that told him how to get to Jim Norton's sailboat. *Name Mariposa, slip thirty-two, Half Moon Bay Marina.* As he checked the directions to the marina, a new idea came to mind. What if somebody was in the car with Jim Norton? What if that somebody got Jim to stop, slugged him, and pushed the car over the edge? Denton realized the

notion was straight out of the movie *The Postman Always Rings Twice*, and laughed aloud at his over-active imagination. But still…

He drove into town and easily found the Half Moon Bay Marina where Jim had kept *Mariposa*. Denton felt the faint vibrations of the Buick's tires crunching over the graveled parking lot. He pulled into a spot near the boat docks and scanned the area for blue Miatas or yellow Hummers.

Nope. Nobody around. He yanked his briefcase from the back seat, exited the car, and walked to the ramp leading down to the wooden floating docks. He found the thirty-two footer rocking gently in her slip.

Mariposa's bird-guano-splattered decks made her seem unloved, abandoned to an uncertain fate. *Needs a wash and wax*, Denton thought as he searched his steno pad for the combination lock number. He twiddled brass dials and was soon below in the neat cabin with its well-maintained teak trim. Denton's nose tickled from the faint scent of mildew, and he sneezed.

He set his steno book on the teak navigation station. But his pen was over the cliff. *Jim must have a pencil or pen in the nav station.*

The brass hinges of the desk-like top of the nav station squeaked as he lifted it. Inside he found Jim's navigational instruments. The tools were made by Weems & Plath, the same as Denton's. He lifted out a seven-inch, nickel-plated divider. Its bright surface flashed in the dim light of the cabin. He examined the course plotter, a combination protractor and ruler that had seen much use. Near the instruments lay several paper navigational charts that bore the pencil lines and waypoint markings of several voyages, including one to Hawaii and back. *Jim was the real deal.* The chart markings reminded Denton of his own voyages, his solitary days at sea, and the recent ones with Sandy at his side.

Denton spotted a green plastic box holding several pencils. Best of all, there was a new-looking black felt tip pen. *I'll take it as a fee. I'm working on Jim's business anyway.* Denton happily snatched it up. The teak top squeaked when he closed it.

Denton looked over Jim's electronic navigation instruments. A Raymarine combination chartplotter and radar, an Icom single-sideband radio for long distance communications, and a Uniden VHF radio for shorter range. *Jim knew what he was doing.*

He opened his steno pad and touched the tip of his new pen to a blank page. The black ink flowed easily. He recorded recollections of Jim's accident scene, including the blue Miata and yellow Hummer.

Finished with his notes, he looked over the instrument panel next to the nav station and flipped on the battery switch to check the voltage. Many boats sank at their own docks, particularly un-used boats whose automatic bilge pumps didn't work because the battery banks were dead. Sure enough, *Mariposa's* batteries were low and needed charging. Denton thumbed on the battery charger and watched its needles flick up, indicating it was working. He'd have Charlotte find out who was supposed to be taking care of the boat and tell them the charger was on.

Pleased with himself, Denton looked around, appreciating the shipshape cabin. His eyes fell on a bookshelf on the port side. It was built into the bulkhead next to the settee that functioned as an eating and lounging booth. He left the nav station, slid across the green cloth seat, and began looking through the several books. There were volumes on navigation, sail trim, and sea routes; all the normal things he'd expect. Then Denton found a book on genealogy research, *How to Find Your Ancestors*.

Surprised, Denton opened the book and riffled the pages. A note on lined tablet paper fell out. It read: "Uncle John, Uncle Clyde, Dad, Aunt Sylvia, and Uncle George." Denton ran the Norton family tree through his mind. This was a list of Asa and Sarah Norton's grandchildren. It included the missing George Norton Schneider.

Denton searched the rest of the book, but found nothing else. Denton slipped the note into his steno book, carefully jotting down the time and place he'd found it, creating an evidentiary authentication, a chain-of-custody that would make it admissible in court if he ever needed it. He'd ask Charlotte to see what she could discover about long gone Uncle George.

Denton climbed up the wooden rungs of the boat's companionway ladder, replaced the door slats, and locked it. He glanced around the cockpit. Next to the wheel lay a red pair of sailing gloves with frayed leather palms and cut-out fingertips. Denton pulled one on. It fit. He clenched his fist. The glove was supple, well-worn. *Just like mine.* He took off the glove and laid it carefully with its mate.

Denton left the boat and walked to his car. He opened the door, but lingered, contemplating *Mariposa.* Her wind-whipped halyards slapped against her aluminum mast, the hollow metal noise playing its part in an atonal marimba-like symphony from the banging halyards of other boats. His mind tried unsuccessfully to decipher this cryptic music of chaos.

He entered the car, the closing door shutting out the boat sounds. As he drove through Half Moon Bay, his mind remained with *Mariposa*—orphaned in her slip, joining other lonely boats in a song of the universe.

His stomach growled. He spied a restaurant, "Pasta Moon," and parked near the entrance. He remained in the car while he called Charlotte.

"Hi, boss, how goes it?"

"Fine. I'm in Half Moon Bay."

"Have you eaten anything? You need to eat, you know."

"No, but I'm parked right in front of an Italian restaurant."

"Okay. Good."

"You know that affidavit Clyde gave me about George Norton Schneider?"

"Yes. Just a sec, let me find it."

Denton could hear the scrabbling of paper, the "thunk" of something heavy falling over. He thought he heard a muffled expletive, then Charlotte's calm voice returned. "Yes. I found his birth certificate and a few other documents that prove he existed, but there's nothing on him since 1944. "

"So what did you knock over, Char?"

"My outbox."

"Oops. Well, check out this George some more. How he died, and so on."

"Okay, but it's easy for you to say, 'and so on.' So what are you having for lunch?"

Denton smiled, appreciating Charlotte's concern. "Don't worry, Sarge, it'll be nourishing."

"I hope so. You need to eat right. You're all set for your meeting at the county coroner's office, where you can review Jim Norton's file *and* interview one Dr. William Herbert, who performed Jim's autopsy. Then at two p.m. you meet Peter Norton's primary care guy, Dr. Albert Smith."

"Yep, I remember. Thanks again. I'm sure it wasn't easy setting those up."

"Who needs easy? But don't be late for Dr. Smith. He's a busy guy."

"So find a doctor who isn't."

"True. Have a good lunch."

Denton caught the aroma from Pasta Moon as he exited his car carrying his steno pad. The garlic-laden atmosphere made his stomach beg. Inside, he chose a corner table. Memories of Skinny, the guy who had tailed him after his court appearance, the blue Miata and the yellow Hummer were fresh on his mind. And what about the red pickup? He remembered Crewcut and Goatee, the two men who had tailed him and tried to kill him on his last case. He preferred to dine with his back to a wall. *I wish I had my lucky briefcase with my pistol,* he thought.

He ordered Spaghetti Alla Puttanesca, a house specialty containing tiger prawns, sea scallops, manila clams, anchovies and a variety of vegetables. He asked for a glass of the house Chianti. He usually avoided a large lunch, but knew he'd be late getting home. The lunch came with a green salad. *Charlotte would be happy.*

He ate slowly, sipping the house Chianti, which turned out to be good, the perfect match for his pasta dish.

Finished, he asked for a cup of coffee and set his steno pad on the table. He pulled out the note he'd found in Jim's genealogy book. Jim's list read, "Uncle John, Uncle Clyde, Dad, Aunt Sylvia, and Uncle George." These were the grandchildren of Asa and Sarah Norton. Now Jim's dad, Peter, was dead. So was Sylvia. George was long gone. That left only John Jr. and Clyde, who were the chief litigants in the lawsuit.

As Denton pondered its significance, the waiter arrived with his coffee. Denton snatched up the note. Explaining coffee stains to a judge would be embarrassing. The cup and saucer clattered as the waiter set them down. "Anything else, sir?"

"No, just the bill," Denton said. That's how life was, always a bill to pay. He read the note again: "Uncle John, Uncle Clyde, Dad, Aunt Sylvia, and Uncle George." What bills had this group paid? What bills were still to be paid in this bitter family feud over money and wounded pride?

Denton tipped back his coffee cup, letting the few remaining drops patter his tongue. He remembered meeting Jim Norton a few times. He'd been tall and blond, with a happy attitude. But that was all over now. Denton thought of the young man lying in the cold canyon, waiting for help that never came. *Mariposa* hung across Denton's memory, alone in her slip, nudging the dock on gentle eddies.

15

Denton left the Pasta Moon and drove through scrubbrush-laden canyons that maintained an ancient solitude despite the intrusion of the highway and its hurried vehicles. The primal mood burst when he reached San Mateo, a nice town, but nevertheless full of modern civilization—the rustle, bang, and bustle he'd tried to escape. He located the neat, modern building housing the county coroner's office and parked his car. He remained seated, gathering his thoughts, preparing for his interview with the doctor who had examined Jim Norton's body. He retrieved his steno pad and read over his notes, adding the comment: "Check for blunt force head injuries."

As he exited the rental car, he spotted a penny lying on the parking lot pavement. His mantra, "Find a penny, pick it up and all day long you'll have good luck," spun through his mind. He knelt and picked it up. It was tails, but he didn't totally believe the idea that only heads was good luck. He pocketed the small coin. Worse case, tails had to be neutral. Probably.

He entered the sand-colored building and was soon speaking to the pathologist who had done Jim Norton's autopsy. Dr. William Herbert listened to Denton with ill-disguised impatience. His washed-out blue eyes squinted in the bright light of his office just off the hospital's morgue. Dr. Herbert wore a long white coat minus the usual stethoscope. *Here's one doc that doesn't need to check his patient's heartbeats.* A boney wrist stuck out of the man's coat sleeve as he pointed Denton to a chair beside a gray metal desk.

Denton noticed age spots on the doctor's downturned head as he read from his report. Thin fingers closed the file, and faint medicinal odors filled Denton's nostrils. *Formaldehyde? Embalming fluid? Companion bouquets to death and decay. The sooner this fuckin' case is over, the better.*

The doctor's pale hand patted the file. "This young man was pretty smashed up. But he did survive for quite a long time after the accident. There are clear signs of hypothermia. In fact, I think he might have recovered from his injuries if he'd gotten immediate medical attention. But lying in cold water induced hypothermia that exacerbated his injuries and led to his death."

Denton made a note on his steno pad. "Did you note any head injuries that could have been blunt force trauma?"

"Yes, of course. Car wrecks often cause blunt force trauma."

"Yeah, but is it possible someone slugged him and pushed him off the cliff?"

With fidgety eyes, Dr. Herbert studied Denton. "Well, it's hard to say. The man went over a cliff. His head took a beating on the way. I suppose anything's possible, but I didn't see any obvious evidence of the kind of thing you suggest."

"I don't mean to suggest, doc. Just asking. You know, checking out the angles. By the way, does the file have the names of the guys who pulled Mr. Norton from the wreck?"

Dr. Herbert sighed and ran a hand over his scalp. "Probably so. Just a moment."

From Dr. Herbert's office Denton went to the information desk and asked where he could find C. Bob Wilkins and Marshall Sunday, the two young men who had descended the cliff to recover Jim Norton's body.

The plump, middle-aged woman smiled, dimples appearing in her rosy cheeks. She could have made money posing for Hallmark Christmas cards. "You must be livin' right, 'cause it's your lucky day. They're right here. Just down the hall at a meeting. It should be over any minute."

Denton slid a hand into his pocket and felt the penny. "Well, I guess I *am* lucky. I'll just wait for them to finish up."

Ten minutes later, Denton sat across a small wooden conference room table from two muscular young men. C. Bob Wilkins was white and blond, and Marshall Sunday was black with an Afro. An aura of good health and strength radiated from them as they gazed expectantly at Denton. Both worked at the San Mateo Fire Department and were proud of their jobs.

"Yes sir," said C. Bob with a southwestern twang, "we roped on down to the creek, Pilarcitos Creek, and we got that poor guy out and brought him on up. I'm sorry he died."

Marshall Sunday nodded. "Yeah, it was pretty routine," he said, wiping dust from the edge of the table. "Like, the roping down wasn't too hard, but that guy was sure busted up. He was lying in cold water for a long time. I don't know how long. He was about dead when we got to him. He could barely speak."

Denton's breath stopped. "What? He was still alive?"

"Just barely."

"He spoke?"

"Kind of spoke. He said some words I couldn't understand, except for the last word that was 'orge' or something like that."

"Orge?"

Marshall looked at the table dust on his fingertips, then wiped it on his pants. "Yeah, something like that. I guess from being down in the *gorge*, maybe."

"Could it have been George?"

Marshall Sunday looked up toward the ceiling, his eyes squinting into the past. "Yes sir, it *could* have been."

16

Denton left the San Mateo coroner's office and walked across the parking lot toward his rented silver Buick Lucerne. It gleamed in the early afternoon sun. As he punched the electronic door opener, he spotted two large men sitting in a yellow Hummer two spaces over.

He froze, the back of his neck tingling. He yanked open the car door and slid inside, slamming the door behind him. He locked the doors. *Take it easy. Relax. That doesn't have to be the same vehicle.* But how many yellow Humvees were there? How likely was it he'd see two in the same day?

He silently cursed the tight airport security that had prevented him from bringing his Hi-Power. His eyes fixed on the two men in the yellow vehicle. Could they be the same guys he'd seen in the red Ford Pickup back in San Diego?

He started his rented Buick and entered Highway 280. As he drove north, he saw the yellow Hummer trailing behind him.

He thought through his tae kwan do routines. After all, he was a third degree black belt. *I can take care of myself... unless they've got guns.* The thought of guns jangled Denton's nerve ends. He'd had enough gun fights to last three lifetimes. Memories of his wounds, of where and how he'd gotten them, made him flinch at the idea of getting into another shootout. *This time I'm unarmed.*

He reached over to his navy blazer lying on the passenger seat and fumbled his cell phone out of its pocket. *I'll call 911. But what will I say?* As he pondered his options, the Hummer exited the highway and disappeared benignly down the ramp, its ugly butt in the air.

Denton's nerves calmed. *Get a grip.* Hell, there had to be hundreds of yellow Humvees in the Bay Area. And the guys in this one couldn't be the ones who had followed him in San Diego.

He exited Highway 280 at Highway 101 and then followed the off-ramp at Potero Road. He located the low building adjacent to San Francisco General Hospital where Dr. Albert Smith had his office. Denton checked his watch. It was two minutes ahead of his appointed time. His luck was holding.

Dr. Albert Smith was short, fat, and jolly. His thin, sand-colored hair was neatly combed, and he wore a stethoscope across his shoulders, signaling that his patients usually had heartbeats. His light gray eyes studied Denton.

"Nice to meet you, Mr. Denton. Let's find a place to talk."

Dr. Smith escorted Denton into an examination room and gestured at the exam table. Denton sat on the table, the white paper cover crackling under his weight. The doctor sat on a small wheeled stool, his stethoscope glinting as he leaned forward.

Dr. Smith glanced at his vintage 1950s gold Bolivia. "Your assistant called and said you wanted to discuss Peter Norton's death. What can I do for you?"

"I know you're busy, doc. Could you tell if Mr. Norton had a long history of heart disease?"

The doctor swung his stool around and grabbed a file. "Let's see, let's see. Ah, not really. He had some arterial plaque build-up, and I'd medicated him with statins and put him on a low-cholesterol diet. I certainly didn't expect a heart attack. But these things happen. Even in men without obvious symptoms. His death was quite sudden and unexpected."

"Unexpected?"

Dr. Smith shifted his weight, his light gray eyes sparkling. "Yes, certainly. My treatment was the usual for a man in Peter's condition."

"Could the heart attack have been caused by an outside agency?"

"Outside agency?"

"Well, poisons, chemicals, or drugs, for example?"

The doctor's small chin sagged, revealing bright white dentures. "Poisons, chemicals, or drugs?"

"Yeah. I remember a couple of murders. That Nevada state controller case. Her husband killed her with some drug that was hard to detect. The death looked like a heart attack. You know what I'm referring to?"

Dr. Smith shut his file. "Yes. That drug was succinylcholine. It's sometimes used in the process of executions by lethal injection."

"Well?"

Dr. Smith stood and ostentatiously looked at his watch. "No, I didn't check for anything like that. Nobody asked me to."

No more the jolly physician.

17

Late August. Madison, Wisconsin.

About the time Denton left Dr. Smith's office, Wisconsin Attorney General Richard Elkin was meeting with his chief investigator, Allen Sanger, a big, well-groomed man in his late thirties. Elkin believed Allen Sanger was the ideal man for this delicate situation. Sanger's muscular body made him formidable, but his soft brown eyes peering through black-rimmed, Clark Kent glasses made him seem innocuous. Sanger reminded Elkin of his favorite high school English teacher. Sanger's regular features and the perpetual eager gleam in his eyes completed the ideal. But Elkin knew the outward impression was misleading. Sanger had killed two men in the line of duty when he was still a lieutenant in the Madison police force. Elkin was confident he would kill again if he needed to.

Elkin handed Sanger the blackmail note he'd faked. "This is the blackmail demand I received."

Sanger studied the paper. His face contorted, and his voice rose. "This is outrageous, Richard. Disgusting."

Elkin replied, "Yes, it is. I'm very worried about my sister. I don't want to put her in danger, but we have to find this person. We have to stop him."

"It could be a woman."

"Right."

Elkin's intercom buzzed and he answered, "Marge, I said not to disturb me."

His secretary, Marge Hawkins, replied, "Yes, sir. But you have a speech in thirty minutes. You need to leave soon to be on time." He noted she kept her voice professionally modulated.

A large diamond in Elkin's wedding ring glinted under the overhead lights as he checked the time. He stood and slipped on his tan suit coat, carefully adjusting the white cuffs of his shirt. Square gold cufflinks with diamonds drew Sanger's attention.

Elkin let Sanger stare, then said, "A present from an admirer."

"Nice."

"Yeah, they are. Anyway, do everything you can to find out who this goddamned blackmailer is, but keep it low profile. I don't want to read about this in the papers. Remember, once I'm governor, you'll be the next head of the Department of Justice. Among other things, you'll command the state troopers."

Sanger's large chest swelled. "Thanks, Richard. I'm depending on it."

"Don't fuck around on this. Get this blackmailer. Preferably, ah… make sure he won't interfere with me ever again."

Sanger kept his face impassive. "No problem, *Governor.*"

"Not yet, Allen. But close, real close."

As Sanger departed, Marge entered, carrying a thin manila file containing the notes for Elkin's speech. She was tall and trim. She wore a red and white blouse with long sleeves that ended with frilly cuffs. Her blond hair was cut short, accentuating the shape of her round face and bee-sting lips. She set the file on the desk in front of him and let her long fingernails scratch across the dark wood as she turned to leave.

"See you later," she said, pausing to let him see how her full breasts strained her blouse. She walked away, moving slowly, swaying her hips.

18

Late August. San Francisco.

As Richard Elkin was leaving to make his speech, Leland Denton's return flight lifted off San Francisco International's tarmac.

Denton closed his eyes and sat back in his seat. The collected images of his day vied for attention. Dr. William Herbert and his absent stethoscope. The smell of formaldehyde. *Mariposa*, lonely in her slip. Jim's worn sailing gloves.

A loud "ding" signaled they'd reached cruising altitude, breaking into Denton's reverie.

A voice asked, "Anything to drink?" Denton looked into the tired eyes of a flight attendant. Long trip, final leg.

He ordered a Jack Daniel's on the rocks and leaned back in his uncomfortable airline seat. He'd struck out with Peter Norton, learning nothing new except that Dr. Albert Smith hadn't checked for foreign substances that could have been the actual cause of death. What was that drug? Succ-something? *The doc sure did turn twitchy.*

But, still, he'd learned something about *Jim* Norton. He now knew that Jim was aware of the mysterious George Norton Schneider who had disappeared in Wisconsin. But 1944? And what about Jim's last words, the reference to "orge?" It could have just

been a sound, or it could have been "gorge." But still, it also could have been "George." Could Jim Norton have been naming his killer?

No, that doesn't wash. Not without more evidence. Besides, how could a guy in his eighties pull off Jim Norton's murder? On the other hand, Denton had seen guys in their eighties slamming tennis balls over the net or whacking golf balls off tees. It wouldn't take much force to slug a guy behind the ear with a rock... or a gun.

Denton watched the land slant away under the wing. Far below, billowing sea fog embraced coastal mountains. Denton unscrewed the top of his miniature bottle and poured the whiskey over melting ice cubes. He took a sip, letting it wash over his tongue and down his throat. *Nice.*

He watched the wing flaps grind back into their slots. The idea that he'd been followed insinuated itself into his reflections. The signs had been there. The blue Miata, the yellow Hummer. Skinny, the guy who'd followed him in San Diego. And the big ugly guys in the red pickup. Were they really following him, or was he getting neurotic? True, the six months he'd spent with Sandy on the open sea had made him unused to traffic. Rhythmic seas had calmed his troubled spirit. The experience of thugs chasing him during his last case had predisposed him to worry about a repeat.

Groping, he turned aside the air vent, blasting cold air into his face. Who would be following him? Who knew about his trip other than Charlotte and Tavita? Clyde Norton did. And it was Clyde who had clued him into George Norton Schneider. But so what?

George keeps coming up, that's what. And that trail leads to Wisconsin. Maybe he should go to Wisconsin and investigate the deaths of William Norton and his Aunt Sylvia.

The seat belt sign bonged. The pilot's voice filled the cabin. "Well, folks, thanks for flying with us today. It's time to buckle up again as we begin our descent into sunny San Diego."

Denton drained his plastic glass just before the flight attendant crammed it into her trash bag. What the hell, it was the end of her day. He was happy for her.

Denton retrieved his white BMW from Charles Lindberg Field and joined the throng of cars leaving the airport. Highway 5 was crowded as usual. He almost turned off to go to Shelter Island and have a drink in *Bruja Loca's* cockpit. He'd make a toast to Jim and *Mariposa*. But he wanted to get home to Sandy. Maybe they'd go sailing on the weekend. Sandy blended with the sea like a marine nymph, all laughter and radiance.

A sense of well-being engulfed Denton as he drove down his own driveway and saw Sandy wave a breezy "hello" from the kitchen window. Her smile reached out to him, welcoming his arrival, his return to those who loved him.

They went to their bedroom, locked Mutt out, and made love, slow and deep.

When they emerged an hour later, Mutt lay on the hallway carpet looking glum. Realizing they had about an hour before sunset, they changed into jogging clothes and put Mutt on his red leather leash for an evening run through nearby Torrey Pines State Reserve. The reserve was one of only two places the rare Torrey pine trees grew, their trunks and limbs gnarled and twisted by prevailing winds sweeping in from the Pacific Ocean.

They jogged up the steep Park Road until they reached the top of the mesa. Denton steered his mind away from memories of the gunfight he'd had here barely ten months earlier. He slowed his jogging pace so Mutt could keep up. Sandy loped along beside him, her blond hair tied in a pony tail and her cornflower blue eyes scanning the scenery around them. At the top, they ran along Razor Point Trail past the rock formation called Red Butte. It looked like a bizarre adobe dwelling. From Razor Point Trail they merged onto Yucca Point Trail and followed it to the edge of the cliff that hung one hundred feet above the beach below. When thugs had chased him down that beach, it had been roiling with storm-generated waves that scoured away the sand and almost claimed his life. But now it was serene. Easy waves lapped white sand. The setting sun cast a long, red swath upon the sea.

"Let's watch the sunset," said Sandy as they jogged in place.

Denton replied, "Okay. Maybe we'll see the Green Flash."

Sandy grinned. They'd both seen the Green Flash several times during their cruise on *Bruja Loca*. They'd sat naked in the cockpit, watching the sun sink into the sea. Just as the sun's last edge disappeared into the horizon, the refraction of the sun's light caused a bright line of glowing green to appear on the last slice of the sun's disk. Exotic. Mysterious. Part of his love of the sea.

Denton told himself the appearance of the bright green line would auger good luck. He wanted to see Sandy's eyes as she watched it. They sat on a rock near the cliff edge, but far enough back for Denton to avoid vertigo. He lifted Mutt onto his lap, and the little dog licked his fingers.

Sandy cried, "There it is," her slim finger pointing to the horizon.

"Yep," he said and watched Sandy's eyes. She was young, undamaged. She still believed in the possibility of a new tomorrow.

Denton knew his own happiness was fragile, mainly preserved by the little white pills he took to allow him to sleep without nightmares. He had rarely needed them at sea, but now he needed them again. *I should have stayed gone.*

As if reading his mind, Sandy whispered, "Maybe you shouldn't have come back, Lee." She slid loving arms around his neck and kissed him. "You're like the wind. A natural element... like the Green Flash."

Tears streaked her smooth cheeks. He wiped them away with his thumb. "No, I'm here. I'm here with you."

Her eyes stared into his.

19

The next morning, Denton roused from the repose of the well-loved. His mind lingered in the nebulous limbo-world between sleep and consciousness. Tendrils of a dream eluded his efforts of recall. He opened his eyes and saw Sandy's sleeping face. Long eyelashes, smooth cheek on a white pillowcase. Her lips were pink without makeup. A few strands of blond hair were caught in the corner of her mouth.

He extended a careful finger and pulled away the fine, golden hairs. The warmth of her body radiated. Sandy exuded a quality that called out to him, to a part of him that ached for human connection. He thought of previous relationships with women. Of how, at their deepest levels, there remained a disconnect. Somehow, something...

Sandy's eyes moved beneath sculptured eyelids. He smelled the sweetly sour scent of her breath. Once, just once, at sea he'd woken from a nightmare. Sandy held him softly and sang him back to sleep. Looking at her now, he remembered how he'd felt. *I don't need a mother. Yet, sometimes...*

But Denton knew his other side, the deep-set internal rage that powered his tae kwan do punches and allowed him to pull triggers. His mind turned away from soft, warm women to yesterday's experiences: Jim Norton's death scene, how the rescuers had found

Jim alive, and the talk with Peter Norton's doctor, who couldn't be positive of the cause of death. The memories were bad omens, portents of violence. How could so many Norton deaths be coincidence? *I should have stayed in the South Pacific*. Reluctantly, he slid out of bed and prepared himself for the work day.

An hour and a half later he was sitting in his big-backed chair staring at his drawing of the Norton family tree, looking for connections.

Charlotte buzzed the intercom. "Boss, it's Bobcat Bill."

"I'm so glad I mentioned his nickname."

"I'm sure. Anyway, here he is."

"Hey, Uncle Bill, how's it going?"

"You didn't tell me your Samoan needed his own barn."

Denton laughed. "Yeah, he's pretty big, but he's usually well-behaved."

"Hah! The first day here he put little wooden owls out all over the house. Says they're good luck that will shield us from hexes, black magic, and for all I know, mosquitoes. He shakes white conch shell rattles and does weird chants. Driving me fuckin' crazy."

"I'll talk to him. You want him to move out?"

"Nah, just tone it down a little. That's all. Did you know he thinks Samoans are related to the Ojibwe? He's been hanging out with John Batiste, an Indian I introduced him to. Batiste lives on the 'Rez,' the Lac Courte Oreilles Ojibwe Reservation, over by Hayward."

Denton thought about it. Samoans and Ojibwe related? Hard to buy, but anything was possible. "Well, I'll tell him to tone it down. I'll probably come up there in a few days."

"Be nice to see you, Lee. We could hang out some, talk about family, and reminisce about those summers we spent together. I'll even introduce you around. You can meet some of Tavita's new Indian friends."

"Sounds good. Remind me what Lac Courte Oreilles means."

"Sure. So the Frenchies find their way up here in the seventeen hundreds, fur trapping. They run into a wad of Ottawa Indians hanging around one of the lakes. Well, these Ottawas think it's cool to cut off their own earlobes; they think it improves their looks. You know, like kids nowadays think nose rings are cute. Anyway, Courte Oreilles is French for "short ears," or "cut ears.""

"Cut ears?"

"Yeah, so the Frenchies name the Indians 'Courte Oreilles.' Then they name the lake—'Lac' is Frenchie for lake—Lac Courte Oreilles after the Indians they met. But the joke is the Ottawa were just passin' through. The local Indians were actually Ojibwe. But the Frenchies don't know one Indian from another. The Ojibwe get named the 'Lac Courte Oreilles Band.' "

"What about the Chippewa?"

"That's another name for Ojibwe. You know how the Europeans always wanted to name everything they saw, even tribes of people who already had their own names."

"Yep. Kind of arrogant."

"Yeah. The Ojibwe were doing just fine without the Europeans."

Denton said, "Bye," and hung up. Then he dialed Tavita's cell phone. It rang several times before Tavita answered.

Denton said, "Uncle Bill says you're putting lucky owls all over the house, shaking rattles, and chanting."

"Oh. But boss, there's a lot of bad signs up here. I have to protect us from bad magic."

"Bad magic... Christ, Tavita."

"Yes, bad magic, boss. You should be here. This guy I met, John Batiste, says the Nortons have some Indian enemies up here. Peter Norton used to come up here to visit his cousin Sylvia and go fishing. He might have messed around with somebody's daughter. Might have pissed off some of the medicine men." Tavita's voice dropped an octave. "His heart attack could have been a hex."

Denton closed his eyes, trying to use Zen training to calm his mind. *Cool pond. Motionless lilies. A dragonfly, its wings catching the sun.* As usual, it didn't work.

"Boss?"

"Yeah. Just thinking. Look, I'll come up, be there in a few days. In the meantime, tone it down with Uncle Bill. He's getting old."

"*Old?* Hah. That guy's not old. He's got several girlfriends. Goes out dancing."

"Girlfriends?"

"Yeh, he's got about three, maybe four. All widows. They're keeping us well-fed. You oughta see the casseroles, the pies, the cakes."

Denton grinned. "Well, good for him. Just tone it down a little, Tavita. It sounds like you've got it pretty cozy up there. All that food. What have you found out about the Nortons?"

"I've got copies of the death certificates and the police reports. Looks like William fell off his boat on a sunny clear day while he was on a big lake named the Chippewa Flowage. He'd been scuba diving. His tank and BC were in the boat, but he was floating face down in his wetsuit, still wearing his mask and fins. He musta slipped and hit his head on the boat when he took off his tank and BC. Had a big knot on his head."

Denton let the vision play through his mind. *Another weird death.* "What could he have been diving for?"

"I don't know, boss. The lake's maybe thirty feet deep there. They have several drownings every summer."

Denton remembered the drownings. "What about Sylvia?"

"That's creepy, too. Stabbed forty-seven times. You know how that goes. Anybody that stabs someone that many times has to hate them. Or be scared of them."

"Yeah. What else you got?"

"They've arrested a guy. An Indian in his late fifties. He's in the Sawyer County Jail in Hayward. Your Uncle Bill got me in to

81

look at him. He hasn't said anything. Doesn't want a lawyer. Just looks at you with his black eyes. Just stared at me. Said nothin'. He's got some weird stuff in the cell with him. A string of cowry shells, a turtle shell rattle, and some other stuff."

"Cowry shells?"

"Yeh, boss. The shells look just like ones we have in Samoa. That's why I'm nervous, why I put out the lucky owls. You better bring Queeg if you come up here."

Denton stared at Queeg guarding the corner of his desk, motionless, basking in sunlight. "Why are they letting him have that kind of stuff in his jail cell?"

"Beats me. They're not as strict here as they are in San Diego or L.A. I suppose they figure 'no harm-no foul.' Besides, it keeps him quiet. Except for the rattles. How are things going in California?"

Denton paused. What had he accomplished? His hand reached for the drawing of the Norton family tree. It depicted surface connections, but not deeper family matters, not the skeletons in closets. The family had originated in Wisconsin. That was where he needed to go.

The sound of Tavita's breathing came over the phone line. "Are you having any luck, boss?"

"I've found out a few things, but I'm thinking the solutions may lie in the past. I think I'll come up, nose around some."

"That's a good idea. Be sure you have that lucky owl I put in your briefcase. Better bring your gun, too. And Queeg."

Denton hung up. Lucky owls. Conch shell rattles. Indian charms. He did his best to keep from thinking about Sylvia's forty-seven stab wounds, but images of dead women with bloody wounds pounded the backs of his eyes. Then there was Skinny the Stalker, the blue Miata, the yellow Hummer, and the red Ford F-150 pickup truck.

He called Sandy and explained his plans.

"That's fine, Lee. My mother's been asking me to visit. I'll drive up to L.A. and stay with her while you're in Wisconsin. I'll take Mutt with me."

"Okay, baby, good idea. Hey, let's go out to dinner tonight."

"Yes, we'll have a little farewell party."

Denton put down his phone, his eyes falling on Queeg. The idol stood impassive in the sunlight, like the hawk that lived in Denton's eucalyptus tree.

20

Late August. Madison, Wisconsin.

Attorney General Richard Elkin delivered the last lines of his campaign speech and listened to the applause. He had them. All the correct phrases and superficial ideas bound together with oratory. "And believe me, fellow citizens, together we'll take back the government, take back your rights, build your future and that of your children and grandchildren! Do the right thing!"

Camera flashes caught his face as he posed, careful to cast his eyes at an upward angle, giving the appearance of seeing far away visions of hope and justice for all. As he exited the stage, his chief investigator Allen Sanger signaled.

"Yeah, Allen?"

"We've called the phone number the blackmailer gave you. It's a TracFone he bought at a Wal-Mart for cash. You buy pre-paid cards to pay for service. It's untraceable."

"Don't you have to give a name and e-mail address to fire one of those up?"

"In theory, but all you actually have to do is input a fake e-mail and other contact information. Then you're all set to go and nobody can trace you." Sanger waited, listening to the applause still going.

Elkin's eyes were cold. "Well, did you call the number?"

"Yeah, I got a muffled voicemail. The message said, 'Hello, Attorney General Elkin, please leave me a message.'"

The clapping went on, becoming insistent. Elkin returned to the stage and waved at the crowd. A crescendo followed. Elkin clasped his hands, raised them to the crowd, then exited. "Was it a man's voice?"

"Probably, but it could be a woman. Like I said, it was muffled. I left a message asking him or her to call. Said we'd pay money."

"And the voice message actually used my name?"

"Yes."

Elkin listened to the applause die away. He had them. "All right. We have to get this asshole. What's the plan?"

"We'll agree to pay, then bust the blackmailer when we deliver the money." Sanger paused, his eyes shifting behind his glasses. "There's a complication."

"Okay, what?"

"The money's to be dropped off tomorrow night at the Middleton Railroad Depot. It's a public place."

"Where the hell is it?"

"It's an old train depot, just a few miles from here in Middleton, Wisconsin."

"Why there?"

"Who the fuck knows, Richard? But I've got a squad over there, staking things out. We'll get him... or her."

Attorney General Elkin wanted the blackmailer dead, not caught. *What if this information came out? What if there's one of those In-Case-of-My-Death things?* But Elkin knew it was best to go along with Sanger.

"Okay. Let's go, Allen," Elkin said, his voice mellowing. "I'll deliver the money."

"You don't need to stick your neck out. I'll handle it."

"No. I'll do it." Elkin had decided what to do. He'd carry his .38 Special, an Air Weight with an aluminum frame. Only the cylinder and barrel were steel. It held just five shots, but that would be enough. He'd make sure the blackmailer didn't survive the money drop. "I want to go. I want to see this person."

On his way home, Elkin stopped at Marge Hawkins' white brick condominium, the last one at the end of a tree-lined cul de sac. He punched a button on his sunshade, and the door of her two-car garage opened. He parked his black Cadillac El Dorado next to her white Porsche Targa and let himself in with the key she'd given him two years before. Why not? He paid the rent. He'd bought the Porsche. Well, technically, the public had paid the bill.

He found Marge sitting on her big white sofa wearing a thin negligee, sipping a martini, and watching gas logs burning in the fireplace. She stood to greet him, and the light of the fire tongued through her negligee. She lifted her glass and moved a bare foot, letting him see the darkness between her legs.

An hour and a half later, Elkin smiled as he started his El Dorado and backed out of Marge's garage. The car purred through the night as he drove home. Marge was hot. Her shuddering body always ready. Like the audience tonight. Ready to be stroked, primed. *Did they know they were being played? I've got this in the bag.* Soon he'd control the state the way he controlled Marge, who would do anything he wanted to do. She was so different from his straight-laced wife, Sally, who wouldn't even get on her knees and let him do it from behind. Yeah, Marge sure was something. *But maybe I shouldn't have told her about the blackmailer thing. Or about the Capone connection.* He'd been stupid, but she'd sucked him dry. The story had spilled out as he'd drifted in the throes of post-sex mindlessness. Burning regret pulsed through him. *I shouldn't have mentioned the Capone thing.*

21

Mid-September. North Wisconsin woods.

Morning claimed the forest. A squirrel chattered. Bird calls mingled with the blue light of dawn. Denton listened, knowing his confrontation with the bear was near. He scanned his refuge of fallen trees and brush, planning his exit. He needed open space for this fight. But bear fighting wasn't covered in his tae kwan do training. *Where do you shoot a bear? The eyes? No, I'd never hit an eye. The heart... but where's the heart?*

He put a comfort-seeking hand on his Browning Hi-Power and stretched his legs, trying to ease his aching back. *Great, a sore back along with the rest of this shit.* His head hurt, his arms were scratched and bruised, and his stomach wound burned. He fought to clear his head, to recall the days before, but fatigue controlled his blurred mind. How had he gotten into this scrape?

It had been easy, like getting into scrapes always was. One move leads to the next till you're waist deep in shit. First, the flight from San Diego's Lindberg Field to Minneapolis-St. Paul. Next, the white Camaro rental car. Then he'd worked up Highway 35 E, heading north, leaving the Twin Cities behind. At Highway 70 he'd driven east toward Hayward.

The further he drove, the more the forest claimed him, closing in on both sides of the road, tugging him back into its depths. At sunset, he crossed the wide St. Croix River that formed the border between Minnesota and Wisconsin. There were two canoes paddling downstream, silhouettes on the sun-flecked water.

What then? He remembered roaring past the "Welcome to Wisconsin" sign, when a long-forgotten excitement had washed over him, evoking memories of laughing vacations, canoe trips, and sleeping under shining stars when he was as green as the forest.

At Spooner, the highway jagged left, then right, and took him to Stone Lake. Just outside Stone Lake, two deer bounded across the highway, their tawny elegance presenting unexpected danger. Denton stepped hard on the brake pedal, momentarily skidding the rear tires. He yanked the wheel and regained control as the deer fled into roadside greenery.

He passed through Stone Lake and exited Highway 70 onto County Road B, which he followed to the end, where he took a right onto North Ranch Road. Then he followed old memories to Uncle Bill's cabin.

There it is. Denton stared, past the windshield and through intervening years, at boyhood memories from twenty years ago. It looked the same. It was built of multi-colored rocks from the local rivers, deposited ten thousand years earlier when the glaciers that created the Great Lakes had made their cold, inexorable retreat. Red, purple, brown, and sand-colored rocks contrasted with log pillars supporting the porch roof. Denton rolled down his window. A scent of pine rode the smoke flowing from the river rock chimney. Strange noises came from inside the cabin. Chanting. The high reedy sound of a flute. A drum. The sound of rattles. This wasn't a part of his childhood.

What the hell? Denton left the car, his feet crunching on the gravel path, his knuckles rapping on the thick wooden door. *Same old door.* As a child he'd had to reach up. No answer. Denton turned the door handle, pushing his way in.

The room was lit by candles and a fire that snapped and popped in the fireplace, smoke-stained from ten thousand fires. Three men danced in loincloths. Tavita blew eerie notes through a recorder, accompanied by Uncle Bill shaking a turtle shell rattle. A bony, gray-haired Indian wearing a cowry shell necklace pounded on a small drum. Tavita held up a fistful of dry weed. *Terrific. Pot, on top of everything else.*

Sweat washed down Tavita's painted face, sliding over the waxy red and black stripes. The intricate tattoos covering Tavita's body from mid-torso to just above his knees completed the bizarre tableau. Tavita threw the weed into the fire, the flame-light shining on his sweating body. Tavita put down the recorder and shook a rattle made of small white cowry shells while the thick scent of tobacco invaded the room. Uncle Bill rattled the stones inside the turtle shell rattle. The bony Indian pounded harder on his rawhide drum.

Suddenly, the eerie music stopped as the three men gawped at Denton, their chests heaving.

"Lee!" Uncle Bill shouted, wiping sweat from his eyes.

" 'Lo, boss," said Tavita. He raised his arm stump, sweaty and macabre in the flickering light. "Meet John Batiste."

Denton's recollections were shattered by a sudden movement in the nearby brush. The bear was rousing. He realized it was almost time to leave his shelter. He'd go in a few minutes, right after he let his aching back rest a little more. Memories of the eerie scene of Tavita, Uncle Bill, and the thin Indian flowed back into his mind.

Tavita and Uncle Bill explained that they'd consulted John Batiste about possible hexes affecting the Nortons. John Batiste's dark eyes shimmered beneath his black painted forehead. A tense smile split the red paint on the lower part of his face. His graying hair formed a long braid down the center of his back. His skin was like old leather. His eyes were suspicious within shadowed sockets.

Those black pupils bored inside Denton, finding some indefinable lack.

Tavita lumbered to the refrigerator, pulled out four brown bottles of beer, tucked a couple under his stump, then shared them around. They all took seats.

Denton took a swig of the Leinenkugle Red. "Mr. Batiste, nice to meet you. So you came over to talk about hexes?"

Batiste's smile softened his eyes. "I know a little bit. Not that much. We're mainly just playing around."

"Yeah, Lee, just goofin' around," said Uncle Bill, tipping his brown beer bottle to his thin lips.

Denton took another drink. He hadn't had a Leinenkugle for twenty years. "What's with the burning tobacco?"

Tavita glanced at the fireplace. "Tobacco is very sacred to the Ojibwe. We were offering it to the spirits."

"The spirits."

Bobcat Bill waved a casual hand towards the ceiling. "Yeah. Offerings so the spirits will treat us right."

Tavita pointed at the several wooden owls placed around the room, their wide white-painted eyes alert for evil doings. "We put out some lucky owls, boss. Better safe than sorry. Did you bring Queeg?"

Denton grinned, thinking of Queeg snug in his bag in the car. "Interesting concepts, Tavita." Turning to John Batiste, he asked, "Mr. Batiste, have you ever heard of the Norton family?"

Batiste glanced away, pretending to search his memory. But Denton had caught the surprise in his eyes and knew the man was stalling for time. "Ah, don't think so. Who are they?"

"Oh, some clients of mine. Several members of the family have died recently. A young man, William Norton, drowned over on the Chippewa Flowage, and Sylvia Norton Smith was recently murdered in her home in Stone Lake. There's an Indian in the Hayward jail that they suspect killed her."

John Batiste's black eyes glistened in the firelit cabin. "Oh, yes. I heard about those things. But I don't really know that guy. He's from another band of Ojibwe. His name is Jack Mathers. Indian name is Red Owl." Batiste's beer clunked on the end table as he abruptly stood, his long braid swinging its shadow across the wall. "Well, gotta go. Thanks for the drinks." He nodded goodbye. As he left, his moccasin-clad feet emitted soft leather sounds, a coda to the eerie ritual that had confronted Denton's arrival. Moments later, an old engine coughed and tires rasped on gravel.

"So what did I say to offend him?" asked Denton, rotating the Leinenkugle in his hands.

"Hard to say," said Uncle Bill. "He's a funny guy. He's a real medicine man of the Ojibwe tribe. He's a member of the Crane clan. He's supposed to belong to an outfit called the Medewiwin. His Indian name is something like 'Dark Panther that Walks in the Forest.' "

"Medewiwin?" asked Denton.

"Supposed to be a secret society of Ojibwe medicine men."

"And you know all this because?"

Uncle Bill's jowls offered stubble and a big Adam's apple bobbing in thought. "Well, Lee, I've been living up here a long time. And... ah, after your aunt died I sort of had a thing with one of John Batiste's sisters."

"A thing?"

The old man's head reared back. "Don't mock me, kid."

"Sorry."

"Anyway, that was fifteen years ago; she's gone now. Passed over to the spirit world three years back. Hey, want another beer? Some firewater from the fruit jar? It's aged two weeks now. Or I've got some Canadian Club. You look cold. Take this big chair by the fire." A gnarled hand shoved aside the drum and rattles. "Need to give Batiste back his drum," Bill muttered. "Let me pour you a civilized drink. How about some Canadian Club?"

"Sure." Denton lowered himself into a brown leather chair and accepted the glass Uncle Bill handed him. Tavita eased down on a nearby couch, and Uncle Bill sat beside him.

Denton swigged Canadian Club. He stared at Uncle Bill and Tavita. "You two look fucking insane." They said nothing, but stared back with innocent eyes. They'd obviously patched up their differences and formed a dubious alliance involving Indian medicine men, fire, tobacco, and noise.

"Nice loincloths, guys—and that face paint, too."

"Just playing around, boss."

Uncle Bill waited it out.

Denton was tired and decided not to push it. *Something's going on, and I'm the odd man out.*

22

Mid-September. Madison, Wisconsin.

"Let's get going." Richard Elkin knew his voice was gruff, betraying his anxiety. But that was okay. He was pleased to let Allen Sanger know he was nervous. It would explain his gun, show why he'd gotten scared and shot the blackmailer.

A street lamp cast its penumbral light across Allen's face, glancing off his eyeglass lenses. Elkin saw that Sanger's eyes were calm behind his black-rimmed frames. He was a man to be wary of. Elkin filed the thought away.

Allen turned the ignition key and drove the black, unmarked Crown Victoria Police Interceptor into the night. Elkin made himself comfortable in the passenger seat, feeling secure in the sturdy car with its V-8 and body-on-frame construction.

Elkin examined Allen Sanger. Six three, about two-twenty. He could become fearsome. More than once, Elkin had felt a twinge when Allen's eyes turned cold. *Those fucking Clark Kent glasses.* "Thanks for taking care of this, Allen."

"No problem." A grin curled up Sanger's thin lips. "Gotta protect my investment. I'm looking forward to being the head of the state police once you're governor."

"You can count on it, Allen. Absolutely."

There was no mirth in Allen's smile, no humor in his remarks. *He's all business. But that's good when it's my business.*

"You know, I've been looking into this since you got that first note. What, six months ago?"

Elkin hid his surprise. *Christ! How much does he know? How could he know?* "Oh, is that so?"

"Yeah."

"I should have told you, but I wasn't sure what to do."

"That's okay." Allen paused. "I came in here one day looking for a report I'd sent you. You'd left the blackmail note on your desk. Not smart. I put it in your top drawer. Anyway, I've been taking some protective action on my own."

Elkin clamped his teeth. "Like what kind of action?"

"Nothing for you to stew over. Just checking things out. Taking care of a thing or two."

Elkin didn't like the evasive answer, but after three years of association, he knew Allen couldn't be pushed. He let it go. "So what's the story on this train depot?"

"Well, it used to be a Milwaukee Road station. Milwaukee Road merged with the Soo Line at some point." Sanger let the tension build. His quick grin was forced. "Does that mean anything to you?"

Elkin shook his head. "Nothing." But it did mean something. There was something about the Soo Line. Some old fact lost or buried through the decades. The politician's mask remained in place.

The Crown Vic cruised along the West Beltline Highway, eating up the twelve-mile trip to the Middleton Depot. When they arrived, Allen Sanger radioed his crew to stay away from the depot until he called back. "I want the place to be deserted for the drop. We'll give the blackmailer a few minutes to scope it out. Then I'll move you in. Don't move until I tell you to."

Elkin studied the depot, a one-story peaked roof structure sitting in the dark beside a length of weed-ridden track. It hunched expectantly in the quiet night.

"You're supposed to put the hundred grand in that trash can by the entrance. Soon as you do the drop, get back in the car."

Elkin nodded, taking his time exiting the Crown Vic. His footsteps found the gravel pathway to the depot entrance. The sound of crunching gravel dominated the night. Close-up, the building's paint job was peeled. Once it had bustled with self importance, busy travelers, fancy luggage, a conductor checking his big railroad watch.

He spotted the trash can and dropped in the package. He moved into shadows formed under the eaves of the depot's roof. He didn't like spending a hundred thousand dollars. Even if it was from a slush fund he'd generated out of funds allocated to the Justice Department. One shot. Problem solved, with the money still his.

Elkin pulled his .38 Colt Air Weight from his coat pocket and held it at his side.

Allen Sanger appeared, his bulk dominating Elkin. "Put that away, Richard. Get back in the car. I've got this taken care of." The black-framed lenses glinted. "Keep your hands clean—you're running for governor. For both of us."

Elkin followed Sanger to the car.

"That was foolish, Richard. You stuck out like a turd on a birthday cake."

Allen Sanger started the car and slowly moved out. A block away, he pulled into an alley and doused the lights.

Elkin said, "How long..."

Three shots cracked in the dark. The car radio came to life. "He's running."

More shots. Then silence. "They'll be chasing him," Sanger said. They sat for ten more crawling minutes. Static and adrenaline pumped over the radio. A voice shouted, "He got away. Disappeared."

"Hell! Did you get pictures?"

"Yes, sir. I'm sorry we lost him, sir."

Sanger switched off the radio.

Elkin's mind whirled with fear. *Now what?* The .38 Air Weight was sweaty in his hand.

23

Mid-September. Northern Wisconsin.

Batiste's abrupt departure left an eerie vacuum in the candlelit cabin. No one spoke. Denton sipped Canadian Club and scanned the room. The small dancing flames reflected off the seashell rattle, the drum. Most of all, he studied Uncle Bill and Tavita. Their red and black painted faces gleamed in the firelight. Denton's glass caught glimmering flames. "You guys supposed to be evil spirits?"

They shook their heads. Tavita replied, "No, this is our war paint. We're *fighting* evil spirits."

Uncle Bill held up a hand, waggling his palm in denial. "Just pretending, Lee. Just playing around."

"I don't believe you."

Tavita's eyes were hooded. "We better tell him, Bill."

Bill shrugged, and the whole story spilled out. He had spoken with his boyhood friend, Sheriff Joseph Nils, who agreed to allow Tavita to inspect Sylvia Norton Smith's house. They'd discovered one porcupine quill necklace and one of small, white cowry shells. Hex signs, a jagged circle and a Thunderbird, drawn on the walls and the floorboards.

"It's possible somebody thought Sylvia was a witch. That she was casting evil spells."

"You mean somebody like that guy they have in the Hayward jail?"

Bill turned in his chair, his arm bumping the cowry shell rattle. It clattered in the shadowed room. "Yes. Red Owl, aka Jack Mathers. He's a Medewiwin, too."

Tavita spoke up. "Yeh. And we think John Batiste knows him better than he admits. He just doesn't want to talk about him."

Denton looked at Bill. "Seems there's a lot to learn about the Indians."

"Yeah. About some of them, anyway."

"All right, so tell me."

Uncle Bill's voice grew low, confiding. "There's a lot to admire about them. The tribe has been here since the sixteen hundreds or even earlier. Their original name for themselves was the *Anishinabeg,* or 'original people.' They fought both the Iroquois Confederacy and the Sioux. Beat them both. The Ojibwe kicked ass. Then along comes Zachary Taylor, never a friend of Indians. When he was President, he signed the Indian Removal Act that ordered the Wisconsin tribes to move west. Instead of dancing around their fires and chanting, the Ojibwe sent a delegation to D.C. to get the Removal Act reversed. Old Rough and Ready Taylor wouldn't give them the time of day. But he died."

Taylor died, thought Denton, *like everybody does.* Death seemed to linger in the corners of the cabin, hiding from the weak light, waiting for the candles to go out.

Uncle Bill drank from a glass of clear liquid. "So Taylor dies and the Indians are walking down some D.C. street and run into a congressman who asks them what they're up to. They explain the deal, and the next thing they know, they're meeting with Millard Fillmore, who succeeded Taylor as President."

Bill grinned, slamming down his glass. "A miracle occurred. Fillmore agreed to rescind the Removal Order. He even allowed the tribe to choose its reservation land in Wisconsin. That's where the Lac Courte Oreilles Reservation came from. The 'LCO,' they call it."

Denton's mood soared. The story was mythological, a real-life example of the "Hero's Journey." An epic of brave men launching a desperate journey to save their people—and winning. "Jeeze, I hope they celebrate a Millard Fillmore day."

"Not that I've heard of."

Denton took a warming sip of whiskey. "What about this secret medicine man society? The Midiw ...whatever."

"Medewiwin," said Uncle Bill. "Who knows for sure, but I've heard they're the real deal. Still practice old rituals, study herbal medicine. They believe in preserving their culture. Some say they can cast spells, lay down hexes."

"Think they'd kill suspected witches?"

"I suppose anything's possible," said Bill.

Tavita held up the cowry shell rattle. "That's what the cowry shell necklace at Sylvia's house could have been about. Some kinda protection against her coming back to get them."

Denton pointed at the carved wooden owls. "So what's the deal with the owls? Are they like my lucky owl?"

"Yes. Those are mine. It's weird, but in Samoa we use cowry shell rattles just like the ones they have here. How did they get cowry shells way up here, so far from the ocean? A lot of Indian tribes had tattoos, like we do in Samoa. And they have carved lucky owls, too. It's not far-fetched to believe Samoans and the Ojibwe are related. I was trying a little Samoan... ah, medicine."

Denton frowned at Tavita, at his grotesque painted face, the lattice of tattoos now revealed by his loincloth. *Do I even know this guy?* "And what's your connection to Samoan medicine?"

"I told you, boss. Back when we first met. I'm descended from Samoan kings."

"I thought that was bullshit."

"No, that part wasn't—just the part about the burning cats. I'm sort of a medicine man back home."

Denton sipped. "If you say so, Tavita."

"No kidding, boss. I've seen strange stuff back in Samoa. This old lady killing is weird. The murderer left hex signs. Keep an open mind. This could be evil spirit stuff."

Denton felt like catching the first plane to San Diego. *Jeezus. Next, he'll be quoting Shakespeare.*

Tavita spread his massive arms. The odd stub of his truncated left arm wiggled in grotesque emphasis. "You know the saying, boss: 'There are more things under heaven and earth, Horatio...' ah... and so on."

"Thanks, I needed that."

Denton shifted his eyes to Uncle Bill, regarding him with the little boy eyes of lost years. His uncle's mouth twisted in a smile, rippling his grease paint. Those carefree days were long past.

24

Mid-September. Madison, Wisconsin.

Allen Sanger knocked, paused a beat, then entered Attorney General Richard Elkin's office. Elkin looked up from a stack of documents. He held a gold pen in his hand.

Sanger's eyes fixed on Elkin's fountain pen. Elkin held it up, letting it gleam. "Behold, my 1974, eighteen-carat gold, Mont Blanc Meisterstuck."

Sanger forced away flashing anger. "Nice."

"Yeah. A gift from an admirer," said Elkin, rotating the pen in his fingers. "This is a real pen, not one of those ballpoint things. Look at its nib. A work of art." The pen's sharp, flared tip was elegantly etched, its edges sharp, like those of a well-made knife.

Elkin set it on the desk and asked, "Did you discover anything about the blackmailer?"

Sanger coughed and handed Elkin several eight-by-ten photographs. Taken at night, they weren't very clear, but Elkin could make out a thin, older man with long, unkempt hair. The man was walking toward the trash can where Elkin had deposited the payoff.

"Who is he?"

Sanger's hands moved out, palms up. "Don't know yet. But he's no spring chicken. Looks like he's in his late seventies, even eighties."

"If he's so old, how did he get away?"

"Some old guys can move a lot faster than you'd think. Besides, he had a hiding place. He knew about a secret alcove inside the old depot. The bastard must have been a railroad man. After my crew chased their own tails all over the area, they went back to the depot. The hidden door was open, otherwise they'd have missed it." Sanger picked up a photo and studied it. "Apparently, he stayed there until sometime this morning. There were several apple cores on the floor."

"Apple cores?"

"Yeah. He must have figured on being followed. Planned to hide there all along."

Elkin checked his gold watch, exposing pearl cufflinks. His voice was a growl. "Yeah. Nice to know all this, but I feel like my asshole has been reamed. The guy escaped with the money. *And* he still has the documents."

Sanger kept his eyes on his shoes. "I'm sorry. I'm doing my best to find this guy."

"Look, Allen. You'd better get this done if you want a future in Wisconsin."

Sanger looked up, his eyes blank slits behind his glasses. "I understand."

"I hope so. Let me know if you manage to make any progress. That it?"

"No." Sanger's face brightened in celebration. "We picked up the blackmailer's trail at the bus station. He caught a bus to Lady-smith up in northern Wisconsin. We lost him after that."

"Maybe you need a new team."

"I do have other information." Sanger waited.

"What is it?"

"He left a note. Here's a copy."

Elkin's blood chilled when he read the note. *Dear Attorney General Elkin. Now everyone will hear about your relationship to Al Capone.*

Elkin realized Sanger had saved this bombshell for last. *Just to fuck with me.* Elkin re-read the note, then looked up to see Allen Sanger's brown eyes studying him. "There's something else, right?"

"I looked into this," Sanger said quietly. "It seems Al Capone had a hideaway near Couderay, Wisconsin, up near where your mother was born and raised. You and your sister were both born in Hayward."

The note crackled in Elkin's hand. "Yes?"

"So do you have any idea what evidence this blackmailer has about your relationship to Capone?"

"No. I just know he claims my mom is Capone's illegitimate daughter."

Sanger fiddled with a stone paperweight on Elkin's desk, lifting it up, rolling it in his hand. He set it down with a wooden clunk. All the while his cold eyes appraised Elkin.

"Ever hear of a family named Norton?"

Elkin ran a thumb along the crease in his suit pants. "Well, yeah. They were from Chicago. Some of them later settled around Hayward." Elkin leaned back and crossed his arms. "There was an old story. That one of them, a young guy, had some business relationship with the Capone gang, knew about my mom. They say that guy disappeared. But other Nortons might know the story."

Sanger's eyes lingered on Elkin. When he spoke, his voice was careful. "That's what I figured. I've been taking some steps."

"With the Nortons?"

"Yeah."

"Take these photos away. I don't want anything like that in my office."

Sanger reached for the photos, his smile derisive. "No problem." Sanger stood. "I'll be in touch once I know more." He turned to leave.

"Allen."

"Yeah?"

"You've taken some liberties. I don't like it."

Sanger's smile disappeared as he squared his heavy shoulders. "Yes, sir. I just thought…"

"I know what you thought."

"Yes, sir."

Elkin watched the big man leave. Anger pulsed. He didn't like being controlled by an employee, especially one that knew his secret. Once he put Allen Sanger into his new job, what then? *Allen might decide he doesn't need me anymore. I better think this through. The thing that gets you is always the one you least expect.*

25

Allen Sanger's face burned as he exited Elkin's office. The last thing he needed was to see Marge Hawkins sitting primly behind her desk, a derisive smile curling her lips. Had she heard his sub-missive self- humiliation, how many times he'd said "Yes, sir" to Elkin? No. The office door had been closed. She was operating on pillow talk. The bitch. Someday she'd get what she was asking for. Things would change when he was head of the state troopers. *One of these days, Marge Hawkins, I'll bend you over that desk and fuck you red.*

"Something on your mind, Mr. Sanger?"

"No."

When Sanger reached his black Crown Vic, parked in its assigned space in the state parking garage, he thumbed the door opener, popping the trunk. His sour mood vanished as he lifted the trunk lid. His eyes caressed the fat package of blackmail payoff money. The joy of the newly rich bubbled within him. The so-called blackmailer hadn't asked for a dime. Not one fucking cent. The idiot wanted to *give* the documents to Elkin without letting Elkin know his identity. Who could blame the guy? This information was like nitroglycerine. It could blow at any time, taking a lot of people down. *But not me.*

Sanger felt like hugging himself. *Well, Mr. Governor-To-Be, you aren't as smart as you think.* It had been easy for Sanger to recruit Mark Scheff, one of his low-life drug informers. He'd told Scheff it was a drug sting and paid the skinny, desperate man with cocaine and cash from a real drug bust. *Now I have the money—and the documents.*

Sanger shoved down the trunk lid. It locked with a reassuring metallic click. *All that money. Tax free.* He climbed into the Crown Vic. He laughed aloud, slapping his knees. *While that dip-shit plays with his fancy gold pen, I'll build my own interests.*

Sanger played it back in his head. How he'd arranged it all. How Elkin had almost fucked things up by trying to waylay the blackmailer with his stupid pistol. *The asshole almost saw Scheff take the package.* Not knowing about the payoff, the blackmailer had simply deposited the documents into the trash can. Sanger held off sending in his team until the blackmailer had had ample time to escape. While the team was wasting time trying to capture the blackmailer, Scheff had snatched the documents *and* the payoff money. God only knew what shadows his team was firing shots at. Later that night, Scheff had turned the packages over to Sanger in return for two ounces of pure coke and five thousand dollars in cash.

It was time to celebrate. Maybe he'd buy a gold pen in the morning. But he needed to roar like a lion tonight. He got a Kleenex from the glove box and methodically cleaned his glasses, shining up the thick, black frames. His smile returned. A gold pen would be nice. Maybe he'd shove it up Elkin's ass some day. Right after he reamed out Marge Hawkins' pussy. *A double play. Man, I'm getting hot.*

He started the car. Tonight he'd screw that little Mexican girl some more. She didn't like it, not the way Sanger did her, but it was either do it or go to prison for selling marijuana. *Man, I hope they never legalize pot. I bet Al Capone shit bricks when they repealed Prohibition.*

26

Mid-September. Northern Wisconsin.

Denton woke with spider-webby dreams clinging to the recesses of his mind. His Uncle Bill, Tavita, and that John Batiste guy dancing to their eerie music. *What a loony bin.* His eyes scanned the bedroom's pine ceiling, looking for the shapes his boyhood eyes had discovered in the swirls of wood grain. There they were. A spitting cobra. A cross-eyed gargoyle. A bear standing on hind legs. An Indian with a tomahawk.

After a few nostalgic moments, he realized the grain-embedded images weren't scary anymore. Too bad how childhood passes away, melting into the inevitability of adulthood.

Denton slid out of bed and pulled on jeans and a black sweater. He yanked on wool socks and hiking boots, then headed for the kitchen. Tavita and Uncle Bill sat at the kitchen table with steaming cups of coffee. They were playing cribbage.

Tavita spread his cards on the table. "Fifteen two, fifteen four, fifteen six, fifteen eight, fifteen ten. And a double run of eight for ten. That's twenty."

Bill's lips moved as he silently checked Tavita's count. "Shit."

Tavita moved his cribbage peg. "I'm out. You're skunked. That's another hundred thousand you owe me."

Denton grinned as he poured a cup of coffee. Tavita was full of surprises. He'd once told Denton, "We're actually well educated in Samoa. *American* Samoa, you know." But cribbage?

Bill shoved the cards into their red box, snatched up the cribbage board, and put the set on a shelf. "Next time double or nothing."

"That *was* double or nothing."

Denton took his coffee to the table and sat by Tavita. "Well, Tavita. Cribbage?"

"Grandma learned the game from an English pirate named Peg-leg Pete."

Bill and Denton's groans filled the room. They clinked their coffee mugs together. "Aaarg. Here's to pirates." "To good cards." "To Grandmas."

Denton enjoyed the camaraderie, suddenly understanding the appeal of putting on war paint and dancing in loincloths. But they had work to do. "Uncle Bill, I've got a plan for today."

Just after lunch, the three of them entered the one-story building that housed the Sawyer County Sheriff's Office. Bill marched up to the receptionist. "I'm Bill Higgins. We're here to see Sheriff Nils."

"Do you have an appointment?" asked the young olive-skinned woman behind the counter. Her hand went to her long black hair as her dark eyes scanned Denton.

Denton smiled at her as Uncle Bill said, "No, but please let him know Bill Higgins would like a moment."

She returned Denton's smile, then glanced at Uncle Bill. Her smile turned to a frown. "Sheriff Nils is very busy, but I'll check." She punched a couple of buttons on her phone and her doubting expression changed to surprise.

"Go right in," she said.

Denton followed Uncle Bill into the pine-paneled office with its bearskin rug. Denton noted the bear's sharp white teeth, then his eyes took in wall-mounted trophy fish and stuffed heads of multi-pointed white-tail bucks.

Sheriff Nils was tall and lean with a weatherbeaten face. "Hell, Bill. Nice ta see ya."

Uncle Bill grasped the sheriff's extended hand and pumped it up and down. "Same here, Joe. Meet my nephew Lee Denton from California."

The sheriff shoved his calloused hand at Denton, his gray lawman's eyes cautious beneath bushy eyebrows. "Nice ta meet ya."

"Same here," Denton replied.

Bill pointed to Tavita. "Meet Afa Tavita. He works with Lee."

Nils looked up and down Tavita's mass. "Yeah, I heard you came by before. You sure are a big one. Are you an Indian?"

Tavita answered, "In a way. I'm from Samoa. *American* Samoa."

Sheriff Nils shrugged and swept a long arm towards a sitting area with a brown leather couch and two matching chairs surrounding a low oak coffee table. "Sit down. What's up?"

"Lee and Tavita are in from California. They're investigating the recent Norton deaths. Some federal judge ordered him to investigate and make a report. A couple of Nortons have also died out in California."

Sheriff Nils studied Denton. "That so? Okay, what can I do?"

Denton smiled and sat up straight. He wanted to establish a good threshold with this man. "Sheriff, I'd sure like to look at your files on the Norton deaths."

"Okay. I'll arrange it." A staghorn-handled knife came out of nowhere. Niles began cleaning his nails.

"Thanks very much. Ah, I'd also like to interview the man you have in your jail." Denton turned to Uncle Bill. "What's his name?"

Bill replied, "Jack Mathers."

The knife point stopped under a nail, then began cleaning again. "Weeell, I'm not sure I should do that." He pointed the knife handle toward Tavita. "He already spoke to Mathers."

Bill nodded. "Yeah, but I'd sure like Lee to size the guy up. He'll be real quick. He won't cause any trouble. I promise."

Denton felt the gray eyes drill him. *Don't fuck with this guy.* "Short and sweet," Denton told him.

"All right, ya don't look like one of those California weirdos."

Denton knew when to keep his mouth shut. *Just smile, boy, just smile.*

Twenty minutes later they were standing outside the jail cell of Jack Mathers, aka Red Owl. Sheriff Nils said, "These gentlemen would like to speak to you. You don't have to if you don't want to. Want to?"

Red Owl said, "One," shrugged, and retreated to the darkest corner of his cell.

"I guess that's a yes." Sheriff Nils' eyes carried a surprising weariness.

Denton entered alone while Uncle Bill, Tavita, and the sheriff waited down the narrow hallway. Red Owl was very still in the dim corner. Denton felt threatened by the stillness, the coiled possibility of sudden violence.

"Mr. Mathers, my name is Denton. Leland Denton. I'm an attorney. I've come out from California to find out what happened to William Norton and Sylvia Norton Smith. The police think you know something about Ms. Smith's death."

Red Owl grinned, letting long seconds tick by, stringing out Denton's nerves. Bad teeth showed in the dim light. "And you think I'll talk to you?"

"I just want to ask simple questions. Do you think Sylvia was a witch or an evil spirit?"

Red Owl's grin grew broader. Not just bad teeth. Missing teeth. He scratched his ribs.

"Are you a Medewiwin shaman?"

Red Owl shifted in the dark, a threatening shadow. "Go away, mister."

"Okay, Mr. Mathers, I'll go. But I'm going to get to the bottom of this. I think you and some of your Medewiwin friends have done something. I promise you I'll get to the bottom of this."

"Mr. Denton."

"Yeah?"

"Don't threaten. It's a sign of weakness."

"Just do it, huh?"

Bad teeth flashed in the darkness.

27

"What an asshole," said Bill as they left the Sawyer County jail. "Where to now?"

Footage of Red Owl's insouciant expression, his dark-pool eyes, played in Denton's head. *Those teeth*. "Doesn't the reservation's community college have a library?"

"Yes."

"Any good?"

"It's fine, depends on what you're interested in."

"I figure it should have something on this medicine man stuff."

"Sure it does."

"Okay, let's go back to your place. I'll pick up my car and go to the library. You two see if you can pry any more information about this Red Owl guy from John Batiste."

An hour later, Denton arrived at the LCO Community College, nestled in the woods, its one-story wooden structure as one with the land. The college had been created long after his boyhood. It was a tribute to the Ojibwe's determination to succeed in a difficult world, to gain power through education.

He passed through a high-peaked *porte cochere*, walking beneath a painted sign bearing the logo of a bald eagle's head with a feather in its beak. The entrance was flanked by pillars that he took to be stylized tree trunks bearing flower stalk symbols. Good luck charms. Inside, he approached the short, dark-skinned woman at the library's reception desk. Her black eyes were friendly as he approached, but they became guarded when he explained his mission.

"We have Internet access, but I suppose you can get that anywhere."

"Yes, that's true. But I was hoping the tribe would have more specialized books on Ojibwe culture. You know—clans, myths, and spiritual practices."

She pointed with a plump finger. "Over there, sir. Those low shelves have books like that."

Denton pawed through the shelves, finally selecting a thick, red book with stories about the host of Ojibwe spirits that inhabited trees, rocks, and animals, spirits that controlled all natural phenomena. There were guardian spirits, an idea that reminded Denton of Queeg, his good luck charm. And the lucky carved owl he carried in his lucky briefcase. *Of course, I don't exactly believe in that kind of stuff. Not exactly.*

Still, he found himself drawn into the mythology and became absorbed in stories of the Windigo, a cannibalistic giant. It was hard to kill a Windigo, but some Ojibwe heroes had managed it. Denton's attention merged into the tale of the Baby Windigo. Apparently, a young Ojibwe baby had surprised his parents by asking the whereabouts of a powerful being named Manidogizik and asserting that he would go visit Manidogizik, the implication being he would kick Manidogizik's nasty ass. The idea of a butt-kicking baby was something Denton could get into.

Once the stunned parents got over the fact that their baby could not only talk, but knew all about Manidogizik, fear filled their hearts, because this Manidogizik loved to kill people who pissed him off—which was most people, most of the time. Well, the night after the baby's precocious pronouncement, the parents woke and found the baby gone. They panicked and ran outside their wigwam, where they found little baby tracks in the dirt. They followed the tracks down to the lake, where they suddenly turned into giant footprints.

Denton pulled his steno book from his briefcase and began making notes. His felt tip pen began to run out of ink. *Shit!* He shook the pen. The ink flowed again. He re-focused on the story.

The baby's parents had freaked out when they realized their baby had turned into a giant. This transformation could mean only one thing—the poor little tyke had tuned into a Windigo. In his transformed condition, the baby was seeking out Manidogizik. But Manidogizik had fifty dwarfs for henchmen, and they attacked the Windigo by flinging rocks at it, rocks that turned into lightning bolts.

Shit! Lightning bolts, Denton thought, jotting down the essentials of the story, fretting that the pen would run dry any second. Then he continued reading.

One lightning bolt hit the Windigo square in the head. He fell with a noise like a big tree falling. The dwarfs swooped in and chopped up the Windigo, who by then had turned into a big block of ice. When the dwarfs left, the baby's parents and other tribe members somberly gathered up the chipped ice and melted it down in a big iron kettle. In the middle of the ice-melt, they found the tiny baby with a hole in his head where the lightning bolt had struck. Then the entire tribe, including the parents, celebrated because the Windigo could have devoured the entire village.

Denton made notes, thinking the celebration was a bit perverse. After all, the baby was dead. But he understood why they'd be happy to have saved the village. *I guess they figured they could have another kid.*

As Denton used his dwindling ink supply to make notes in his steno pad, he sensed attention from other library patrons. The woman at the front desk, in particular, watched him closely and seemed to be writing things down, possibly the books he was consulting. Denton sent her a nice smile and returned to his reading.

Not only did the historic Ojibwe believe in a large number of spirits, both good and evil, but they also believed in ghosts and witches. Denton recalled the many Joseph Campbell books he'd read. He thought about how Campbell, and others before him, had believed there were primordial myths. They adhered to the idea that something genetic existed in humans that gave rise to similar myths all over the earth. Ojibwe myths were similar to those in other cultures. *Now I'm getting the Ojibwe versions.* These stories had power, conveying community ideals of self-sacrifice and courage.

Denton opened his briefcase and took out the big-eyed wooden owl Tavita had given him the year before. Whatever urge had produced this owl in Samoa was also at work in northern Wisconsin. And that's what Bobcat Bill and Afa Tavita were doing with John Batiste—playing an ensemble of similar myths against one another. Tavita was expressing his mythology himself by shaking his cowry shells with John Batiste's. And who knew what Uncle Bill was up to?

Denton remembered Uncle Bill's long, intimate relationship with an Indian woman. Maybe she'd passed on some stories. Or even spells. What woman didn't?

Denton decided to page through one last book, then call it a day. He chose the biggest one left, a thick, cloth-covered volume. He thumbed through it until a chapter about Medewiwin rituals caught his attention, and he began scanning the paragraphs. He started making notes on his steno pad. *Medewiwin (also spelled Midewin and Midewiwin) derived from a Native American term for Grand Medicine Society. A super secret society.*

He underlined "super secret." Now this was interesting. A secret Indian medicine man society, and it used cowry shells, just as Tavita had said. Denton read the section twice, his mind racing. He made quick notes. *Sacred cowry shells. Used by Medewiwin. Found in numerous burial sites in North America. Way before Columbus. Shells grow only in the South Pacific. Presence in America can't be explained.*

Denton stopped reading. The Ojibwe cowry shells really could have come from the South Pacific. Tavita might be right in his belief there was a connection with Samoans. Denton read on, making more notes. *Medewiwin advanced from one degree to another through initiation. Higher degrees consisted of instruction in special mysteries of Medewiwin and in the properties of rare herbs, the nature of poisons.*

Denton double-underlined the word "poisons" and checked his watch. It was almost five. Time for the library to close. He wrote faster: *Medewiwin recorded secret information on birch-bark scrolls.*

A shadow fell across the book. Denton looked up as John Batiste took a chair across the pine library table. "Hello, Mr. Denton. Having a good read?"

The interruption had startled Denton. "Oh, hi, Mr. Batiste, or do you prefer to be called Dark Panther?"

Batiste emitted a low chuckle. "John will do. Looks like you're reading up on our spirits and what all."

"Call me Lee. Yeah. That dancing stuff you guys were doing got me interested. You wouldn't happen to be Medewiwin, would you?"

Batiste grinned. "Oh, we do that stuff some, but it's mainly for cultural entertainment. We don't actually believe in it these days. It's like the Grimm Brothers' fairy tales. Stories for kids."

Denton looked into John Batiste's deep-set eyes. They glittered at him from eye sockets darkened by the angle of the overhead lights. Batiste's gray hair, now unbraided, fell long across his shoulders. He looked like he could cast hexes or put poison in your food. "I'm sure that's true, John. I'm just interested. Seems like you Ojibwe used to kick some ass back when you fought the Iroquois and the Sioux. I read in that book over there that Ojibwe means 'cook until puckered.' "

Batiste kept smiling, but his face remained humorless. "That refers to the way we used to cure our moccasins. We boiled them till the seams puckered. That made them more waterproof."

Denton replied, "Yeah, I read that too, but some books say the phrase refers to the way you used to cook captives. *Well done,* you might say."

Batiste shrugged. "Just stories made up by white missionaries who wanted to make our culture look bad. Don't believe everything you read."

Denton said, "I take everything with a grain of salt."

"Good. Well, I gotta be going… just happened by and saw you. Thought I'd say hello."

Denton nodded. "Yeah, what they call a felicitous coincidence."

28

After Denton left the library, he drove towards Bill's cabin, staring through the windshield, thinking of the Baby Windigo, of good and evil spirits inhabiting the dense woods surrounding the narrow black-topped road. Long shadows of night began to finger across the lush greenery. The woods took on a sinister cast, so different from the way he'd viewed them as a boy. Old memories swept over him. A fishing trip and a campout with his dad, who had died in an airplane crash when he was twelve. Camping with Uncle Bill. Swimming in the Couderay River. He thought of tawny-skinned Marie, the Indian girl he'd adored when he was sixteen. Hurried motions in the moonlight, soft kisses, shining tears.

At the intersection of Highway 27 and County K, he decided to stop at the Trailways Inn for an early and solitary dinner. Charlotte would be happy to know he was eating. He scanned the wine list, but he was a long way from Napa Valley. He chose a Jack Daniel's on the rocks and a T-bone, cooked medium, with cole slaw and French fries. As he waited for his food, he scanned the quaint room with its low wooden beams and pine board ceiling. Stuffed fish hung on the walls. He recognized bass, Northern pike, walleye, and muskie. He'd caught all those as a kid.

His steak had come as he finished his drink, and he said yes when the waitress asked, "Another Jack?"

He dug into the steak, suddenly ravenous, recalling he'd skipped lunch. When the waitress returned for his empty plate, he ordered a piece of rhubarb pie and another Jack Daniel's. *Rhubarb pie. I haven't had that since my grandma made it.* He looked forward to the sweet, yet sour taste of the pie. The whiskey seeped into his brain. *Whoa, I'm getting a little buzzed.* But when the pie and Jack Daniel's arrived, he relished them both. "Whiskey and rhubarb," he said to the glass-eyed Northern pike looking down from the wall.

"The bears are here," called the waitress, pointing at the far window.

Denton joined several patrons who rushed to the window to see the bears that had come to a red wooden feeding station fifty yards down the hill. Denton watched the two black bears. He'd forgotten how big they could get. One of them stood on its hind legs, staring up at the window. It had to be seven feet tall. Denton caught a glimpse of sharp white teeth as the other bear bit into the leftovers put out by the owners of Trailways. *I wouldn't want to run into one of those guys.*

Denton finished his drink and exited. He stood on the well-trodden wood porch, rubbing his stuffed belly and breathing cool evening air. It smelled... woodsy. Pine. Dew-wet grass. He shivered, glad he'd dressed warmly. A faint flash within low clouds on the horizon foretold bad weather. He recognized the rain smell in the wind.

He climbed into the rented white Camaro. An eerie impulse urged him to take his Browning Hi-Power and its clip of Hornady XTP hollow points from the glove box. On the flight up, he'd had to unload the gun and check it. The pistol was cold in his hands. He ejected the clip and checked the hollow-mouthed shells. He palmed the clip back in with a satisfying click. He slid it back into the glove box, cocked and locked. His concealed weapon permit would be recognized in Minnesota through reciprocity, but not in Wisconsin. *You'd think a state with thousands of hunters and millions of guns would allow concealed carry for those who got checked out and took the course.* He drove

carefully, not wanting to be arrested for speeding with elevated alcohol and an illegal weapon.

He eyed the speedometer, keeping the needle on fifty-five as
he worked his way to County B, then to Uncle Bill's place on Big
Sissabagama Lake. Darkness claimed the landscape, and Denton
switched on his lights. A deer dashed across the road, just missing
Denton's car. *Shit!*

He sat up straighter, his hands gripping the wheel, his eyes trying to penetrate the black nothingness beyond the reach of his
headlights. His head buzzed with whiskey as he steered over uneven blacktop, avoiding deep potholes.

Relief flooded through Denton when he drove up to Uncle
Bill's cabin. He switched off the car, rolled down a window, and
inhaled the night air. The faint smell of a wood fire rode in from
across the lake. He heard leaves riffle in the gentle breeze. A pale
quarter moon offered itself, revealing the still waters of the Big Siss
and lighting up a stand of white birch beside Uncle Bill's dark cabin.
But rain clouds were sliding across the moon, dimming its hold on
the night sky. A squall was coming.

The place is pitch black. They must be out. As he opened the car
door, the dome light flashed his eyes, stealing his night vision. He
remembered to take his gun from the glove compartment. The car
door closed with a metallic click. He slid the gun into his waistband
and searched for the rock that hid the house key.

A crunching noise. Something moving at the side of the cabin.
His brain recorded a second quick flash of movement, a shading
against the night. He shook his head to clear away the buzz. It must
have been a residual image from the car light.

The moon lifted itself above the trees, casting a tree-shaped
shadow of light and dark. Another movement. This time from the
right. Rhubarb and whiskey churned in his stomach.

A figure rushed at Denton. A man swinging a weapon that
glinted in the moonlight. Denton's tae kwan do training took over.

He side-stepped under the swing, grabbed the man's arm and used his momentum to fling him away into the darkness.

Denton backed against one of the log pillars supporting the cabin's porch roof. *Protect my back. Stay ready.* As Denton's night vision returned, he saw the man he'd thrown rise from the gravel walkway and rush back at him. At the same time, another man came at Denton. Denton pulled his Hi-Power, thumbed off the safety, and pulled the trigger. The muzzle flash lit up the red and black paint on his nearest attacker's face. The tall man wore an eagle feather in his hair and swung a tomahawk at Denton's head.

Denton ducked under the arc of the tomahawk and fired his gun at another rushing figure. The tomahawk buried its sharp steel into the wooden pillar beside Denton. More figures charged at Denton and he fired his pistol, left and right. *Go down, you fuckers.* Then he ran for it, plunging into the thick forest, fighting his way through trees and undergrowth.

Voices yelled in pursuit. A crashing of brush followed his blind stumbling through the forest. Then the sounds were drowned in thunder and slashing rain.

Lightning ripped the dark as Denton slipped and fell, his fear urging him back to his feet, propelling him through the night. *Finger off the trigger. Finger off the trigger. Calm down. Remember your training.* He fell into a creek and splashed his way out. Then he ran into a large tree, the impact knocking him down into the wet undergrowth. He lay there, gasping for breath, big rain drops smacking his face. The gun was heavy in his hand. He pushed off the safety. *Christ! Remember your training.* Lightning revealed a nearby stand of trees where a large tree had fallen, bringing down smaller trees and creating a wooden pile of refuge.

He squirmed his way deep into the timber, shoving farther and farther in until he was able to put his back against the wide trunk of a still-standing maple. There he lay, pistol still warm from firing. Rain found its way in. He shivered from cold and fear. The fear drove away the last tenuous grip of alcohol. He could think.

Indians? Trying to kill me? Tomahawks? He remembered the long-bladed knife that had been thrust at him. His exploring fingers felt a warm wetness. A sweet smell of blood in the dank branches. His face burned from scratches, and his forehead hurt from when he'd run into the tree. Scraped knees. Elbows sore. How bad was the knife cut?

The rain abated. He checked his Hi-Power, amazed he'd shot only four times. Nine hollow-points left. He laid the pistol on dry pine needles and pulled up his knees, putting his arms around them, huddling into himself for maximum warmth.

His mind spun, seeking reason and finding none. *Indians?* The squall passed and the woods dripped water from leaves and tree branches. Drip drop, drip drop. Denton's tired mind let go, deadened to fear and confusion. Drip drop, drip drop. He fell asleep.

He dreamed he had been seized by painted Indians. A black cast iron cauldron hung over a crackling wood fire. Men wearing wooden animal masks danced around the fire, and naked dark-haired women stirred the thick liquid inside the cauldron. The women chanted, "Cook until puckered… cook until puckered." Large men with eagle feathers and black painted faces seized Denton and dragged him to the steaming caldron.

Firelight shone on the Windigo baby's grinning face.

29

Mid-September. Madison, Wisconsin.

Allen Sanger sat in the parked Crown Vic watching John Norton, III's wife Liz carry groceries from her Chevy Tahoe into her fancy home. It was warm for September, and she wore a thin summer dress. The sun revealed her shape as she walked up her front steps. She looked pretty good for a woman in her late thirties, possibly early forties. Real good, actually. He wouldn't mind a piece of that.

John Norton, III emerged from the garage, pushing a lawnmower. Norton pulled the starter cord twice and the machine roared, slicing discord into the homey scene.

Sanger watched Norton mow and thought about Mrs. Norton and the way the sun had revealed her body. He'd sure like to… but then he got down to business. Was this guy the so-called blackmailer? Sanger chuckled at how he'd had to repeat "blackmailer, blackmailer" over and over to get his mind right. He didn't want to make a slip in front of soon-to-be-Governor Elkin. The man was a sleazy son-of-a-bitch, but a passport for Sanger. *I'll have pearl cufflinks. And a gold pen.*

John Norton, III looked much younger than the man in the blurry photos. But that could have been a disguise. There was a resemblance, but there were other Nortons, ones he hadn't visited yet. He'd find some of the younger Norton women, make them suck his dick like he'd made those other women do.

Three years, three long years since the night he'd slipped into the young blond woman's bedroom. His collection of lock picks had made it easy. He'd straddled her and woke her with his knife at her throat. The memory aroused him. Better than being top cop. Better than anything. Once he was in charge, he'd have a whole gaggle of broads who needed to be brought to their knees. Where they belonged.

His glasses began to steam up. *Christ.* He cleaned them off, wiped away the women and got back to the surveillance. He allowed a lingering thought of the young blond woman. He'd come in her mouth. She'd sobbed as he squeezed her throat until she swallowed it. He could see the disgust in her eyes. It was so good. So good. He'd put his face close to hers and shouted, "If you report this, I'll kill you and your whole family." She'd shut her eyes against the power of his voice, against the evil he'd produced.

As far as he knew, she'd been too scared to ever call the police. And as a highly placed law enforcement officer, he would have heard about it if she had.

The pretty woman in the yellow dress reappeared on her front porch. The wind blew the dress against her. She probably worked out, probably had a tight ass and wet pussy. He wanted her, wanted to rub her full, wanton lips with his dick. Maybe she liked it in the ass.

Yeah, there were also Nortons living in California. Even some granddaughters. He'd look them over carefully before choosing.

30

Mid-September. North Wisconsin woods.

Sunlight chased away the blue light of dawn. Denton lay on his back, his eyes staring into a crazy lattice-work of branches. His head throbbed. He closed his eyes and stretched tired legs, pulled a knee into his chest to ease aching back muscles. It was time to move out.

The snorting of the night before re-claimed his attention. "Wuff, wuff," like an oversized dog. Something big moved in the brush, but he saw nothing except innocent sunlight filtering into his refuge. He summoned his tae kwan do training. *Breathe, concentrate on your tanjun, summon your Ki. Let Yourself be Yourself as you face the Other.* Power surged into his body, into his gun hand.

Denton kept his pistol on safety as he crawled out of his nest. No damned twig would fire an accidental round into him. He exited into a small clearing, stood, and backed away from the pile of timber. His thumb pulled off the safety.

A heavy movement in the brush. The entire pile shook. Dead leaves spun down through filtered sunlight. Loud snorts. The bear was coming. Would the 9 mm be enough? No matter. It was all he had. Within his skull, the headache pounded. *Should I run? Where? No, you can't outrun a bear.*

He squinted against violent shafts of sunlight, preparing for the inevitable. Boyhood stories of raging bears reeled in his aching head. He spread his legs and crouched, the pistol held in both hands. *The Weaver stance. Take careful aim. Squeeze the trigger. Give him the rest of the clip.*

Twenty feet away, a massive black bear emerged into the sunlit clearing, twigs and leaves clinging to its humped back. It spotted Denton immediately and rose on its hind legs, a throaty roar issuing from its huge head. Yellow teeth, purple tongue, brown eyes. The small bright eyes stabbed at him. It had to be seven feet tall. Claws protruded from black paws.

He took a breath. *Showtime*, he thought.

Denton pointed the heavy gun. Iron sights on the bear rendered the gun small, too small. Denton's throbbing head grasped the truth. He could die right here. He shifted aching knees, rolled stiff shoulders, then reassumed his fighting stance. *We'll see.*

With surprising grace, the bear lowered itself to all fours. It strolled away, deeper into the woods. Denton's heart still raced as he watched it retreat. An odd disappointment flooded through him. The challenge unmet. The victor unknown. He put the Hi-Power back on safe and tucked it into his waist. His headache vaporized. His fighting tension drained away, leaving him hollow. *I could have taken him.*

Denton contemplated the small clearing, watching morning dew glitter the grass, hanging from tree branches, shimmering like fresh hope. For a few minutes Denton allowed the scene to exist, simply to be without further intrusion. But like the bear, he had things to do. It was time to get to home base.

To do that, he had to find his way out of the forest. As a kid, he'd heard stories about people becoming lost in the woods and wandering aimlessly until they starved or died of exposure. But that was long ago, before county roads crisscrossed once limitless forests. When he was a boy, he'd gone into the woods and tried to get lost, but he always found his way to a road. He knew he'd reach a road now if he could avoid walking in circles. This was different from navigating the open ocean, which had no landmarks. All he needed to do was pick a tree silhouetted against the rising sun glowing in the eastern sky. Then he'd pick another guiding tree, then another until he hit a road.

He trudged on, pushing away branches, stepping over fallen trees and kicking through underbrush. Twenty minutes later he emerged onto the blacktop of County Road F. Putting the sun on his left pointed him south towards Big Siss Lake.

Birds chirped and butterflies flitted in happy sunlight. He ambled along the edge of the road, his boots kicking gray gravel along the roadside. A small, dusty cloud rose, stinging his nose and making him sneeze. It was good to be alive this wonderful morning, the kind that made birds twitter and grass reach for the glowing sun. The hollow rapping of a woodpecker echoed through the woods. Denton's library reading had mentioned that the sound of a woodpecker foretold the arrival of a friend. That would be handy.

Denton liked woodpeckers, but wondered why the repeated battering didn't scramble their brains. It was like knocking your head constantly against a wall. Maybe woodpeckers had a special casing around their brains. Like football helmets. Still, all they had to do was eat bugs. Being crazy wouldn't matter.

A battered brown pickup stopped beside Denton. A young, dark-haired girl with long lashes and black eyes said, "Need a ride?" Perfume wafted odd in the mix of pine and dust.

Denton looked her over, noticing long tight braids, white teeth, smooth tan skin, straight nose, and full lips. She wore some kind of uniform, with dark olive drab trousers and a khaki shirt.

He said, "Sure. Thanks."

"Nice gun."

He looked down. His gun was still in his hand. "Ah... I can explain."

"It's okay. I'll let it go for now. Not really my beat. Climb in."

"Thanks."

The passenger door opened with a dry screech, and Denton found his passenger seat occupied by a raccoon. Wordlessly, the young woman shoved it off the seat.

"Don't mind Sue-Sue, she's tame. Have a seat. She'll stay out of your way."

Sue-Sue's claws were long and sharp, but Denton had just faced a bear. Still, he cringed when the raccoon climbed back onto the seat and snuggled up next to him. He wasn't ready for the close proximity of clawed, furry animals.

"My name's Lillian Deerfoot. Sue-Sue likes you. That means you must be nice." She studied Denton's cuts and bruises critically. "Where to, handsome?"

Deerfoot, Deerfoot… sounded familiar. But Denton couldn't retrieve it from his fatigue-clouded mind. He gave her directions.

"Oh, yeah. I've heard of Bobcat Bill. I bet my uncle knows him."

She pushed the accelerator and the truck rattled and coughed its way towards Bill's cabin. Denton leaned back and closed his eyes. He heard Lillian's hypnotic voice telling him about herself as he tried to clear his mind and erase the angst of the long, cold night.

As the truck slewed and jerked along, Denton learned that Lillian possessed a master's degree in zoology, worked for the Wisconsin Department of Natural Resources, was single, and thought the slight bend in Denton's nose was cute, especially with his light blue eyes.

"I never saw eyes that shade of blue. That's probably where the expression 'White Eyes' came from. You know that's what the Indians used to call the Europeans, back before the invasion? So do you think I'm pretty? Would you like to take me to dinner Friday?"

The question yanked Denton's eyes open. Quick dark eyes met his glance. He couldn't lollygag around with this woman, even if she was friendly and beautiful. Even if she did like his nose. Hell, he was in danger. Besides, Sandy Jones would be pissed. He meant to say no, but never got around to it as Lillian told him how happy she was to have her job with the DNR, how she loved the animals she worked with, and how nice it was to have a gorgeous new friend.

She pulled over to the side of the road where County F intersected with County CC. The car came to rest next to a tall oak post with a dozen arrow-shaped signs nailed to it. The signs pointed in various directions, showing the way to local resorts. Lillian said, "See all those resorts, all those places tourists come to? But not that many people actually live here."

Her eyes pinned him. "I don't get taken out to dinner much."

The knife slice seared his belly as he turned toward her. He meant to say no, but... the way Lilly looked at him, the softness in her dark eyes... "Sure, dinner Friday."

Lilly's smile lit up Denton's heart. She put a light hand on his shoulder, the touch electric, and her soft voice said, "Better make it seven. Around here, the eateries shut down by nine."

"Okay."

"Better leave that gun in the cabin."

"Yeah."

Lilly drove on, her young face glowing with happiness. Sue-Sue snuggled against Denton, emitting a sound of contentment. *Do raccoons purr?*

Lilly deposited Denton at Uncle Bill's front door and, as she drove away, shouted out the truck's window, "Pick you up at seven Friday." A slim hand twiddled fingers as the truck disappeared onto County F.

Denton was still standing bemused on the front porch when Tavita and Uncle Bill emerged and peppered him with questions. Where had he been? What had happened? Was he all right?

But Denton held up a restraining palm and said, "Coffee. Food. Quick."

Fifteen minutes later Denton was finishing his third cup of coffee and mopping up the last of his fried eggs with a slab of toast. "Thanks, Uncle Bill."

"You're welcome. Now tell us what happened. Why are you so messed up? What's that line of crusted blood on your belly?"

When Denton finished his story, Uncle Bill and Tavita said nothing.

"Jeeze, boss. Indians? Tomahawks?"

"Yes."

"But, boss..."

Uncle Bill interrupted, "They say the Medewiwin can send Warrior Spirits."

Denton's eyes hardened. "Meaning what, Uncle Bill?"

"Sounds like that's what you're talking about."

"You don't believe in Warrior Spirits."

"You'd be surprised what I believe in. What I've seen."

"Do spirits produce knife cuts like the one on my stomach?"

"Let's see it."

Denton pulled up his shirt and showed the jagged red line. "Ow!" Denton jerked away as Uncle Bill ran a coarse finger over the cut.

"That could be a scratch from a tree branch," said Uncle Bill.

Tavita peered at it. "Yeh, boss. Hard to tell."

"Well, look at the post on the front porch. There's a cut from a tomahawk."

The three trooped outside, cold air covering Denton's exposed belly. He pointed to the post where the tomahawk had buried its blade. "See, that's an actual cut from a real tomahawk."

Uncle Bill looked. "A cut, sure 'nuff." Bill's finger explored it.

"Okay, see?"

"But Lee, that could be from days ago. Some kids messing around. I don't inspect these posts every day."

Denton gave up. It did sound insane. "So what do Warrior Spirits do?"

Uncle Bill scratched his chin, an audible rasping across bristles. "Don't know exactly. I think they just scare folks. I suppose they can do some bad stuff, but I never heard of anybody getting chopped up."

Tavita's stump waved in emphasis. "Let's ask John Batiste."

Bill nodded. "Yeah, let's go inside and call him."

Batiste. As Denton followed Bill and Tavita inside, he imagined John Batiste's flat, black eyes, his unfriendly stare that could turn a library ugly. He didn't trust the man, but that didn't matter much. Investigations involved asking questions and evaluating the answers. "Sure, why not?"

Bill put a gnarled hand on Denton's shoulder. "Take a seat, Lee. I'll call him."

Denton sat, sinking into the softness of the sofa. Bill's concerned face looked down on him. Something about the way the shadows fell on Uncle Bill's face contorted his features, jogging Denton's memory. "Uncle Bill, do you know Clyde Norton?"

Bill turned away, reaching for the phone. "Sure. At least I did when we were kids. We went to junior high together, back before his parents moved to California. What about him?"

"You guys resemble each other a little."

Bill laughed, the moment of rippling shadows melting away. "Well, that's bad news. I recall him as being kinda weird looking." He rubbed his scalp and dialed John Batiste's number.

31

Denton's stomach wound burned. His eyes lost focus as Uncle Bill waited for John Batiste to answer his phone. Bill's form was silhouetted against window light. He looked like a Spirit Warrior.

"No answer."

No answers. Denton's coffee energy drained away. *No answers.* Sleep was what he needed. Sleep beneath clean sheets on a soft bed. But first, he had to wash off his accumulated grime, to stand naked beneath a hot shower.

He undressed, examining his tired body as he did so. Bruises and scrapes covered him like poorly drawn polka dots. His leg and back muscles ached, and the cut on his stomach was infection-red, screaming for attention. He reached for the door of the white medicine cabinet, pausing to scan the tired face in the mirror. Dark strands of hair hung across his forehead. His light blue eyes held no life. He pushed the cabinet door open, his face flashing away, and pulled out the red and white bottle of Tylenol Extra Strength tablets. He turned the sink's water tap, palming a handful of still-cold water into his mouth and swallowing three Tylenol. The tablets scraped his throat as they went down.

He turned on the shower and placed his hands against the plastic outside of the stall, leaning on it while the water became hot. Then he stood beneath hot water, soaping and rinsing off. He let the liquid warmth caress the back of his neck as he contemplated the dirty swirl of grime surrounding the drain. His mind chased stark, fleeing images. Gun flashes in the night. Painted faces. The tomahawk. The long-bladed knife across his skin. Cold hours in the brush pile.

He couldn't focus. He was practically sleeping standing up. *Get to bed, grab a couple hours' sleep.*

As he toweled off, Denton examined the inflamed gash across his stomach. He opened the medicine cabinet, found a half-used tube of Neosporin, and slathered it on the wound. He daubed it indiscriminately on other cuts and scrapes. His finger probed the long wound. It did look as if he'd been scratched by a branch. But he remembered the knife, its metallic arc. Could it have been a dream?

He replaced the Neosporin. As he closed the medicine cabinet, his face appeared in the mirror. He looked better. His eyes were alive, his face no longer pale. He combed his dark hair.

He wished Sandy was there. She'd hold him close, reassure him. He would sleep warm against her soft body. He wondered how she was, how Mutt was doing. He needed to call. Later.

He tried to summon Sandy's image, but it was Lilly's dark eyes that emerged. Lilly—who had captured him as he shuffled along his lonely road.

He never should have left the South Pacific. *What bullshit. I'm a fuckin' lawyer, not a commando.* He slipped on a green pair of shorts and a tan T-shirt. He needed sleep, but knew it wouldn't come without his white pills. He unzipped a side pocket on his bag and extracted his brown bottle of white pills. He put three into his mouth and palmed water from the tap.

He slipped into bed and lay staring at the ceiling. *Will I have to eat these damn things the rest of my life?* He felt chemically induced sleep closing in. He'd face the rest of his life some other time.

The high-noon sun heated the small bedroom. Denton stared at framed prints on the pine-sheathed walls. Two fishermen beached a red canoe as a third kindled their campfire. One flannel-shirted fisherman held a stringer with four small fish. They all stared as an American eagle snatched a huge fish from the lake.

Beside that picture was a framed prayer. "Now I lay me down to sleep/I pray the Lord my soul to keep/But if I die before I wake/I pray the Lord my soul to take." The poem had scared him back then. He'd worried about dying in his sleep, about the Lord snatching his soul. Where would he take it? But now, Denton barely remembered his younger self. He might have had a soul worth taking then. But now his soul, if there was such a thing, was tainted. The Lord, even if there was a Lord, wouldn't want it.

Denton tried to picture that young kid, but couldn't. He was a dead boy that Denton used to know.

White-pill magic claimed Denton. He dreamed confused movies with Spirit Warriors throwing dead fish, slapping his face with strings of cowry shells. A beautiful young woman, dressed in full Ojibwe ceremonial regalia, pushed the Spirit Warriors away, throwing back the fish. He searched for her face, but she kept it averted.

She caressed his cheek and kissed him, shoving her tongue into his mouth. She pulled away. He saw black eyes, but an indistinct face. Her small hand clutched a staghorn-handled knife with a long, blood-spattered blade. Then he saw her face clearly. It was the Cuban woman he'd killed. Terror engulfed Denton as her red lips twisted, as she screamed and plunged the knife into his chest.

Denton woke in panic, one hand held high in self-defense, the other tangled in bed sheets. But the room was empty. He'd recognized the scream. It was the same scream he'd heard in his sleep ever since Grenada.

He checked his watch. It was three fifteen in the afternoon. The second hand made its inexorable rounds, the same way it had during the firefight in Grenada when the Cuban woman aimed Hem's service pistol at him. Then the watch's second hand ticked off the nano-second he needed to stop his finger from pulling the trigger. But the gunshot had thundered in the small room as the 9-mm round splattered into her chest.

He fled the bedroom and went into the kitchen, where he poured two fingers of Jack Daniel's. He chugged it down, then poured another as quick heat flooded his guts. He sat at the kitchen table and reached for his briefcase with its documents of another reality, of problems he still had a chance to solve.

He retrieved a stack of files, and his photos of the Norton clan spilled out on the table, a profusion of frozen faces, staring eyes. Some lay face down. The Jack Daniel's worked on him. *Ally-ally-oxen-free. Come out, come out, wherever you are.*

Clyde Norton was face up and so was his daughter, Joan Norton. Asa II's face was down. So was John Jr.'s. But John III and Mary were face up, John's photo on top.

Denton began arranging them in rows. He turned them all up. Then he turned them all down. *Get a grip, Denton.* He shoved the photos back into his briefcase and pulled out his drawing of the Norton family tree.

His cell phone rang. He stared at the phone, annoyed, still grasping the family tree. Nortons branched down the page. *But the leaves are dying.*

He opened the phone. The caller ID said it was Charlotte. "Hi, Char."

He heard excitement in her voice. "Lee, someone just tried to kill Asa Norton and his girlfriend at their home in San Francisco."

"What?" Jack Daniel's burned as he got focused.

"Yes, a guy with an automatic pistol waylaid him when he went to his car and took him back inside. He made Asa stand against the wall and told Marylyn to take her clothes off and bend over the table. She refused, and he pushed her over to the wall with Asa. Then he tried to shoot them."

Denton's mind raced as he grappled with the information. Uncle Bill and Tavita came into the room and began pelting him with questions. Denton put his hand over the mouthpiece. "Shut up, you two, I'll tell you in a minute. Let me listen."

"Boss, you there?"

"Yeah. Tell me the rest."

"The guy wasn't used to the automatic, or he forgot he had a shell in the chamber. Anyway, he worked the slide, which ejected the round in the chamber. He panicked and kept working the slide, ejecting bullets until Asa punched him. The guy fell to the floor, and when he tried to get back up, Marylyn hit him in the head with a cast-iron frying pan. She made All-State on the UCLA women's tennis team. Apparently she's preserved her forearm technique— the guy's in a coma at St. Luke's Hospital. She probably knocked his brains across the net, if you know what I mean. They don't know if he'll regain consciousness. He has a Wisconsin driver's license. His name's Mark Scheff."

A Wisconsin license? "Christ. Where are Asa and Marylyn now?"

"They've gone to Clyde Norton's house. Joan and Mary Norton have gone there, too. The police have put a watch on Clyde's house."

"Good." Denton glanced at the family tree still in his hand, his mind running through the frozen photo faces.

"Lee. Do you think you should come back out here?"

"I don't know what I could add there in California. Police protection should be enough for a few days. They've put detectives on the case?"

"Yes. This Scheff has a long record of car thefts and small-time robberies. The kind of guy who'd do murder-for-hire. Scheff recently deposited five thousand dollars into his bank account. Of course, he can't be questioned unless he wakes up."

"Yeah, a hired shooter, it sounds like."

"Is everything okay up there? Ya gotta worry about this Wisconsin connection." Charlotte paused.

Denton hesitated. He knew her pauses. She'd detected something in his manner. He'd better fill her in. But Bill and Tavita hovered, eager for information. "Let me brief Tavita and Uncle Bill. I'll call you back in a few minutes."

"Fine. But boss, I can tell something's going on."

"I'll call back."

32

As Denton ended the call with Charlotte, Tavita and Bill closed in and claimed seats at the table. "Tell us," said Bill.

Denton explained what had occurred as Tavita and Bill listened, their eyes anxious. "This is some serious shit," Bill said. "I'm gonna clean my shotgun. Find my old service pistol."

Tavita rose to his full six feet three, his mouth a stern line under angry eyes. "I saw a baseball bat in the garage."

Despite his concern, Denton smiled at his newly formed army. "Okay, gentlemen. Let's take precautions, but this happened over fifteen hundred miles away."

Bill shook his head. "The attack on you happened right out there on the porch."

"Ah, so you see the light?"

"Yes. We need a defensive perimeter. We need to be alert."

Tavita and Bill left on their defensive missions. Denton realized he needed to tell Charlotte about the Indian attack and called her back.

"Okay, Char, your intuition is still working." He told her about the assault on him, adding, "Bill and Tavita said it could have been Spirit Warriors sent to scare me." He said it like a joke, then waited for her Marine sergeant's skepticism.

"Like Indian Spirit Warriors?"

"Yeah."

"You don't sound too good, boss."

"I'll manage."

"Spirit Warriors?"

"Okay, I admit, I'd had a few drinks, but I didn't imagine it."

"Boss, maybe you should come home."

He sensed the concern in her tone. "Nah. I'm fine, but don't mention this to Sandy. I don't think they were spirits either. I think they were real Indians trying to scare me. Why they want to go after me, I don't know. But I'll find out. You know how it goes—when you're getting close to the solution, the bad guys react. Their reactions reveal things."

The concern in her voice increased. "Swinging hatchets and knives at you is a pretty strong reaction. They were trying to do more than scare you. Please be careful. Carry your gun."

Denton knew she was right. "Don't worry, I'm carrying. But Wisconsin doesn't have a concealed weapon permit system."

"Better to get arrested for carrying than get your scalp lifted by Spirit Warriors."

He needed to lighten the mood. "So true. I wonder where Spirit Warriors go when they aren't chasing gringos or whatever they'd call me?"

Charlotte's chuckle came over the wire. "Probably the unhappy hunting ground."

Denton laughed. He was lucky to have Charlotte. She always perked him up. And she mothered him just enough.

She said, "Good news. Judge Sands ruled in your favor on the Motion for Summary Judgment. He held that there were issues of fact that gave you a right to trial *and* that the Rule Against Perpetuities didn't invalidate the will under Wisconsin law."

Denton had forgotten about the pending ruling. The news of victory was sweet. "Good. I wasn't too worried, but you never know."

"Oh, Mary Norton wants you to call her. Ready for the number?"

"Yeah."

Charlotte rattled off the number, and Denton wrote it on his steno pad. "Well, well, boss. *Another* woman?"

"Okay, at ease, Sarge. I don't need a mother."

"Hah. That's what *you* think. I assume you know how to call Sandy at her mom's."

33

Denton remained at the table, staring at the handwritten digits of Mary's phone number. Charlotte's mocking words choked the room, like the smell of piss on a fire. *Well, well, boss. Another woman?*

He punched in Charlotte's number, his stiff finger beating sharp clicks on the small keyboard of his cell phone. Who the hell was she to lecture *him*? But a millimeter above the last numeral, his finger halted. Then he pressed the off button. Charlotte had a point.

His mind turned to Mary. Soft blond hair; clear, caressable skin. Lips damp and red without makeup. Her hazel eyes held an aura of naiveté, as if innocence itself lived within her. But Denton knew of her several relationships with men, and the business acumen with which she'd invested her trust funds. He'd been drawn to her from the moment they met, but he knew the dangers of having an intimate relationship with a client.

Denton's eyes fell upon the Norton family mug shots strewn on the tabletop. Mary's eyes looked into his. Like cards abandoned after a hand, he gathered them up, then slid them into his briefcase. Mary's face disappeared with the rest.

That was how it had to be. Besides, when he'd met Mary, Denton had just married Jane, who later ran off with his law partner, Kap. That was after James Gridley, Jane's ex-husband, had shot Denton in the stomach. Denton's hand felt through his shirt for the puckered scar beside his bellybutton. The old wound lay just below the new gash across his stomach. Then he felt higher up for two scars from bullets that had hit his chest during the shootout in his last case. *Was that barely a year ago? The ole bod's taking a beating. And now I'm up against fuckin' Spirit Warriors and bony old medicine men.*

He looked out the window at the sunlit green lawn, the trees, the placid lake. The sour mood seeped away, and he pulled in a lungful of afternoon air, then let ballooned cheeks whistle it out as he dialed Mary's phone number.

Mary's voice came on the line. "Thanks for calling. Can I get back to you in just a second, Shirley?"

Denton hung up. *Shirley?*

Three minutes later, his phone rang and Mary's soft voice again flowed over the wireless network. "Lee. Sorry. Gustav was right there. I'm in the bathroom with the shower going now."

"Sounds like fun."

"Well, it's not, Lee. You've heard about that horrible man who attacked Asa and Marylyn?"

"Yes. You need to be very careful, Mary. And Joan does too. I think your family has a stalker."

"I realize that. Did you hear that nasty bastard wanted to have sex with Marylyn? Right there in the kitchen. He wanted her to bend over the table with all her clothes off. He was going to do it to her. Right in front of Asa." Her voice sounded excited, as if she was visualizing the scene.

"Ah, yeah… How's Gaston?"

"Gustav. He's an asshole. He thinks you and I are doing it. That's why I called. To alert you."

Denton decided to be perverse. "It?"

"You know. Sex. He's been following you. I had to go to L.A. last week. He heard you were going up to San Francisco and decided you and I were meeting at a hotel. Somewhere in between, I guess."

"Does he envision a kitchen table being involved?"

She giggled. "Oh, Lee. Stop. You're being a wise ass. I remember how you got when we were dancing that night at the Top of the Mark."

He remembered, too. She'd been like a feather in his arms, and the warmth of her young body had radiated into his. They'd glided as if on ice. He'd gotten excited and knew she felt him. He'd moved himself away, his eyes on hers.

Denton searched for a suitable response. All he found was, "Well?"

"Well, never mind… for now. But Gustav went up to San Francisco. He rented a car and followed you. But of course, you weren't meeting me."

"What kind of a car?"

"I'm sure you don't expect me to know that kind of thing. But it was a Miata. He was bragging about how fast he drove it through the mountains. He told me all about it to prove how much he loves me."

Denton's mind retrieved the memory of the blue Miata whizzing past as he stood at the edge of the cliff, looking down into Pilarcitos Creek where Jim Norton had crashed. *The prick Miata guy was Gustav.* "So, fair maiden, did that prove his love and eternal devotion?"

Her pixie laugh tickled his ear. "No, he proved he's a total asshole."

34

Mid-September. Madison, Wisconsin.

Richard Elkin was checking his correspondence when Marge entered. She wore a professional-looking gray suit with pink pin-stripes. A pink handkerchief peeked from the breast pocket of her jacket. She watched him watch her as she strolled to his desk.

"Hi, baby," he said, his voice a whisper.

She smiled and touched a hand to her hair. "I can read your mind. Same here. But later." She handed him a fax. "This is from Stan Collins. He said you wanted copies of anything on the Internet about anybody named Norton. This is about a home invasion at the San Francisco home of Asa Norton II. Some guy broke in and was going to kill him and his girlfriend. The guy's in a coma now. The girlfriend bashed his head with a cast iron skillet. Cracked his skull."

Elkin's chest was tight as he read the fax copy of a *San Francisco Chronicle* article outlining the incident. *Shit! This has to be Allen's work.* It was hard to breathe. He felt Marge's eyes boring into him. *Gotta calm down. Make a joke.* He pushed out a chuckle. "Man, that lady must be some girl."

Marge tugged at the hem of her jacket, a move that stretched the fabric taut against her ample breasts. "So am I. Remember that."

Elkin caught the intriguing aroma of the expensive new perfume he'd given her. "Remind me to keep you away from frying pans."

Elkin heard a heavy knocking at his door. Three staccato raps. Allen Sanger stood in the doorway. His eyes looked worried behind his heavy-framed glasses. *He's seen the newspaper report. He wonders if I've seen it.*

"Come on in, Allen. Thanks, Marge."

Marge and Sanger passed one another as she left. She didn't give him a glance.

Sanger lifted his nose like a hunting dog. "She's wearing new stuff."

"Stuff? That's a hundred an ounce."

Elkin waited for a response, but Sanger knew when to shut up. Elkin held out the fax. "Have you seen this article, Allen?"

Elkin watched Sanger as the man peered through his Clark Kent glasses. *He's not surprised.* "Is that someone you hired, Allen?"

Sanger frowned. "No comment. Besides, if it was, it's better you don't know anything, Mr. Attorney General. Or should I say Governor?"

"Allen?"

"Don't worry about it, sir," Sanger interjected. "I doubt that creep will leave the hospital alive. I'm checking out the Nortons for you to see if one of them could be the blackmailer. I'm sorry Marge bothered you about that incident."

"Don't be hassling Marge, Allen."

Sanger took a seat in front of Elkin's desk and ran his big hand down the crease in his trousers. "I won't, sir. I understand the situation well enough."

"Don't play me, Allen. Talk straight and do your job. That's all I want for my money."

Sanger stood and spread his hands with his palms up. "No problem. I've got to run some errands. I'll be away for a few days."

Elkin's eyes followed Sanger as he left, his large body surprisingly graceful. *I'm losing control of this situation. I may have to do something about Allen. But what?*

Elkin consulted a small red address book, then dialed a number.

A voice answered. "Yes?"

"Do you know who this is?

"Yes."

"We have to rework our plans."

"No problem."

35

Mid-September. Northern Wisconsin.

Denton's hand carelessly held his cell phone while Mary Norton's laughter still played in his ears. He set the phone on the table, twitched his fingers, and set it spinning like an awkward child's toy. His still-frayed nerves jittered with the plastic-on-wood clatter. The spinning stopped and the phone pointed at him. It seemed to signal, "You're It, pal."

So the Miata guy was Gustav. It was nice of Mary to warn him. Or was it? Maybe she was covering her ass. After all, Denton had stared directly at the Miata as it passed him on the cliff. Gustav would realize Denton might have recognized him. What if Mary had sent Gustav? What if Gustav was supposed to ram him off the cliff with the Miata?

Denton stared at the pointing cell phone. He shoved it with his forefinger and set it spinning again. He was still "It" when the spinning stopped.

Cold, clammy ripples assailed his neck. Mary's giggle ran through his mind, but now it seemed forced, out of sync with the gloomy tapestry of death now hanging over the Norton clan. And the deaths of her father and brother had moved her to a higher inheritance tier.

He opened his briefcase, pulling out the Norton files. He flipped through them until he found his hand-drawn Norton family tree. The drawing was now crumpled, and he smoothed it out with his palm. Brown coffee stains claimed a corner. Midnight oil.

He studied names and relationships. Photos ran like a video. Empty eyes, frozen smiles. Each name represented a life, young couples moving on, children laughing in new dawns. The older generation living into their eighties, not disappearing into life's sunset, instead hanging on to assets while the younger generation waited patiently. Or were they patient? Were they even waiting?

Any heir might want to kill any other heir. The motive could be to gain the inheritance, but that might not be the motive. Families could have long-term animosities, lots of skeletons hanging in closets.

Denton's pencil doodled crooked lines on his steno pad, searching for connections. The top two tiers of the family tree were gone. That left Clyde Norton's tier and the one below it. Denton tapped his pencil tip on the circles he'd drawn earlier. Peter Norton, Sylvia Norton Smith, Jim Norton, and William Norton. All dead.

His pencil tip left small dots that logic couldn't connect.

But, best guess: the attack on Asa and Marylyn meant someone was going after that tier of heirs, taking out the great-grandchildren. Jim Norton was dead in his car crash. William Norton had drowned. Now, Asa was almost killed. If Asa had died, the surviving great-grandchildren would have been Joan, Mary and John III. But Asa, Joan and John III wouldn't inherit anything as long as Clyde Norton and John Norton Jr. were alive.

On the other hand, Mary Norton had already inherited a full share due to deaths of her father Peter and her brother Jim. Perhaps sweet Mary wasn't so sweet? But there were other potentials. Like the guy he'd dubbed "Skinny" who had followed him from the court hearing in San Diego. Someone could have sent him. Hell, Mary could have sent him. *And what about the yellow Hummer, and the red pickup?*

Mary's lovely face came into his mind. The idea of Mary-the-Killer didn't jibe. After all, she'd gain little by Asa's death because both Clyde and his daughter Joan would still be alive. Mary wouldn't inherit from Asa under those circumstances.

Still, it was possible she'd already gotten what she wanted, that the attack on Asa was a ploy pointing the finger away from Mary. His pencil tip tapped her name. And what about Mary's mother, Alice? While Alice couldn't inherit, she could receive whatever Mary wanted to give her.

Denton scanned the rest of the family tree diagram. He focused on Clyde and John Norton Jr. Each would gain a lot with the death of the other. And the deaths of the other's children.

Nothing. I'm getting nothing concrete. The dots weren't connecting. Disgusted, Denton dropped the pencil on the table. He stood, stretching his back, feeling the belly wound protest, then bent over to touch his toes. He was sore, but he needed to work out. He took off his shoes and assumed his tae kwan do stance.

He breathed deeply, measured breaths, calming his spirit, clearing his mind of family photos, empty eyes, frozen smiles. *Let go. Let go.*

Which kata *to do? The* won hyo *always calms me.* Denton's hands flashed and he moved into a right cat stance for a double knife hand strike. Now the forward stance, a middle spear hand strike. *Fuckin' Spirit Warriors! Control your breathing; put your hip into it.* Denton was soon lost in the process, his body expertly flowing from one movement to the next, his feet striking out in high kicks, his hands chopping at imaginary throats. *Come on, Red Owl. Okay, Gustav. Fuck you, yellow Hummer guys.*

Finished, he assumed the closed ready stance, his feet together, his left hand at chin level, covered by his right fist. He kept his mind clear, empty of thoughts of death. *Breathe in. Breathe out.*

Reality seeped back in. He allowed his surroundings to focus. Tavita stood by the entrance door, his brown eyes carefully watching Denton.

" 'Lo, boss. You're very good at that. You could have beat Mike the Mugger."

Denton smiled. "That's the guy you whipped for the heavyweight title back when you were wrestling, right?"

"Yeh. He was the king of the hill till I showed up. But now…" Tavita held up his left arm with its missing hand.

Denton shrugged. "That was a terrible thing, losing your hand and your wrestling career. But now you're a successful legal assistant and a licensed private investigator. These will be longer-lasting careers than wrestling would have been."

Tavita smiled, his smooth tan face displaying its dimples, his brown eyes shining. "True, boss, but nobody shot me when I was wrestling."

Memories returned of his last case, the Security Life case. Insurance Commissioner Stubbs had asked him to help with a financial audit, to get hard numbers. Both Denton and Tavita had been shot by a would-be assassin. Denton forced a grin. "True enough, but you *were* stabbed."

Tavita laughed. "Point for you, boss. Speaking of being an investigator, Charlotte ran down a couple of guys up in the town of Mercer who might have some info on George Norton Schneider. Uncle Bill's lending me his truck so I can drive up and talk to them. Charlotte already set up a meeting for tomorrow morning."

"Good. Maybe it'll lead somewhere," Denton said, snuffing an urge to invite himself along. He needed to allow Tavita to work on his own, to prove what he could do. Or what he couldn't do. The Capone connection seemed tenuous, another dead end. But the past had a sneaky way of connecting itself to the present. All possibilities had to be explored.

36

Mid-September. San Francisco, California.

During his flight from Madison to San Francisco, Allen Sanger's fingers clawed into the arms of his coach class seat. The airliner tipped a wing, flying low over the ocean as it approached LAX. He held his breath as they slammed into the runway, became airborne, then thudded to Earth again. He'd already stained the armpits of his light tan suit jacket, sweating while trapped inside a tin tube, suspended at thirty-five thousand feet. But he couldn't trust this job to anybody else.

As the plane's engines reversed thrust, shoving him forward against his seatbelt, his thoughts returned to the botched attack on Asa Norton II. *I never should have hired that little prick, Mark Scheff.* Scheff was supposed to tail Asa Norton, not kill him. Check up on him, see if he could have been in Wisconsin dropping off the Capone documents at the Soo Line depot. *Instead, Scheff gets brained with a fucking frying pan.*

The airplane jerked to a stop at its gate. He had the seatbelt off before the loud "ding" signaled permission to leave his seat. Sanger slid into the aisle along with a crowd of other passengers and waited for the exit door to open. The wait grew longer. Sanger was pressed against a pretty young woman from the next row up. He felt her youthful ass against his thigh and felt a stirring. He'd follow her if he didn't have to take care of Scheff.

The pilot's voice informed them the gate crew had not been ready for their early arrival and there would be a short wait. A communal groan went up. His thigh felt the woman's ass as people jostled with their carry-on baggage. Then angry black eyes were challenging him.

"Always the same," he smiled, "hurry up and wait."

The woman shifted away from him, unsure of what had happened. People kept shoving.

Sanger fidgeted, anxious to get his rental car and make his way to St. Luke's Hospital. He had no plan. He'd figure things out when he got there.

An hour later he exited his Pontiac rental car and slipped on his tan suit coat. He straightened his red tie and composed himself. He rehearsed his short story: *I'm Mark's brother. In from Wisconsin. Anxious to see him.*

He squared his shoulders and walked into the hospital. He adopted a broad smile as he neared the information desk. He adjusted his glasses and smiled as he asked for Mark Scheff. "I'm his older brother. Just in from Wisconsin."

The elderly woman smiled. "He's in ICU, sir. Eighth floor. Room 812." She pointed a thin, shaking finger. "That elevator bank. Welcome to St. Luke's."

Sanger entered the elevator. He was followed by a young Hispanic attendant pushing a gurney carrying an unconscious, sheet-wrapped woman. An IV dripped clear liquid into a needle impaled in the back of her hand. Only her pale face was visible. Not much life in this one, not like the woman challenging his leg pushing against her, her black eyes hot.

Sanger punched the eight button and asked, "What floor?"

"Eight also."

Sanger politely held the elevator door as the young man pushed the gurney out of the elevator onto the polished green linoleum.

Sanger scanned the long, sterile hallway. Ash-colored doors, bright ceiling lights, calming art prints lining the halls. He watched the attendant and gurney disappear around the corner. Sanger checked the room numbers. He saw 812 only five rooms down, on the left. A nearby sign marked a convenient exit stairway. Sanger sidled up to the closed door of 812, turned the knob, and opened the door.

The room held two beds, one empty and one occupied. Life support equipment crowded around the occupied bed where Scheff's face lay upon a white pillow, an oxygen hose in his nose. His head was swathed in bandages. An IV stabbed the back of his hand. Blips of light danced across nearby screens. The already skinny young man now seemed stick-like.

Sanger stared, anger roiling inside. This pathetic bundle stood between him and the top cop job with the new governor. Sanger wanted to smash his fists into Scheff's face, pounding it to mush. Sanger's thumb pushed up one of Scheff's eyelids. His eyes were rolled back. Maybe Scheff was seeing his brain full of bone splinters. *Is that what you're doing, you worthless shit?*

Sanger slid back to the door and surveyed the hallway. Empty. He returned to Scheff. *You stupid fucker.* Sanger placed his wide palm over Scheff's mouth and pinched his nostrils shut. Scheff's body heaved with surprising primal strength. His lungs fought to suck air. But he was dead in scant minutes.

Sanger gazed at the dead face, its oxygen tube lopsided. Sanger straightened it out. *This has to look normal.* Scheff looked the same as when he was alive. What was the thing that had departed? Like something you could catch in a bottle. Like a firefly. But now it was gone forever. *Too fuckin' bad.*

A sharp electronic buzzing interrupted Sanger's thoughts. The machines protested Scheff's demise. *Time to run.*

Sanger exited the room and dashed to the stairwell. As the stairwell door closed behind him, he heard running footsteps in the hall. Thirty seconds later, Sanger left the hospital. It had been so easy. The road to Top Cop was still his. Now he had to suffer another airplane ride before he took care of other problems. Annoyed, he wiped at some spots of IV fluid on his light tan jacket.

37

Denton's eyes blinked in the sun-filled cabin room as he stared at the illuminated dial of the bedside alarm clock. It read 8:30. He rolled over on his back and stared at the pine ceiling. Despite his aches, cuts, and bruises, he felt refreshed from his night of dreamless sleep. White pills had their benefits. Someday he'd be free of them, but not yet, not while the Nortons had him twisted into their net.

He slipped out of bed, pulled on his shorts, and went to the kitchen, where he found Uncle Bill finishing up a plate of bacon and eggs. Bill gestured with his coffee cup. "Well, you look a lot better today. Have some coffee?"

"Sure."

"Want me to fry up some eggs and bacon for you?"

"Not yet. Did Tavita go up to Mercer?" Denton stood at the counter, pouring coffee into a chipped white mug bearing a Marine Corps logo. "*Semper Fi,*" it proclaimed.

Bill eyed the mug. "Ah, yeah, he did."

"Do you know those guys he's meeting?"

Bill drained his cup. "Yeah, vaguely. Hey, it's almost nine. I've got a date with Lorraine. She'll be here any second."

155

A gentle tapping at the front door resonated through the cabin. "There she is now," said Bill. He jumped to his feet, tucked in his red and black flannel shirt, swiped a palm along his hair, and moseyed to the door.

Denton followed and spied a gray-haired woman opening the squeaking door with a practiced motion. She was slim and pretty, in her mid to late fifties, with a smile on her tanned face. She entered with an elegant ballerina movement. Denton half expected a pirouette.

"Lorraine Culbertson, meet my nephew, Leland Denton."

She toed her way to Denton and they shook hands with dainty ceremony. Denton re-calculated; she was probably in her sixties. Still, quite young compared to Uncle Bill. "Oh, I'm so glad to meet you at last. Billy has told me all about his famous nephew."

Billy? "The pleasure is all mine, Mrs. Culbertson."

"Oh, do call me Lorraine."

They exchanged a few pleasant irrelevancies, and then Lorraine hooked her arm in Bill's. "We gotta make tracks, Billy." Bill followed meekly, and she twiddled her fingers over her shoulder at Denton as they left.

The front door squeaked shut. Denton sat at the table and took a drink of coffee. Caffeine-laced heat warmed him. *Time to call Sandy.* He retrieved his cell phone from the bedroom and returned to the kitchen table.

"Lee. You just caught me. I'm on my way to work."

"Work?"

"Yes, Mom has a friend that owns a local insurance agency. His assistant is out having a baby, and he needs a temp. I'm filling in for a bit."

"A bit?"

"Yes, silly. I told Albert I'd work until you finish up in Wisconsin. It's wonderful to hear your voice. How are you?"

Denton assured her he was fine and dandy and making progress on the case. He didn't mention the Spirit Warriors, the bear, or Lilly. The soft tones of her voice made him ache to be with her. They ended the call with mutual "I-love-you's," and he felt high, happy in the cool of the morning, remembering Sandy's warm, eager body.

Then the idea of insurance agent Albert and Sandy's job at his agency intruded. Sad memories of Denton's former girlfriend, Ricki, choked his thoughts. Ricki had also gone off on a new job. And Ricki never returned.

In the early afternoon, Denton was rigging fishing rods when Tavita returned from his trip to Mercer.

"Hey, boss. Goin' fishing?"

"Yeah. You come too."

"Don't you want to know about my meetings?"

"Yes, but how about we go fishing? You can tell me while we're out on the lake."

Tavita held up his stump. "Fishing is a little difficult for me, boss."

"Nonsense, I'll bait your hooks. We'll raid Uncle Bill's worm box and go out for some crappie and bluegill. It'll be fun. We'll have a fish fry."

An hour later, Tavita pulled in his tenth fish, a large crappie. He swung his pole over to Denton, who unhooked the fish, saying, "I can certainly see that the loss of your hand is a handicap. For me, that is. I barely have time to bring in my own fish because I'm so busy unhooking yours and putting new worms on."

"Your idea, boss."

"So true. Nice out here, isn't it?"

"Yeh. I used to fish back in Samoa. Sit in a boat for hours thinking about stuff. Remembering stuff."

Denton's rod arced, and the monofilament line twanged with tension. "Got a big one," Denton yelled, and hauled in a large-mouth bass. He held it up for Tavita to see. "Well, here's one for your memory banks."

Tavita smiled. "I've got bigger ones than that to remember, boss."

"Yeah, I suppose you do. I've seen those big groupers and sea bass out in the South Pacific." Denton slipped the fish onto their stringer, re-baited his hook, and slung out his line. He watched the red and white bobber rise and fall on small lake ripples. "Memory's most of life, isn't it? I mean, you're never in the present. When the future comes, it shoots right by and becomes the past. It's only memories that we keep."

An eagle soared overhead. Both men watched it without speaking. The eagle's high-pitched "screeee" pierced the air.

Tavita rested his fishing rod on the edge of the boat. "That's what my tattoos are. They're signs of the things we Samoans remember. They show respect for our ancestors, honor those who came before."

Denton eyed the intricate tattooing. "I bet that hurt."

"Yeh. It took months. But I was in training to be a chief. And a kind of medicine man."

"So why'd you leave?"

"I was in line for chief because my uncle, who was chief, had no kids. His wife died, and he remarried. His young wife had twins. That made me third in line. Then she got pregnant again."

"So you became a wrestler."

"Yeh." Tavita held up his maimed arm. "And you know how that worked out."

Denton nodded, fiddling with his line. "You go where fate takes you, Tavita. Just think, if you'd stayed in Samoa, you'd be kissing all those cousins' butts. You'd never have met Charlotte... ah, or me."

Tavita's eyes twitched away. He concentrated on bringing in his fishing line, holding the rod in the crook of his left arm, using his good hand to check the health of his worm. "Yeh. True. Say, I meant to tell you what we found out about George Norton

Schneider, that Norton cousin who disappeared back in the 1940s after he delivered a package to some mobsters."

Denton shrugged. "I guess there wasn't much to find out."

"Actually, there was."

Denton swatted at a fly buzzing around his head. "Okay, what did you find out about Cousin Georgie?"

"Remember he rode the train from Chicago. Delivered the package to a guy in Couderay."

"Yeah," said Denton. "That's what—maybe twelve miles from Capone's hideout?" He put his hands against the small of his back and stretched aching muscles. "Anybody know what was in the package?"

"Maybe. Could have been records, like duplicate books for some of Capone's operations. It could have been cash."

Denton twitched his fishing line and watched a bluegill wriggle free, a flash of gills and gold. "Okay, but who's telling you the stuff about the package?"

"Charlotte located these old guys up in Mercer, Wisconsin, where Al's brother Ralph had his place. I met them this morning. They worked in Ralph's auto garage. One of them, Ruben Myers, claims he was the driver of the car when George handed over the package."

Denton put the lid on their worm can. "Interesting. That would have been in 1944. What does he say was in it?"

"Ruben says he overheard Al tell Ralph it was financial records."

"Makes sense."

"Ruben also says Al told Ralph the package had birth records."

Denton glanced quickly at Tavita. "Birth records? Whose?"

"He didn't know."

Denton's mind played with Tavita's story. "Let's head back in so I can write this down."

"Good idea, boss. I have some notes, too."

Denton pulled the starter cord on the five-horsepower outboard. It started with a billow of white smoke. "Interesting, Tavita. Very interesting." Denton steered back to Uncle Bill's cabin.

Ten minutes later, Denton and Tavita were sitting in Adirondack chairs sipping from brown bottles of beer. Tavita's yellow legal pad lay on the wide arm of his chair.

"So what happened to George?"

Tavita's hand ruffled his black mop of hair, then flipped through his notes. "Not clear. He did some work around Capone's hideout for a year or so. And he made some trips back and forth to Chicago during the same time period. Then he disappeared." Tavita looked at his beer bottle, as if the answer was hidden in the brown glass. "Some say he's buried somewhere in the woods around the hideout. Others say he's wearing concrete shoes at the bottom of that forty-acre lake at Capone's place."

"And these someones are...?"

"Well, one was Ruben Myers, an Indian who lives in New Post. His dad, Gaspar Myers, ran a little hotel in the town of Post." Tavita checked his notes. "Ah... it was named the Thayer Hotel after the original owner. Ruben claims the hotel could still be accessed for quite awhile when the new lake was filling up. Ruben's dad, Gaspar, told him that George stayed there. Then supposedly George was killed. But a few days later, Gaspar's driving Capone's big Packard that he was taking care of while Capone was in prison. Gaspar passes a car on the road, and guess what?"

Denton shrugged. "I couldn't possibly."

"George was driving. When George saw the Packard, he took off. Nobody ever saw him again."

"Is Gaspar still around?"

"Nope. Dead twenty years or so."

Denton spotted the eagle soaring back across the lake, its white head and tail lit by the sun. He watched the wide-winged raptor swoop to the lake surface, its sharp talons poised. "That's pretty weak evidence. The worst kind of hearsay."

"You mean because Ruben's saying what Gaspar said."

"Yes. There's no way to know if Gaspar was reliable or if Ruben got the story straight."

The eagle snatched up a fish, leaving a slash of white water that quickly disappeared. Hunter and prey skimmed away.

"Hope that's my bluegill," Denton said. He tapped Tavita's shoulder. "Look how peaceful the lake looks, how fast the water hid the place the eagle grabbed the fish." Denton sipped his beer. "Still, hearsay can be true."

Tavita sat forward in his chair. "That's right, boss. And that reminds me of something." He used the nub of his left arm to steady the legal pad on the chair while he flipped though its pages. "Just a sec. Here it is. Gaspar said George Norton left some stuff at his hotel in Post."

"Left some stuff? Like what?"

"Ruben told me Gaspar only knew it was something in a steel box. With a lock."

The hair on the back of Denton's neck curled; cold tingles rippled his shoulders. "A locked box?"

"Yeh, boss. That could be important, right?"

"Well, hell yes. If George left a locked box, that's where his Capone stuff is."

Tavita nodded. "Sure, boss, I know that—but we can't get the box even if it's still there."

"Sure we can. We'll just go over and ask for it. If Ruben Myers won't let us look at it, we'll get a warrant." Denton smiled. Lose a bluegill, gain a locked box.

"But, boss, Post has been twenty or thirty feet underwater for years."

Denton glared at him. "You held that back."

"No, I didn't."

"What a pisser."

"Yeh. That's what I thought."

38

Mid-September. Northern Wisconsin.

"Post is underwater? Under the lake?"

Tavita smoothed his notes with his stump. "Yeh, when they dammed up the Chippewa River, they flooded... ah, more than fifty-six hundred acres. That included the village of Post. Let's see, the Indian name was Pahquahwong. The water of the Chippewa Flowage is twenty or thirty feet deep where Post used to be."

Denton gazed into Tavita's brown eyes. He reached for his still-cool beer. "Well, so much for trotting over and checking out Gaspar Myers' basement."

"Right, boss."

"That flooding must have pissed off the Indians."

"Yes, it did. They resisted the Wisconsin-Minnesota Light & Power Company for years. But then the U.S. Congress passed the Federal Water Power Act that allowed the takeover. That ended the dispute. For then, anyway."

Not for the first time, Denton was impressed with the thoroughness of Tavita's research and investigative ability. "Good work."

"Thanks. Anyway, they finally settled the argument. The power company agreed to build a whole new village, with houses, a church, a school. And to move the Indian graves to a new cemetery on higher ground that wouldn't be flooded."

"So that's where the name *New* Post came from."

"Yeh. But the power company didn't do all it promised. A lot of graves were never moved. During the next several years, bodies would float up, coming out of their coffins."

Mental images of drowned bodies demanded Denton's attention. He mumbled, "And the sea gave up the dead which were in it... they were judged every man according to their works."

Tavita leaned closer. "What was that? You okay, boss?"

"Yeah. Just something I remembered from a long time ago."

"You look pale."

"I'm okay. What a fucked-up thing for the power company to do." Denton's thoughts shifted to William Norton's body floating in the same lake. "Hey, didn't William Norton have scuba gear when he drowned?"

"Yeh. And they found him floating face down in the water near where Post was. He could have been diving on the sunken village. There's a bunch of buildings down there. Even an old jail... and the hotel."

Denton stared at high cumulus clouds. *Graves. Dead bodies. Not a big leap to ghosts.* The approaching sunset smeared the clouds pink, blue, and mauve. "I wonder what's happened to whatever William had in the boat with him. His scuba gear and all."

"The sheriff's office has it. Everything got impounded along with his boat. Possible evidence."

Uncle Bill walked out on the porch, carrying a beer. A smile seamed into his weatherbeaten face. "Hey, guys, whassit?"

"It's *whassup*, Uncle Bill, and we need to see your pal Sheriff Nils again."

With the grace of a younger man, Bill moved into an empty chair. "No problem, but what for? He's not going to let us see that Jack Mathers guy again."

Uncle Bill's face from Denton's boyhood shimmered away the older man's wrinkled visage. Denton saw the man as he had been during warm boyhood summers. He'd been strong, protective. Available when Denton woke frightened in the night. Bill was old now, but Denton sensed power still throbbed in the man. "No. The sheriff has William and Sylvia Norton's personal effects. I need to see them. Judge Sands in San Diego told me to give him a report on the deaths. Sands is a federal judge."

Bill took a swig of his beer and wiped his mouth with the back of a thick-knuckled hand. "Not a problem. But you know Joe Nils is gonna know whatever you find out."

Denton said, "No problem." But how far could he trust Sheriff Nils? Unbidden, an Indian corpse floated across Denton's mind, slowly twisting, rising into the justice of sunlight.

39

At 9:30 the next morning, Denton arrived at the Sawyer County Sheriff's Office lugging his brown leather lucky briefcase. Its beat-up appearance was a symbol of his expertise, of knowing what the hell he was doing. The entry lobby was empty except for two men in jeans, flannel shirts, and scuffed leather boots. They looked like they'd come in from a farm, maybe a logging operation. Denton felt out of place, wishing he'd worn chinos with a sweater instead of his bright tie with his stand-by blazer and gray slacks.

He explained his business to the chubby, dark-haired receptionist. She consulted a list. "Yes. Please have a seat. Someone will come for you."

Denton was escorted to the sheriff's office by a woman deputy sheriff whose khaki uniform fit tight. She was tall, well-built, and pretty. Long blond hair, high cheekbones. She wore little, if any, make-up, and Denton thought she looked like the kind of woman who might ski bare-breasted in the moonlight, like a Viking queen, nipples honed sharp. She scanned Denton with green eyes of a faint Asian cast. She didn't seem impressed with what she saw. She'd probably read his mind.

Sheriff Joseph Nils was still big and beefy, but now he wore a .357 Magnum in a tooled leather holster strapped around his waist. "Come on in, Mr. Denton. Nice to see you again."

Denton smiled and stuck out his palm. Sheriff Nils seized it in a massive fist. Denton strained to deliver a respectable handshake, but doubted he had done so. "Thanks, Sheriff."

"Hell, son, call me Joe."

"Sure, Joe. I'm Lee."

"Okay, Lee. I guess you met Sherry here," said Sheriff Nils, pointing at Denton's escort.

"Yes. Sort of." Moonlight bathed the snow; skis hissed.

"Well, Sherry here is gonna take you to one of the interview rooms, where she's put all the stuff we found in William Norton's boat. The boat's in the impoundment yard if you want to see it. Nothing interesting on it, but if you want to see for yourself, just ask Sherry here."

"Thanks."

Sheriff Nils slapped Denton on the back. "Another mystery in the North Woods. Have fun figuring it out."

Denton turned to leave, but Sheriff Nils said, "One thing, Lee."

"What's that?"

"You can look, even touch. But don't fool around with anything or take anything unless you get my permission."

"No problem, Sheriff, ah, Joe."

"Follow me," said Sherry, her crystal eyes slicing into his as she pointed. "Along this hall, Mr. Denton."

Denton stared back, delivering his best boyish grin. The corners of her lips twitched, a concession to yet one more male with the hots.

"Call me Lee," he said, but she was already striding away. Denton trailed behind, clutching his briefcase, until they reached a door with a sign proclaiming it to be Interrogation Room Two.

Sherry gestured at a scarred wooden chair. "Have a seat, Mr. Denton. I'll have the material brought in to you."

Before Denton could reply, she was gone. A damned annoying habit she had. He sat at one end of the rickety table that looked as if it had been leaned on by too many big men. He spotted a camera in the far corner. A dingy one-way mirror was built into one wall.

The room exuded isolation. He took a chair, setting his briefcase on the table. Its scarred leather blended with random scratches and cuts on the tabletop. He was a long way from San Diego, confined in a tiny wood-paneled box inside a small-town sheriff's office. But unlike his desperate predecessors, he was free to leave.

He opened his briefcase and pulled out his steno pad and new felt tip pen. He was jotting down the date and time when two hefty deputies carried in three cardboard boxes and an aluminum scuba tank. The tank clanked when they set it down by the table. They left without a word.

Denton was still making notes when Sherry appeared in the doorway. "That's the stuff. My office is four doors down on the left. Please see me before you leave."

"Thank you," Denton said quickly, before she could leave.

"By the way, your pen's leaking."

Denton looked at the black stains on his fingers. When he looked up she was gone, like a ghost. He tore a sheet from his steno book, wrapped the leaking pen in it, and tossed the wad into a gray metal trashcan standing in a corner. He turned back to the table. Where to start?

He hefted the steel scuba tank and checked the inspection date information stamped into its side. It was current. He worked the valve, and a powerful rush of compressed air escaped. The tank was fine. He pulled open the boxes and searched for the regulator. He found it in the third box. It was a comparatively new Sherwood. In addition to the primary regulator, the rig had an octopus that provided a second mouthpiece to breathe through if the primary regulator failed. It pays to be careful. He checked all the air hoses. No problems.

Denton connected the apparatus to the steel tank and turned on the air. The gauge flung its pointer across the dial. Nine hundred pounds of air left. Denton mentally calculated: if the tank had been full, it would have held about three thousand pounds of air. Say the lake was thirty feet deep; then the twenty-one hundred pounds of air William had used would have given him a bottom time of at least forty minutes, likely more than that.

Denton eyed the primary mouthpiece, last used by a dead man. Denton put it into his mouth, catching the familiar vibration of air against dry rubber. It tickled his lips for a second as the air flowed steadily. Then the octopus. It flowed easily. Denton took several breaths, checking for the taste of rust or other foreign materials. None.

Then it hit him. *Shit! This air could be poisoned.* What a fool he'd been. As his brain settled down, he realized he'd already be feeling the effects of any poison. Or would he? He sucked in several deep breaths of room air, evaluating the condition of his lungs with each. *I'm fine. Christ, what a fuck-up!*

He dug through the other boxes. Two life jackets, a small fire extinguisher, fins, snorkel, buoyancy compensator vest, weight belt, fins, dive booties, and assorted other equipment, including a big dive knife with a sharp, serrated blade. A waterproof zippered bag, like a small briefcase, yielded William's driver's license, a credit card, thirty dollars in cash, a ballpoint pen, and a folded, white sheet of paper.

Denton pulled out the pen and clicked it. Dead Nortons were keeping him in writing gear. The pen's blue ink flowed as smoothly as the air from the tanks. A decent pen with no current tendency to leak.

Denton laid it down and picked up the folded sheet of paper. It was a drawing. A kind of map with a few black lines that crossed one another at a central point. Roads, most likely. There were several drawn shapes, like distorted circles. He saw that the shapes had writing on them, but he had to strain to read it. One said "Desire Lake" and another was labeled "Pokegama Lake." He'd never heard of either. Small black squares were drawn on the paper, some in small clusters and some sitting alone along the black lines.

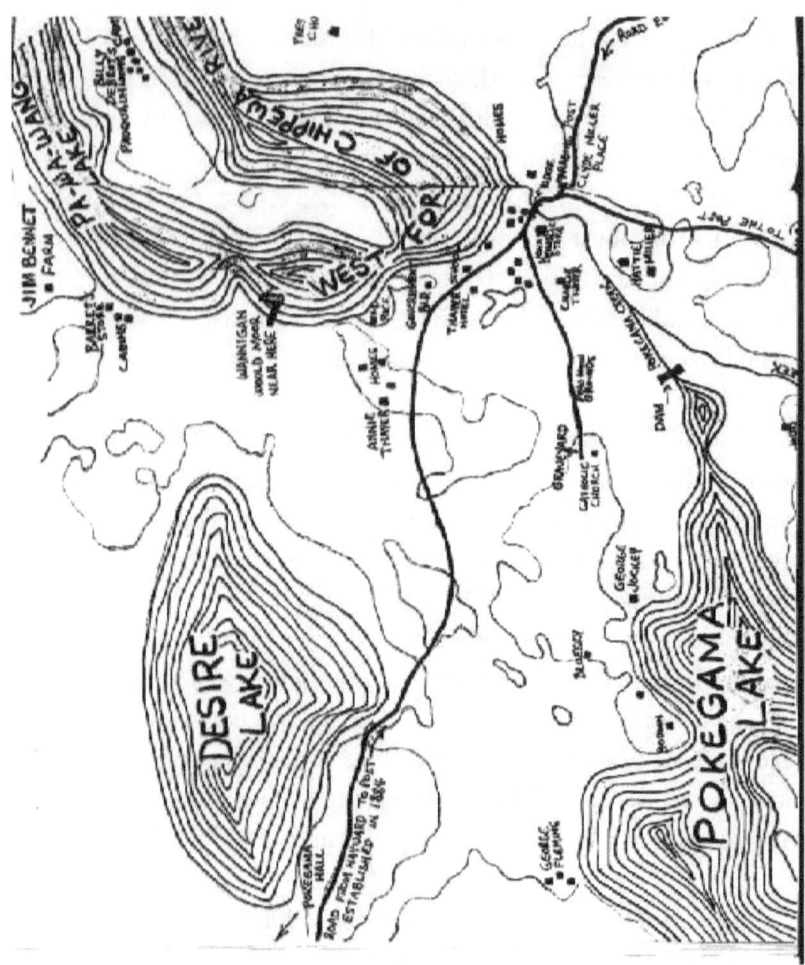

Puzzled, he left the room, walked down the hall, and tapped at Sherry's door. Her green Asian eyes looked up from a file she was reading. "Yes?"

He showed her the paper. "Have you ever heard of Desire Lake or Pokegama Lake?"

"I think Pokegama Lake is part of the Chippewa Flowage, but I never heard of Desire Lake. Let's ask Sheriff Nils."

Denton followed Sherry to the sheriff's office and showed him the paper. The sheriff pulled a black plastic pair of reading glasses from his desk drawer. "Just a sec. I need these cheaters."

He slipped on the glasses and looked at the paper. "Yeah. I saw this in that William Norton stuff. It's a map of Post and the area around it back in the years before they built the dam that flooded the area and made the Chippewa Flowage. Desire Lake and Poke-gama Lake were there before they built the dam. Once the valley flooded up behind the dam, those old lakes became part of the Chippewa Flowage." The sheriff peered over his lenses at Denton.

Denton gently extricated the paper from Sheriff Nil's burley hand and stared at it. "What did you think this meant when you found it?"

The sheriff removed his glasses and shifted in his chair, getting comfortable. "Well, hell. It's obvious. William was diving into the sunken village. Maybe just to do it, maybe looking for something. Who knows? See those little squares? Those are houses and other buildings." Sheriff Nil's tapped the map with his self-manicured finger. "There's were the school was. A store here. The old hotel and even the graveyard. All submerged."

Denton leaned over, peering at the map details. "When did all that go underwater?"

"Well, let's see." The sheriff's sat back, his eyes elevating to the ceiling. "Well, they finished the dam in the mid-1920s, but it took quite a while for the water to cover the village. I'm not sure when it actually went under. Hell, it's thirty feet deep there now. Every now and then, a board or something floats up. You know, the power company never got around to moving the dead from the graveyard. Years ago, bodies used to float up."

"Yeah. I heard about the bodies."

Sherry interjected, "Right. I expect some are still down there."

Sheriff Nils rubbed his square jaw as he evaluated Denton. "You know, that part of the lake is kind of a spooky place. Lots of folks avoid it."

Sherry nodded her agreement.

Denton realized they were serious. "Spooky how?"

Sheriff Nils shook his head. "Oh, dunno. The place is just kinda weird."

The three of them were silent as they thought about it. A male deputy stuck his GI buzz-cut into the room. "Almost time for the meeting, Sheriff Nils."

The sheriff nodded and waved the man away. Denton broke the silence. "Could I get a copy of this map?"

"Sure. Sherry, would you make him a copy? Is that all? I've got a meeting."

Denton said, "Yes, that's it for now. Thanks a million, Joe."

"Sure." Nils' blue eyes probed. "Tell Bobcat Bill I said he owes me one."

Denton watched Sherry as she tried to make his copy. She punched a button, but nothing happened. She leaned over and read the message in a small screen on the copier. "Gotta change the toner."

She opened the toner door. Her taut body bent and twisted as she replaced the black cartridge. Denton's mind traveled far from toner problems. She didn't look back, but her words carried over her shoulder. "I know what you're thinking, Mr. Denton, but I've got a boyfriend that I like a lot. He's twice your size and mean as a snake."

"Sorry. So, who's the second prettiest woman in town?"

The plastic door of the copier clicked shut. She faced Denton, the fading corners of a smile still apparent. But her eyes held something he couldn't read. "Mr. Denton, everybody up here knows there are bad spirits in that part of the lake."

"I respect that."

The copier glowed green and spit out Denton's copy.

Sherry's soft hand gave Denton the warm white paper. "All those dead people under the water. Bodies floating up. William Norton never should have dived there."

40

Sherry's dire comment hung over Denton as he left the sheriff's office with the old map folded in his blazer pocket. He'd left William Norton's pen on the interrogation room table. After all, William wasn't his client. Now it was time to go to the impoundment lot to check over William's boat, the second dead man's boat he'd be on inside a month. He felt sour at the prospect. And pretty Sherry's doom and gloom didn't help things.

He stepped down the hallway and smiled at the receptionist as he approached her desk. Dimples appeared in her round cheeks when she grinned back. He pegged her as matronly youthful, a mild woman. Then he saw the collection of skeet shooting trophies that dominated her desktop.

"You just go on down that hallway and out the double doors at the end. Then you'll be in the impoundment lot and you'll see the boat. It's the only one there."

Denton entered the graveled lot and spotted the red, eighteen-foot Lund sitting on its trailer parked against the high chain-link fence. She was imprisoned, abandoned by her owner, as bereft as Jim Norton's *Mariposa* back in her slip in Half Moon Bay.

Her aluminum hull was covered with the dust of neglect. Denton's hand wiped a clear swath of red paint that gleamed in the sun. He patted her 90-horsepower outboard, a Mercury four-stroke. It was rigged with tilt and trim, just the way he would have bought it. Denton carefully checked the undersides. No dents or other damage. The upper hull was fine, too. *Well, William didn't fall off because of a collision… or a ramming.*

Denton clambered aboard, his movements producing hollow thuds against the aluminum. A careful search revealed nothing. *What could have made William Norton fall into the lake? If he fell, that is. A push would explain it, but who could have done that?*

All he had was speculation, no real clues. Despondent, Denton turned to leave, then spotted the depth finder mounted at the steering console. It was a gray Humminbird 580 GPS. His mood escalated a few steps. This was a global positioning satellite unit, probably with charts of the local waters. What if it had a chart of the Chippewa Flowage? What if William Norton had left some waypoints on the unit?

Eagerly, Denton slid into the driver's seat. *I hope the battery still has a charge.* He poked the instrument's power switch. The unit lit up with a friendly beep. His finger stabbed the menu button. An electronic chart of the Chippewa Flowage flared. Several Xs had been entered on the chart. Denton scrolled through the menu until he retrieved the list of waypoints, a list of entries that gave the latitudes and longitudes of the Xs William had put on the electronic chart.

Denton shoved a hand into his blazer pocket, yanking out his copy of the hand-drawn map and comparing it to the electronic chart. *Yep. He's entered marks for various places in Post, sites over fifty years underwater.*

He had to call Uncle Bill. *Gotta get a boat with a GPS.* As he pulled his cell phone out of his briefcase, he felt the weight of his Browning Hi-Power in the concealed weapon compartment. He'd been lucky the sheriff's office hadn't run him through a security machine.

His fingers searched for the phone, but found a stubby pencil. Then he felt the cold disc of his lucky penny. Finally, he got the phone and dialed Uncle Bill's number. He practically jitterbugged while the phone rang. Finally, Bill answered. He seemed out of breath. Fearing a heart attack, Denton said, "You okay?"

"Ahhh, it's you. Well, don't worry about it. Whadda you want? And make it quick."

Denton explained about William Norton's waypoints and that he needed a boat with a GPS. "Just a minute," Bill said. Faintly, Denton heard him call out, "Do you still have that boat with the GPS?" A woman's voice answered. Uncle Bill came back on the line. "Yeah. Lorraine has one you can borrow."

"Thanks. You two doing exercises together?"

"You could say that. Bye."

41

As Denton drove away from the sheriff's impoundment lot, he felt like singing. At last, solid clues to... something. First, Tavita's story via Gaspar Myers about a locked steel box left in the hotel that was now underwater. Next, GPS waypoints on William Norton's boat proving he'd searched for something in the sunken town of Post.

Denton came to a stop sign a block away from the sheriff's office. His eyes surveyed the main downtown section of Hayward. He still needed a decent pen, so he parked and scoured the stores. He entered a souvenir shop, one he'd been in as a child. A display of pens gleamed amid other tourist regalia that also begged Denton's attention. His fingers slid over smooth plastic tubes. His thumb worked the buttons: *click-a-de click, de click.* Like tiny steel wheels on railroad tracks. He liked the yellow one with a red heart and the logo, "Heart of the Muskie Country."

His father's voice echoed, "We'll go muskie fishing. We'll catch a big one, son, catch a real big one. A fifty-incher." Denton felt soft paws of melancholy. He knew they held embedded claws. *Think of something else.* His desperate eye caught a Smokey Bear poster. Only Denton could prevent forest fires.

Forest fires—rangers. Lilly Deerfoot. It was Friday. He had a dinner date with Lilly Deerfoot. Melancholy pattered away, chased by Lilly's brightness.

He bought the Muskie Country pen, then hopped in his car. As he drove he sang an old Ian and Sylvia song, "The Renegade." It was about an Indian who vowed to drink his own liquor, to find his own way, sing the old songs. What were the words? Something, something, then "I leave you to your white man; I curse their church that tells us that our fathers were wrong." His baritone echoed within the car, but the rest of the words eluded him. Only the road noise from his tires broke the silence.

What was it John Batiste had said? Something about stories made up by missionaries to slander the Ojibwe. *Oh, yeah. The cook until puckered stuff. Ouch!*

He arrived at the cabin and entered to find Tavita and Uncle Bill chatting with Lorraine Culbertson. Bill greeted Denton, slipping his weathered arm around Lorraine's shoulder. "Lorraine says you can borrow her boat. It was her late husband's."

Lorraine beamed white teeth and let her pale eyes rub Denton's body, appraising him. "Hello, Lee," she said. "Billy says you want to take the boat to the Chippewa Flowage. That's where my husband Chris used to fish for Muskies."

Denton grinned. "Thanks, Lorraine. You too, *Billy.*"

Bill harrumphed and said, "The boat has a fine GPS chartplotter. But don't forget your big date tonight."

Tavita emitted a thin giggle, but said nothing.

"It's not a *big* date." Denton smiled into Lorraine's bemused eyes. He glanced at his watch. "Well, I gotta get ready. Thanks again, Lorraine."

He glanced over his shoulder as he left the room. Bill and Lorraine were walking towards the porch, arms around each other. Tavita moved to the couch, carrying a beer.

Time to shower and get presentable. It *wasn't* a big date, but a guy's got to be clean and neat when he goes out. Soon he was pulling on khaki pants and a white dress shirt left open-collared, without a tie. Brown loafers and a navy blazer completed his ensemble. He checked the mirror, saw the guy in the Dewar's scotch ad staring back, and chuckled. *Okay, a bit duded up, but you'll do.*

He re-entered the living room to find Bill standing alone at the window watching the lake lie smooth in the calm of the evening. He saw Lorraine's form in the distance, approaching her cabin.

Bill turned and looked him over. "You sure are duded up, nephew. Trying to impress your date?"

Tavita pitched in, "Yeh, boss. I hear Lillian's a babe. And she's single."

Denton's blazer suddenly felt heavy. "You two can put a lid on it. I'm just going out with her because she cornered me into it. Besides, she can help me meet the Indians around here."

Bill laughed. "Not painted ones, I hope. So it's research, eh? I'll just bet she's got some stuff you want to go over."

"Yeah, *Billy*? I'm thinking you and Lorraine have been covering a few points of your own."

Tavita's odd giggle rang out. "I guess I need to find a girl-friend, too. So I can fit in with you ladies' men."

Denton pointed his finger from one to the other, then dropped it and laughed. "Okay, okay. But still, you never know what a diligent investigation might turn up. Besides, I'm looking forward to getting an evening away from you two."

Uncle Bill said, "Well, you better get on out to the porch and wait for her."

Denton shook his head. "You got it all wrong. You have to treat women the right way, and I insist that my escorts come to the door and meet my relatives. Especially my old, fat ones."

Uncle Bill and Tavita laughed, pulling Denton further into their merriment. Denton feigned a finger shake. "Bobcat Bill, re-member your manners. No farting."

Another round of laughter was smothered when they heard a rapping at the oaken front door. "Uncle Bill. You answer," said

Denton, assuming a casual pose in the nearest chair. Sandy wouldn't like it, but Dewar's would be proud.

Uncle Bill's jaw dropped when he saw Lillian Deerfoot. She wore tight jeans and a bright-beaded, buckskin jacket. Her long black hair fell softly on her shoulders and shimmered in late sunlight. Her full lips smiled, and her contralto voice caressed. "Hi, I'm Lillian Deerfoot. You must be Bobcat Bill."

Uncle Bill sucked in his stomach. "Yes, the very one. And what part of heaven did you just come from?"

Bill bowed her into the cabin. Denton maintained his pose for a second, then stood. "Meet my associate, Afa Tavita."

Soon Lillian was seated in Bill's most comfortable chair, chatting with Tavita. "I beat Mike the Mugger for the title before I became associated with Lee."

Denton cringed as Tavita explained his theory that Samoans and Ojibwe were related and Bill rushed back and forth from the kitchen offering Lilly snacks.

"I just bought these crackers. They're from England. The cheese is fresh Wisconsin cheddar."

Lillian's happy eyes shifted between Bill and Tavita, vamping it up, enjoying the game. She nibbled at the cheese and the corner of a cracker. "Mmmm, so good. But Bobcat Bill, don't you spoil my dinner. Lee, we have reservations at the Moon Cow out on Highway 77."

Denton knew a cue when he heard one. "Well, we'd better shove off, Lillian."

"Call me Lilly," she said.

As they walked down the front steps, she slid an arm through Denton's, looked up at him, and said, "I like your Uncle Bill and Tavita."

"So I noticed. I suspect they liked you, too."

She glanced up at him. "You must be six-three, huh?"

She tightened her pressure, and Denton felt her soft breast warm against his arm. "Ah... no, only six-two."

He eyed her beat-up DNR pickup. "I'll drive."

"Of course you will, Leland."

"Call me Lee," he said, ushering her to his rental car.

The Moon Cow Diner turned out to be a converted red barn with the picture of a brown cow jumping over a yellow moon. They both ordered steaks, and Denton, happy there was a decent wine selection, ordered a bottle of Rutherford BV cabernet.

Lilly smiled at him, a trace of seriousness in her eyes. "I hear you're involved in that lawsuit between the Nortons," Lilly said.

"How did you know?"

"My Uncle John Batiste told me. He said you're a famous law-yer out in San Diego."

"Well, I'm from San Diego. He got that part right."

Lilly played with her silverware, nudging forks and spoons that flickered silver in candlelight. Her eyes were radiant. "I think you're..."

The waiter arrived with the wine and made a production of uncorking the bottle. The Moon Cow had style, even if it was self-conscious. While Denton wondered what Lilly had been about to say, the waiter offered Denton a sniff or two of the cork, poured a taste of wine in a glass for Denton's approval, then poured each of them a glass.

Now that it was just the two of them, Denton raised his glass to Lilly, and she raised hers. Denton said, "Here's to a nice evening."

Lilly's smile produced alluring dimples. "And here's to..."

The waiter arrived with a basket of fresh baked bread. As he departed, Lilly sipped her wine.

"Mmm, good," Lilly said. "Did you know my great-great-aunt was a Norton?"

Denton's mind fumbled, then chased after the concept. *Deerfoot. That's why the name was familiar. Asa Norton's wife's maiden name was Deerfoot.* "You mean... ah... Martha, no, Sarah Deerfoot?"

"Yes, my great-great-grandfather was Sarah Deerfoot's younger brother. Michael was his name. I guess I'm some kind of cousin to your Norton clients."

"I suppose, but I can't figure that stuff out past second cousin."

"Me neither, but I meant to mention…"

The waiter returned with their salads, carefully setting them down before he left.

Between hungry bites Lilly said, "Did you know my Uncle John Batiste's Indian name is Dark Panther that Walks in the Forest?"

"Yeah, my Uncle Bill told me that. Bill said your Uncle John is a Mede-something, a medicine man."

"Medewiwin. Yes. He's a very powerful medicine man. He knows all the healing herbs and plants. And he knows about curses too."

"Curses?"

"Yes, he says a curse has been put on you, Lee. A bad curse. Dark Panther wants to help."

"*I'm* cursed?"

"Yes, Lee, it was…"

The waiter brought their steaks, gave them each a sharp serrated steak knife, asked if they needed anything else, then left.

Lilly's black eyes watched the waiter go. She lifted her steak knife and tested its edge with her thumb. "Sharp."

"The curse?"

"Red Owl cursed you when you came to the jail. Uncle John wants to help you."

"How?"

"He can make a counter-curse. A protection spell to keep evil away, to chase away the Spirit Warriors." She deftly sliced into her steak, red flowing from the gash. A wet drop remained on her lip as she chewed and swallowed.

Denton stopped eating. Within him sizzled an urge to wipe the red liquid from her mouth. He stared into the blackness of her eyes. They seemed to grow larger, wider, drawing him off balance. "Whoa, what are you doing?"

"Why, nothing, Lee, just thinking how handsome you are. I heard you have a girlfriend. A beautiful blond woman with light eyes that you think you love. Dark Panther told me about her."

"That's true, Lilly."

"Maybe someday you'll love *me*."

Denton thought how truly beautiful this young woman was. Her smooth olive skin, her long shining hair, and her joy of existence. Her eyes were spellbinding. Through them, he could swim into her soul, he could...

Denton dragged his mind back. *No! Something's going on here. Something I don't understand.* "How does your Uncle John know there are Spirit Warriors after me?"

She took a large bite of steak. This was no cracker to be nibbled. "This is good. I'm glad I ordered mine rare. Better eat yours before it gets cold." She chewed in silence, then put down her knife and fork. "Look, I'll ask Dark Panther to come and see you tomorrow. You can ask him yourself. I'll come too."

"Sounds good."

"You ordered rare, too, didn't you?"

"Medium."

Silence flowed in candlelight, then moved into Denton. Lilly's face dissolved in flickers that licked the tablecloth, fondling Denton's mind.

42

It was one-thirty Saturday morning, and Denton lay electrically awake, staring at the faint moon glow against his window curtains, trying to remember coming home from his evening with Lilly. His brain fluttered like a falling leaf as he tried to remember how his date had ended.

No matter what, there would be no white pills, not if he had to stare at the ceiling till daylight. A wind gust rattled his window, twanging his nerves. A loon called, the lonely tone piercing his mind. What was it about Lilly? What force drew him?

Long after the moonlight faded, Denton fell asleep. He dreamed of Grenada. Of how he'd shot the Cuban man who had aimed Hem's service pistol. Of the Cuban woman who had retrieved the pistol when the man dropped it—and how he'd shot her, too. Images swirled. Gouts of blood from her shattered chest. Her manic scream and red, twisted lips. He pushed the dream away, calming his ripping heart, leaving Grenada in boiling clouds of time.

Then he dreamed of Lilly, beautiful Lilly. They were naked in the woods, lying on dead leaves, making urgent love. Panting, shifting images in faint light. Lilly's high wail as she climaxed. The pounding of his heart. Spurting into her. His body joining hers, their essences melding.

He woke with a start, in a sweat, the dream spinning in his mind. *That never happened. Not with Lilly. Just a dream.*

He felt sweaty, but more than that… gritty. He got out of bed, then stood under a hot shower, letting the water lash his body, washing away the night sweat, the grit. Pictures replayed against the vaporous cloud of steam.

"You have a curse on you," Lilly said.

Then she was gone.

43

Mid-September. Madison, Wisconsin.

Attorney General Richard Elkin stared out his office window, watching low gray clouds whip the rainy horizon. Allen Sanger was overdue, a bad omen because the man was never late. Itchy impatience clawed Elkin's mind. He was reaching for his desk phone when Sanger appeared at the office door, brown eyes flat behind his heavy, black-framed glasses.

Sanger rapped a ropey knuckle against the door frame. "Ready?"

Elkin lifted his gold watch. "I've been ready for the last ten minutes."

"Yeah? Well, I had to cover some bases. Anyway, I've got some information from a contact in Hayward. There's this lawyer named Leland Denton in from California, investigating the Norton deaths."

"And what's his interest again?"

Sanger caught the "again" and hesitated. Did Elkin already know about Denton, or was he simply confused? *No, how could he have heard of Denton? Let it pass.*

Sanger approached the desk, his bulk projecting over Elkin like a bad tomorrow. "He's handling litigation involving the Norton estate. It's a lot of money. Millions. Some of the Nortons have been having fatal accidents. This Denton doesn't think they're accidental. He's trying to figure out who's killing who."

"Whom."

"Okay, *whom*. I'll bone up on grammar when you're governor. Anyway, Denton's asking questions about a guy named George Norton Schneider who supposedly worked for your grandfather Al."

"Don't say that. You know I don't like that reference."

Sanger shifted his feet. "Sorry about that. But I think our black-mailer is a Norton. And this Denton might come knocking on your door one of these days."

"Allen, please sit down. You're making me nervous leaning over me that way."

Sanger's wide face threw a mirthless grin. "Yeah, sure." He lowered his bulk with a swooping grace.

Elkin's annoyance ebbed with Sanger out of arm's reach. But the big man had a new attitude, a new aura of disrespect. "Allen, are you involved in these Norton deaths?"

Sanger's laugh was low and mean. "Well, it's about time you wondered about that, Mr. Attorney General and Governor-to-be."

"Now I need to know."

"Why ask me? They look like accidents to me. All but that old lady who was killed by the crazy Indian." Sanger handed over a photo. "This guy, named Red Owl. He killed her, and now he's in the Hayward slammer."

"Why would an Indian kill a harmless old lady?"

"From what I hear, he thought she was a witch. Thought she put a spell on him or something. Probably gave him limp-dick."

Elkin didn't react, and Sanger's eyes didn't blink as he returned Elkin's steady gaze. After a few seconds, Elkin looked away and shoved the photo toward Sanger. "All right, Allen. Take this away. Keep me up to date."

"I still need to find out precisely *whom* is blackmailing us," Sanger said. "That's an accident waiting to happen."

When the door closed behind Sanger, Elkin sat quite still. A manicured hand played with the gold letter opener lying in an elegant gift box, then fiddled with his gold pen. Norton deaths, a loose, but inevitable chain twisting back... all the way to grandfather Al.

"*Your* grandfather Al," Sanger had said. What if Sanger blabbed? The concept turned his lungs to ice. And now this new disrespect. Sanger needed watching.

Elkin's eyes returned to the coiling clouds out on the horizon, beyond the refuge of his windows. Below he saw normal citizens hurrying to their normal chores in this busy capital of Wisconsin's government, the government he'd soon control.

Normal citizens? Yeah, and they could turn on me in a second. Was Allen out of control? How much of a threat was this Leland Denton? What should he do? He'd figure it out. He always found a way, a way to slide into the cracks of opportunity no matter how small or twisted.

He examined the golden letter opener, a gift for his wife Sally. She got as much mail as he did, what with all of her anti-pollution and animal rights causes. He peered at the engraved initials, "SME," Sally Moran Elkin. He'd been taken with young and beautiful Sally Moran back when he was the most eligible bachelor in the state. Her family's fortune was nice, too. But Sally's sexy looks disguised a Puritan sexual response that didn't manifest itself until their wedding night. He was a fool not to insist on a test drive. And now? Now, they only did it a few times a month—whenever her sense of duty spread her legs. *What the hell, I've got Marge.*

He polished the golden knife blade on the sleeve of his expensive Egyptian cotton shirt and placed it in its silk-lined gift box. Tomorrow was her birthday.

Elkin's mind drifted to the blackmailer. *Fuckin' asshole. Who could he be? How could he possibly know I'm a Capone grandson?* The situation confronting him wasn't a bit like a chess game. That was a cliché for spy movies. No, it was all about timing and managing a random flow of events and information. Information like Grandpa Capone, and the identity of people he'd recruited over in Hayward, people who'd told him about Denton when he'd first arrived from California.

When the phone rang, he ignored it.

What should I do about Allen Sanger? And when?

44

Mid-September. Northern Wisconsin.

Saturday morning chill enveloped Denton as he left the shower, putting away his visions of Lilly. He quit trying to recall the details of how he'd gotten home as he vigorously toweled off. The terrycloth stung his penis. Jangling alarms seized his brain. He bent to inspect the precious flesh. *Goddamn, it's red enough to glow.* Last night's dreams of Lilly swept back, weakening his knees.

He sat down on the closed toilet lid, head in hands. *How could I have been out in the woods fucking Lilly? What about Sandy?* He hadn't drunk much, only a couple of glasses of wine during dinner. But he couldn't recall anything between finishing dinner and lying in his bed feeling confused—nothing except his dream. He wished it was only a dream, but his raw penis told him otherwise.

He dressed slowly, slipping on fresh Levi's, a black t-shirt, and a red-and-black-checked flannel shirt. He pulled on wool socks and laced up his brown leather boots. *Man, oh man. I've got problems now.*

Tavita was in the kitchen when Denton went in to fetch a cup of coffee.

"Boss, you're looking tired. How was your date?"

"It... was... not... a... date."

Tavita raised his arms, the fingers of his good hand spread. "Okay, boss, just joking."

"Well, don't joke about it. I don't want you or anybody else, like Sandy for instance, getting the wrong idea."

"Sure, boss."

Denton poured a cup of coffee, the gurgling sound loud in the silent room. The toaster emitted a metallic click as he put in a bagel. "Good. Weren't you going to find out more about that Red Owl guy?"

"Yes. He's gotten a lawyer. A bail hearing is set for Monday."

"Super. What else?"

"Well, lessee. He's a member of the Ghost Lake Band of Ojibwe. He's in the Bear Clan and is a well-known traditionalist. He even speaks the Ojibwe language, Anishinabe. He believes in all kinds of spirits that inhabit trees, rocks, animals, birds. Just about everything."

Denton's bagel popped up, but it wasn't done. "Why don't these toasters ever do a bagel the first time?"

Tavita watched Denton sink the bagel back into the toaster. "Now it'll probably burn."

Denton shrugged. "Ghost Lake, huh? That seems appropriate. Does he do curses or hexes, that kind of stuff?"

"Oh, yeh. That's the kind of stuff he's known for. Lots of folks around here are scared of him because of that."

Denton sipped his coffee. "Lilly said he's put a curse on me."

The smell of burning bagel permeated the room. "Shit," muttered Denton as he set his mug down and pushed the pop-up button. The hot bagel burned Denton's fingertips and he dropped it in the sink. He flashed a self-conscious smile at Tavita. "Red Owl must have put the Burning Bagel Curse on me."

Denton fixed another bagel and drank two cups of black coffee. His mood improved, then shadowed with guilt as he thought of Sandy. Things would work out. He could explain to Sandy. *The thing with Lilly was an accident, after all.* But Denton immediately realized that a plea of accident wouldn't work. He could imagine himself in the witness box, Sandy standing before him in a severely dark business suit, conducting cross-examination: "*So Mr. Denton, you don't recall the event, but you assume you must have tripped and somehow your dick ended up in this young lady now sitting in the front row of the courtroom? By the way, sir, is that a contented smile on her face?*"

No. The best defense was to keep his mouth shut. He would stay away from Lilly. Absolutely away.

The doorknocker echoed through the house. Tavita went to the door, and from the kitchen, Denton heard Tavita's greeting. "Oh, hello, Lilly."

Thoughts of flight flashed through Denton's mind, but there was no place to go. The lake. But images of a thrashing swim dissipated in the knowledge that he had to face reality. *Oh, what the hell.* He shoved himself to the front room to greet Lilly.

He watched Lilly's dark eyes grow soft. Sunlight beaming through the eastern windows danced in her hair. Her jeans and beaded buckskin jacket hugged her tight, showing the alluring curves of her body, a body he knew. "Hi, Lee," she said, giving him a hug, sneaking her lips against the hollow of his neck in a wet kiss. Her perfume was light and erotic.

Lilly turned to Tavita, "Hi, Afa. Where's my friend Bobcat Bill?"

"Oh, he's down the road seeing one of his... ah, visiting a neighbor. I was just leaving to meet them." Tavita smiled as he left, his exit calm, unhurried.

As the front door shut behind Tavita, Denton and Lilly stood alone in the sun-filled room. Lilly moved close, looking up into Denton's eyes.

"Lilly. About last night. I must have lost my head."

She smiled. "It was wonderful."

Denton kept silent.

"Ah," Lilly said, "you're thinking of the light-eyed one. Sandy?" Her fingertips caressed his cheek. "Lee, your relationships are with the wind, the water—with the elements. You need to be free."

"But I'm with Sandy."

"For now. But I am the daughter of the wind, and you live in the wind. I didn't expect to love you, but I do. You will live in me."

Her steady eyes were serious. Argument was futile. He'd said what he had to say. He would do what he had to do. But what was it she'd just said?

"You didn't *expect* to love me?"

"No, not when I was sent to you."

"*Sent?*"

"Yes, by someone, someone I think Red Owl knows."

"Red Owl? What's he to you?"

"He is Medewiwin, a powerful medicine man. I am Medewiwin, too. You didn't think I was just a zoologist, did you? Not after last night."

She put her arms around Denton and pulled him against her straining body. He felt her heat radiate into him. "I have things to tell you, Lee. Things you need to know."

45

On Monday morning, Denton and Tavita drove to the Sawyer County courthouse. All of the parking spaces were filled with pickups and ATVs.

Tavita said, "Looks crowded, boss. Fifteen minutes till Red Owl's bail hearing, and the place is mobbed."

"Yeah," said Denton.

He found a spot a block away by a green park with a small lake and a playground. Denton envisioned Sunday mornings with dads pushing swings, kids with pails playing in the sandbox. As they approached the small courthouse, he watched the Stars and Stripes snapping atop its tall mast.

Tavita said, "It's a lot different from our San Diego courthouse."

Denton had seen justice meted in small, ugly buildings and travesties practiced in shiny edifices. "Same justice, though. Hope so, anyway."

Denton glanced up at the American flag at the top of its tall white mast. "Wind's picking up." The one-story building's wood entrance was flanked with faux river stones. It looked rustic, yet exuded a sense of law and order. Denton spied a penny lying beside the entrance. It was a heads. Good luck for sure. He snagged it and slid it into his pocket.

The crowd of citizens made it easy to find the packed court-room. "No seats," Tavita said, then pointed. "The back row," he added and led the way, his bulk squeezing down the row of citizens like toothpaste, making just enough room for two more.

Denton eyed the courtroom, observing the American and Wisconsin flags flanking the judge's bench, an empty witness stand, and two counsel tables now occupied by nervous attorneys. At one counsel table, Red Owl sat stiffly beside a lean, white-haired man in a charcoal-gray suit. The lawyers' hands fussed with documents already littering both tables.

Denton empathized with them. This was a big deal, and the air was heavy. Every breath seemed humidified by human sweat. A steady murmur of voices filled the background.

Denton felt sticky, even dizzy. He closed his eyes and thought of Lilly's lips close to his ear, her soft voice whispering.

"Red Owl wants you to go away, Lee. He'll hurt you if he has to. He'll even kill you or have you killed."

"Why?" he'd asked her, but she didn't know. She only knew what her Uncle John Batiste had told her… a man from Madison had hired Red Owl. Batiste had said the man might call Lilly, too.

"What man?" Denton had asked.

A door opened in the back of the courtroom, and the voices stilled. Denton opened his eyes and watched a dark-haired woman enter with a stack of papers. She set the papers on the clerk's desk beside the judge's dais, then left the way she'd come. The voices resumed.

Denton's mind returned to Lilly. She'd said, "I don't know, but that man from Madison phoned me. He told me to look for you on the road the other day. To pick you up and become friends with you. That the welfare of the Tribe depended on it."

Denton had felt anger's hot rush. "He ordered you to have sex with me."

"No, of course not. Only to be your friend. To report what you were doing."

Denton had shoved her away, his hands pushing her shoulders. Tears sprang into her eyes, rolling down her smooth cheeks. "I'm sorry, Lee. I only did what I was told. And I didn't see any harm in it. But the night we went to dinner…" Her hand grasped his, sharp fingernails in his palm. "I realized you lived in the wind, that we belong together because I am the daughter of the wind. Our spirits were together in olden times. I love you. You are for me. I am for you."

She had turned away and run out the cabin door. He'd listened to her pickup engine cough, then the grinding of her gears, the roaring of her engine. Gravel rattled against the front door.

The court clerk bustled back into the room, sorting more papers. Then Circuit Judge Joseph Williams entered and the clerk shouted, "All rise." Denton's packed row managed to ooze to its feet, then pack itself back down when the clerk yelled, "Be seated."

The Honorable Judge Williams called the case, and Red Owl rose to his feet. He twisted his thin torso so he could look out at the crowd. Haunted eyes found Denton's and stared for long moments until his lawyer pulled at his sleeve.

During the hearing, Denton's thoughts remained on Red Owl's piercing eyes. *What's he got against me? Well, fuck him.* Denton wasn't going to worry about some skinny old man and his stupid curses. Denton's fingers found the shape of the penny through the twill fabric of his slacks.

Denton's mind remained on Red Owl's intense glare while the lawyers went through the usual arguments over bail. The prosecutor asserted Red Owl was a flight risk, particularly in a murder case with such an innocent victim brutally murdered. No, claimed the defense counsel. The man had family, an entire tribe in the area, and would not be a flight risk. What was more, he had little in the way of financial resources, so the bail should be low.

"Bail is denied. This is a capital case. Indeed, the defendant's own safety is at risk outside of custody."

The judge stood and the clerk shouted, "All rise." Tavita lurched out of his seat, and the entire row of people expanded before gaining their feet.

"That guy sure gave you a mean look, boss," said Tavita as they exited the courthouse and walked down the incline towards their car. "Hey, boss, let's get a Hayward sweatshirt." Tavita pointed at the row of shops lining both sides of Main Street.

Denton nodded and followed Tavita to one of the stores. He stayed out on the sidewalk while Tavita shopped. A tourist crowd had swarmed the town. Denton stood in front of Tremblay's Sweet Shop where, behind a large window, an elderly woman used a long wooden paddle to stir fudge cooking in a big copper kettle.

Denton scanned the crowd. Three swarthy men stood in the center of the sidewalk, an island parting the tourist flow. Two pairs of black eyes glared through the crowd. One's lips moved, speaking to the others, then glared at Denton with startling blue eyes. The other two nodded. A slim and lovely Indian woman about Denton's age approached the blue-eyed man. She said something to him, then left. Something about her seemed familiar.

He was wondering whether he should confront the men when Tavita came back, carrying a plastic shopping bag hung over his stump. Tavita yanked out a purple coffee mug bearing the yellow logo *Hayward: Heart of the Muskie Country*. "That's for Char. And I got you a sweatshirt, boss."

Denton looked it over, feeling the soft cotton, hating the black color. "Thanks, my favorite color." He gestured down the sidewalk. "Check out those three guys."

"What guys?"

Denton looked for the men. They were gone.

46

As they drove back to Uncle Bill's cabin, Denton's mind was on the three men who'd stood brazenly in the street, letting him see they were watching him. Were these guys his Spirit Warrior enemies? What about the one with blue eyes?

Tavita's voice claimed his attention. "It's nice up here, boss."

"Yeah." He glanced at Tavita, who was staring out the window at the dense forest, its trees speed-blurred. "Not much like Samoa, is it?"

"No, but the drums and cowry shells are almost the same. I feel a connection."

Denton's cell phone rang. Charlotte's voice flowed through background static.

"Hi, Lee. How's it going?"

"Hard to say. But bail was just denied for the guy that may have killed Sylvia."

"That's good, right?"

"I suppose. What's going on in sunny San Diego?"

"The office is under control. This is a good time for you to be gone, because most of your cases don't heat up for another few weeks."

Tavita said, "Tell her I said Hi."

Denton handed the phone to Tavita. "Go ahead, tell her yourself."

As Tavita and Charlotte talked, Denton concentrated on his driving. He didn't want to eavesdrop, but he couldn't miss the softness in Tavita's voice.

After a few minutes, Tavita passed the phone back to Denton. "Thanks. She wants to talk to you again."

"Lee, I meant to let you know I called Mary Norton and told her you'd turned on the charger at Jim's boat. She'll have Gustav take care of it. Also, she's agreed to have her father's body exhumed for additional testing as to cause of death. And best of all, Clyde Norton wants to come to Wisconsin to meet with you. He has some ideas about the long-lost George Norton Schneider."

"When?"

"In a couple of days."

"Okay. I really have no desire to see the guy, but he's paying the bills. I suppose we have to humor him."

"True, and he pays promptly, unlike some of our clients."

"Do you know where Clyde Norton is, as in physically located?"

"No. He's not at his office." Papers rustled. "They say he's taking several days off. He called on his cell phone to ask about meeting you."

Charlotte's steady efficiency brightened Denton's mood. "That's odd. I wonder what he's got on his mind."

"You'll know pretty soon."

"Yeah. I'll bet it's got something to do with that affidavit he gave me about George Norton Schneider. And..." Denton's voice trailed off as an idea formed in his mind. "Uncle Bill has a speakerphone. We'll be at the cabin in a few minutes. Tavita and I will call you back and the three of us can conspire."

"Sounds mysterious."

"I'm beginning to see a pattern here."

"Roger."

47

Mid-September. Madison, Wisconsin.

Richard Elkin signed a last letter and slid it into his outbox with the others. He checked his gold watch. It was almost time for Allen Sanger to call. But would he call on time or make it a point to be late, asserting his new attitude of disrespect? *He's not going to be indispensible much longer.*

The phone rang. *Right on time.* "Richard, it's Allen. I've got a line on the blackmailer. He's definitely an older guy who knows about railroads. One of our agents questioned the woman who runs the Middleton Railroad Depot where we had the money drop, remember?"

Elkin's mind replayed the blackmailer's sudden flight, gunshots in the night. "Like I could forget that total fuckup."

"All right, all right. Anyway, the woman described a guy in his seventies or eighties who was hanging around the Middleton Depot. He was a former railroad man—back when they had steam engines. One thing led to another, and she showed him the secret room."

"Interesting." Elkin's fingers pushed at a memo pad and reached for his pen.

"Yes, and she also got his car plates. A brown Honda Prelude."

Elkin's heartbeat quickened. "Then we've got him."

"Almost. The car is registered to a Howard Charles. I sent a man to the registration address, but it's a vacant lot in Wausau."

"Shit!"

"Calm down, Richard. We found a police report from the Ladysmith police. The blackmailer's car was in a fender-bender on Highway 8 in Ladysmith. That's about fifty miles from Hayward. He may be heading that way. I'm on the road, just south of Ladysmith. I'll find him and take care of things."

"Good. Make sure you do." As he hung up, Elkin's heartbeat settled. Ladysmith was also about fifty miles from Al Capone's hideout. Could the fly be coming into the parlor?

48

Mid-September. Northern Wisconsin.

Denton and Tavita returned to an empty cabin. Denton found a note on the kitchen table. "Bill says we're having steaks tonight. He's gone to the store."

"Great. I sure can't complain about the food around here."

"That's because you've got Uncle Bill and all his girlfriends giving you groceries."

"Can't knock that, boss."

"Yeah. Let's call Char."

Denton sat at the kitchen table and turned on the speaker. Tavita took a chair as Denton dialed his San Diego office number.

Charlotte's voice filled the room. "Boss?"

"Yes. Tavita's here too."

"Hi, Char," said Tavita, his voice smooth and soft.

"Hi, Afa," she replied, her voice soft and careful.

Jesus, get a room, Denton thought. "Okay, here's what I think. Someone in Madison, Wisconsin—the state capital, by the way—has hired local tribe members to run me off. To hurt me if they have to."

Charlotte asked, "How do you know?"

Denton flashed a keep-your-mouth-shut look at Tavita and said, "An Indian friend of mine told me. She was asked to help them by spying on my activities up here. But she changed her mind."

"So it's an Indian *lady* friend?"

Denton affected a dramatic sigh. "Yes. Her name's Lilly. But the point is, the guy I think killed Sylvia Norton Smith must be one of the group that tried to co-opt Lilly. The Ojibwe tribe members are honest, hard-working people, but all groups have their bad apples. It would have been easy for guys with local knowledge to approach William Norton while he was on the lake, then hit him in the head and roll him into deep water. "

"Yeh, makes total sense," Tavita said. "Char, I've met Lilly and think she can be trusted. I've also seen this Red Owl guy who probably killed Sylvia. He's a bad one."

Denton added, "And don't forget Lilly's uncle, John Batiste. He could be implicated too."

No one spoke as they mulled things over. Denton pulled a few file folders from his briefcase. The stack of Norton photos fell from one of the files and lay scattered on the tabletop.

Charlotte broke the silence. "Maybe you can introduce this Lilly to Sandy."

"Charlotte?"

"Yes, boss?"

"I get the point. Stifle, please."

"Yes, boss."

Denton had been idly spreading the Norton photos out on the kitchen table, but now they drew his close attention. "Hey, did you ever notice how much Clyde, Peter, and John Jr. look alike?"

Tavita leaned toward the photos, his stump exploring. "Yeh, they sure do. They look more like brothers than cousins."

Denton pondered the resemblance, but it really didn't mean anything. Cousins sometimes looked like brothers. "Well, no big deal. I think the way to crack this case is to lean on this Red Owl and any other locals that are involved. I'll go talk to the prosecutor and see if he'll help. Char, anything else?"

"No. Don't forget Clyde Norton's coming up there."

As the call ended, Uncle Bill came in carrying two brown paper bags of groceries. "Hey, grab these; I've got two more in the truck."

Denton took the groceries and began arranging them on the counter, lining up several red and white cans of Campbell's chicken with rice soup. He was aligning cans of pork and beans when Uncle Bill arrived with two more heavy bags, ruining Denton's careful rows of canned goods.

"Well, well, *Billy*, what's making you actually *buy* food instead of getting it from your lady friends?"

"Lorraine told me that we're going steady. That's gonna cut down on the free meals."

Denton and Tavita congratulated Bill, who blushed and got busy putting a head of lettuce into the refrigerator. "We'll have a big salad tonight with those steaks," he said, pointing at several T-bones next to the sink.

Denton again noticed Uncle Bill's resemblance to the Nortons. He walked to the table, where his briefcase sat on a chair, pulled out his stack of photos and shuffled through them. "Uncle Bill, you look a hell of a lot like the Nortons. Come see."

Uncle Bill's gnarled hands rummaged, sorting things inside the refrigerator, then emerged holding a jug of fruit punch. "Just a sec. Want some fruit punch?"

"No thanks."

"I'll have some," said Tavita.

Denton watched Uncle Bill pour two glasses, the sun flashing in the red liquid. Bill handed one to Tavita, then turned to Denton with a broad smile that wrinkled up his face. Uncle Bill clinked glasses with Tavita, took a swig, then walked toward Denton and the photos now spread out on the table.

"Well, Lee, I wouldn't be too surprised at a resemblance. I told you we were kids together. I think we're third or fourth cousins, something like that. I never had much interest in looking back at the family tree." Uncle Bill shoved the photos around. "Yeah, there's some resemblance. But it's a big family. Not that surprising."

Denton started to reply, but the gravamen of what his uncle had said suddenly hit home. *If Uncle Bill's related to the Nortons, I am, too.* His hand went to the Norton photos lying on the table. His eyes probed the faces. "Hey, if you're related to these folks, I'm also related."

Bill scratched his jaw as he pondered the idea. "Ahhh… yeah, in a very distant way. My grandma—your great-grandma—was a Norton, but your mom and I were Higginses. You're a Denton. That makes you a… hell, I dunno what. An umpty-eighth cousin three or four times removed or something like that." The old man counted on his fingers. "Hey, Lee, do you think I'd be in line to inherit something from the Norton will?"

"Not unless you knock off six or ten heirs in line ahead of you."

Bill smiled and took a sip of red punch. He cocked his head into an odd angle, made a squinty-eyed evil face, and said, "Hell, I suppose I'll have to watch out for *you* from now on."

Denton chuckled and replied, "You bet your ass you do. Not to change the subject, but how do I get to John Batiste's place?"

As Uncle Bill gave him directions, Denton saw the older man was distracted. *I know that look—he's calculating odds, counting cousins. This case is complex enough without bringing in a bunch of cousins.* Was there a danger the uncle who was such an important part of his childhood could become a wild card? He shook away the idea. "But listen, you two. Let's get some dive gear and go over to the Chippewa Flowage. See if there's anything underwater where William was diving."

Neither man seemed enthusiastic. Tavita sipped his fruit punch, his eyes on Bill.

But Denton was excited, rolling the idea forward. "Great! I'll get up early and drive to that dive shop next to Trailways Inn and rent some dive gear. Uncle Bill, you and Tavita borrow the boat and tow it to the lake. You've got a trailer hitch, right?"

Bill's face remained impassive. "Sure, I've got a hitch."

Tavita spoke up. "Get me some gear too, boss. I'm a certified diver, more than six hundred open water dives."

The news that Tavita could scuba dive didn't surprise Denton. As an experienced certified diver himself, he knew the lack of one hand would not be much of a problem. "You got it, Tavita, but I doubt they have a wet suit to fit you."

"Don't need one, but get me six pounds of lead."

"Fine. You guys haul the boat over to the launch. Say at ten."

Uncle Bill scratched his head. "Well... all right, Lee. Which launch?"

"You tell me."

"The one on County CC. Ten a.m."

Denton asked, "Isn't that close to Capone's hideout?"

Uncle Bill swallowed the last of his punch, his big Adam's apple chugging. "Quite close."

49

Denton was enjoying the morning as he drove along the narrow highway to the Chippewa Flowage boat launch. The approach of fall was casting reds and yellows into the greenery. His cell phone rang. It was Charlotte.

"Hi, boss. Can you hear me okay?"

"A bit scratchy, but I can hear. What's up?"

Her voice became maternal. "Don't be mad, but I'm worried about you."

Here it comes. A lecture about Lilly and Sandy. "And why's that?"

"Afa says you're not sleeping well. He hears you moving at night. Groaning. Like you're having bad dreams."

Denton said nothing, giving control to the phone static.

"Lee. Please don't be mad. I'm worried about you. You've been shot, I don't even know how many times. Or how many fights you've been in. Now you've been assaulted by who knows who… or what. I've seen Marines with post traumatic stress."

Harsh sunbeams flashed in Denton's eyes as he passed a gap in the woods.

"I'm just worried, Lee. There must be something I can do."

He raised a palm to shade the light away; focusing on the twisting, pitted road.

"Okay, Lee. I'll let you go. Please take care. Let me help if I can."

The phone went dead.

Denton would talk to Tavita about this bullshit, but now, he summoned his tae kwan do. *Breathe. Stay calm. Concentrate.* A few minutes later, he spotted the sign for the boat ramp and turned left onto a gravel trail.

A motley collection of vehicles, some almost rusted out, others with camouflage paint, were crammed into the woods. Empty boat trailers spoke of boats on the water. Dense green trees and brush surrounded the concrete ramp that sloped into the calm waters of the Chippewa Flowage.

Denton parked his rental and walked to the shore. The lake surface stretched smoothly to adjacent shorelines. A bird sang twiddling notes that hung in still air—a song of innocence enhanced by the placid water. But these waters had claimed William Norton's life. They'd experienced the outrage of bodies rising from abandoned graves, symbols of promises broken.

Sherry the deputy sheriff's voice played back. *"Everybody up here knows there are bad spirits in there."* A sudden puff of wind riffled the lake's surface. Something might have moved just below.

Denton's dark emotions were replaced by exhilaration, a joy of the coming adventure into the unknown. *The visibility underwater should be decent.* The "viz" was his major worry. He knew how morning calm could turn into a windy day. Wind would stir up the water and mix it with silt, turning the water to dirty mist. This was going to be difficult enough without groping through murky water trying to find an old building. Who knew what kind of wires, nails, old pipes, and other stuff they could blunder into?

His thoughts turned to a dive trip to Truk Lagoon in Micronesia, far out in the South Pacific. He'd been elated to go to that diver's Mecca where dozens of Japanese ships had been sunk by an American air raid during World War II. The experience of diving on sunken ships that were still full of war equipment, including bombs and other munitions, was the best underwater adventure he'd ever had. He was amazed at how well things had been preserved, even after over sixty years underwater. He'd found paper songbooks on one wreck and amused himself by turning the saltwater saturated pages. In the hold of another sunken ship, he'd sat in the cockpit of a Japanese Zero, imagining the havoc it could have caused had it survived. Denton had worked at the instrument panel's toggle switches. Some still functioned. What sort of man might have flown it, pressing its red machine gun button and sending death through the skies? What children and grandkids were alive because it was sunk? Fate played its little games, butterfly eddies of ultimate consequences.

He'd learned on that dive to be careful when entering the wrecks, to elude the wide variety of snares awaiting an unwary diver. The darkness inside a ship lying one hundred twenty feet under the surface was as dark as it could get. He carried two underwater lights, but knew even then not to penetrate too far inside unless he ran a guide rope from the entrance. A too-strong kick with a dive fin could throw up a dense fog of silt that could make even the most powerful dive light useless.

Images curled into his mind of bright soft corals that fluttered in his passage as he feather-finned his way into the bomb-shattered control room of one of the ships. He was one hundred forty-five feet below the surface as he eased down a companionway. Suddenly, he couldn't move forward. He tried to back up, but couldn't do that either. Momentary panic hit, but his dive training took control. He thought, *Be calm. Stop. Think.* He reached back along his regulator hose. It was snagged on something.

He held his breath, removed the regulator from his mouth and turned so he could look at the problem. A hook-shaped broken pipe had trapped his hose. He freed it and put the regulator back in his mouth, pushing the purge button to clear the water so he could breathe.

He sure didn't want a similar experience here at the Chippewa Flowage. He might not be lucky a second time.

Denton unloaded the dive gear and began assembling it. His eyes surveyed the area, looking for observers. What about those guys in Hayward? They could have been local Indians. Probably were. If William Norton had been murdered, they were prime suspects. He glanced at the small waterproof gear bag that held his wallet, car keys, and his Browning Hi-Power. It also held Queeg, his good luck charm.

He connected the regulators' first stage valves onto the two tanks and tightened the connections. He turned the tanks on and breathed through the mouthpieces. Good. He turned the tanks off and pushed the purge buttons to ease pressure in the regulators and hoses. The sun's warmth would expand the air inside them, possibly breaching a seal.

He pulled on his wetsuit and strung eight pounds of lead weights onto the weight belt. He left the remaining weights in a pile for Tavita to use on his weight belt as he saw fit.

He was reaching for his dive mask when Uncle Bill and Tavita arrived, towing the boat behind Bill's truck. The boat was aluminum with a red stripe, an eighteen-foot Lund much like William Norton's.

"Wow, Uncle Bill, that's a nice boat."

"Yeah. Ralph bought it two months before he had his stroke. Killed him in seconds. A complete tragedy."

Tavita said, "And now Bill's comforting the poor widow."

Uncle Bill waved a hand in dismissal. "It's been two years since. Lorraine's been lonely."

Denton folded his arms across his wetsuit-covered chest. He was about to make a comment about Uncle Bill and Lorraine "working out" together, but thought better of it. He didn't have room to talk. "It was very nice of her to lend us the boat. Let's get it launched."

Denton and Tavita guided Uncle Bill as he backed the boat trailer down the ramp until it was tongue deep. Denton climbed aboard, unhooked the strap holding to boat to the trailer, and threw the bow line to Tavita, who tied it to the dock. Denton shoved the boat off the trailer, and Tavita pulled the boat to the dock while Uncle Bill parked the car and trailer.

Denton admired the automatic efficiency of their teamwork, as if they'd been doing this together for weeks. He retrieved the slip of paper with William Norton's GPS coordinates from his gear bag. It lay next to his pistol. His fingers brushed the gun's cold metal. He wished there were waterproof nine-millimeter pistols.

He zipped the bag, turned on Lorraine's GPS, and entered the coordinates: 45 degrees, 54 minutes, 73 seconds north. Then 91 degrees, 9 minutes, 12 seconds west.

That's where William Norton dove, where he died. We'll see what's there.

A slight breeze kicked in as they loaded their gear. Clouds gathered on the horizon as Denton maneuvered away from the boat ramp, hoping the wind wouldn't rise. They passed beneath the County Road CC Bridge with its spots of cracked concrete and visibly rusting rebar. When he passed Rudy's Island, he turned southwest till the GPS began beeping, signaling they were nearing the mark. With careful eyes on the GPS, Denton motored slightly windward and signaled Tavita, who tossed the eighteen-pound anchor overboard. The anchor shattered the still calm surface and plunged to the lakebed as Tavita let the anchor rope slide through his palm.

Denton yelled over the noise of the two-stroke engine, "Let out about two feet of anchor rope… one more. Okay, tie it off. We're there." He tested the anchor line, making sure it would hold. "All right, here's the deal. After sixty years plus, we can't expect the buildings down there to be in very good shape."

Tavita held up his index finger. "But I've dived on saltwater shipwrecks that were that old, and they were well-preserved even in salt water."

Denton nodded. "Yeah, me too. That's what I was getting to. There's every reason to think there'll be stuff still down there. But there'll be all kinds of wire, nails, loose boards, and other shit to be careful of. And don't forget the signals we went over. Okay?"

Tavita held up his hand, thumb and forefinger forming an O. "Okay."

Five minutes later, Denton and Tavita had their dive gear on, the air turned on, and were perched on the side of the boat ready to go. Denton told Uncle Bill, "We've got three thousand pounds of air. At thirty feet, we can stay down quite awhile. I've set my dive timer for forty minutes. If we don't surface within five minutes after that, we're in trouble."

Bill frowned and said, "What'll I do then?"

Tavita laughed. "Start worrying."

Denton adjusted a strap on his black buoyancy compensator vest. He handed Tavita an underwater flashlight and shoved another into the pocket of his BC. He grinned at Bill. "If neither one of us is up by then, call the dive shop and tell them what's going on. They'll know who to call. Ready, Tavita?"

"Yeh."

"Remember, if we lose sight of each other—and we probably will—don't look for me. Take care of yourself."

"Yeh."

"Go."

They somersaulted backwards into the lake and fin-kicked toward the bottom. The water was clearer than Denton had expected. *The viz is probably ten or twelve feet.* As Denton descended, Tavita swam porpoise-like beside him, a powerful force at home in this element. Denton's ears popped. At thirty feet the pressure would be twice what it had been on the surface.

Rising pressure tightened Denton's mask. He blew through his nose, forcing air out of his mask, equalizing the air pressure inside. Then the mask began leaking from the top. Irritating drops of water fell into his eyes and accumulated at the bottom of the mask. *Too bad*

I don't have my own mask. Renting dive gear was always a crap shoot. He'd just have to keep clearing water from his mask by lifting its edge and blowing through his nose.

A bare, silt-pudding bottom loomed in depth-dimmed light. Denton and Tavita adjusted the air in their buoyancy compensators until they were neutrally buoyant, hovering inches above the bottom. The tip of one of Tavita's fins scratched the bottom, sending up a brown plume.

Denton checked his wrist compass and pointed their course. Suddenly, his plan seemed hopeless. They'd be lucky to even find the hotel, let alone discover William Norton's path. But you don't know if you don't try.

Denton signaled a halt, then made a square with his index fingers. This was a prearranged signal meaning they would separate and search in a square of twenty yards a side. The idea was they'd meet on the last leg of the search square. If they found nothing they'd move the search square to the west and try again.

Tavita signaled "Okay" with thumb and forefinger. Tavita's calm brown eyes told Denton he'd chosen his dive buddy well. They separated, and Denton swam the first twenty yards. William Norton must have searched this same area. The waterlogged stump of a tree loomed at the brown edge of visibility. Had William Norton seen it, too?

He did a second twenty yards, gliding just above the silted bottom. Still nothing. As he began the third twenty, he saw it. The ghostly white glow of a large cement foundation. Excitement bloomed in Denton's chest. *Fuckin' A, this could be it! What luck!* He might have found the basement of the old hotel. Denton worked his way along one wall. *So what am I looking for? Best to look for something recently moved or altered.*

Denton turned a crumbling corner and froze.

Ten feet ahead the water roiled with arms, legs, and scuba gear. He recognized Tavita's bulk in the middle of the fight. Two men in wetsuits and hoods were attacking Tavita. One of the men maneuvered behind Tavita and slid an arm around this throat, and the other man ripped off Tavita's mask and pulled at his regulator. Tavita's eyes bulged, their whites bright in the dim light.

Denton pulled his dive knife and was there in seconds, severing the air hose of the man choking Tavita. The severed air hose spewed air bubbles, dancing through the water like a crazed eel. The black-suited man released Tavita and swam for the surface.

Tavita shoved the other man away. Tavita glanced at Denton, held a clenched fist at his chest in the out-of-air signal, and swam upward.

The other hooded diver moved warily toward Denton, holding his own dive knife. Eddies of stirred silt rose from the bottom, alternately revealing, then hiding, the man's silver-gray wetsuit. Denton swam to clear water and waited for Graysuit. Denton saw the man's eyes shining behind his dive mask. The eyes were blue. His fins stirred up bottom muck as he attacked Denton.

Okay, fucker. Underwater knife fighting was another subject not covered in Denton's tae kwan do courses. But this was no time for finesse. Denton stiffened his right arm, the knife-point held straight out. He swam at Graysuit, kicking fins powering his lunge. As they collided, the edge of Denton's left hand knocked away Graysuit's weapon, and Denton shoved his knife into the man's throat.

A cloud of air bubbles engulfed Graysuit as he dropped his knife. Both hands went to his throat. He kicked for the surface, passing through his own exhales. A widening trail of blood chased him up.

50

Mid-September. Northern Wisconsin.

Allen Sanger concentrated on the unfamiliar blacktop road as the Crown Vic flew past lush forests south of Ladysmith. Elkin's parting shot seized his thoughts. He laughed. Elkin was so dumb. "Make sure you do," Elkin had said as he ended their phone call. *Make sure you do. Make sure you do.* It must be nice to sit on your ass and leave the grunt work to others, others who can actually get it done. But Sanger was going to have the last laugh in *this* game. He'd gotten the blackmail money, and now he'd get the blackmailer.

He glanced at the piece of paper with the blackmailer's license plate number. It was a brown Honda. He'd catch up soon. After that, it would be the gravy bowl for him. As chief of the state police, he'd theoretically be under Elkin's thumb, but not really. The new gov would be busy; too much else to keep up with.

Things would sure be different. Now Elkin was getting prime pussy from his secretary, and probably other women. But what was he, Allen Sanger, getting? Nothing he didn't pay for. Or brutalize for. Women were afraid of him. They saw something.

His eyes were glued to the snaking white center line, but his mind was on the past. *When did it all start?* He'd been just another normal kid. Neither his father nor mother had beat him, or fucked him. What had happened? One night, he'd been walking near his college dorm when he saw a girl coming towards him on the walkway. He'd seen her in class, was drawn to her full, red rose lips. Her sweet ass looked juicy as she walked. He'd moved behind a tree to watch her, then followed her to her dorm, trailing her inside until she entered her room.

He leaned against the wall, telling himself to go. But he couldn't leave. He tied his handkerchief across his face and knocked on her door.

She was foolish enough to open it. She got what she deserved. He did her for a long time. He left her sobbing as he delivered his warning, "You report this and I'll cut your face. I'll cut your tits off." She'd kept quiet.

He got an erection as he remembered the panic in her eyes when he did it in her mouth, and later, her sobs as he gave it to her in the ass. His hand went to his cock, but then he began to cry.

He tried to stifle the tears but couldn't. He realized he was out of control, still doing these things that he couldn't stop. But why try to stop his true nature? Why not let his inner self feed? His sadness disappeared. *I'll take care of the blackmailer. Then I'll go see that Norton woman in Madison, the one with the thin dress. I'll give it to her like she's never had it. After that, I'll go back to California.*

51

Mid-September. Northern Wisconsin.

Denton watched Graysuit swim desperately for the surface, chased by a cloud of his own blood. Denton followed, keeping his eyes on the struggling man. As the man rose, his body became still. Graysuit and his blood cloud became silhouettes against the sunlight. Death and his flowing black cloak.

Denton omitted his safety stop at fifteen feet and popped to the surface, rising inside the turmoil of his own air bubbles. He looked frantically for Tavita and the other attacker.

"Here, boss."

Tavita was ten feet behind him, his hand held against blood flowing from a shoulder wound. Denton shouted, "You all right?"

"Yeh. He cut me a couple of times, but not bad. Thanks, boss, you saved my bacon."

Denton spotted Graysuit floating on the water halfway between them and the boat. Uncle Bill stood on the boat waving and pointing at a second wet-suited man trussed to a boat seat.

Denton pointed at Graysuit. "Let's check this guy out."

"There's blood all around him. He hasn't moved. I'll get him."

They swam to the boat, Tavita pulling the inert form of Graysuit with him, like a hunter returning with a dead seal.

Bill helped Denton scramble aboard and the two of them hauled in Tavita, then the dead man. They placed the man on the floor of the boat. His dead blue eyes stared into the sun.

Denton turned to Bill. "Are you in one piece?"

Bill held up the boat's red fire extinguisher. "Sure I am. I saw all these air bubbles coming up. Then this guy surfaces with a cut air hose. I helped him into the boat and the bastard tried to push me overboard. I whacked him on the head with this, then hog-tied him."

Denton noticed one of the boats he'd seen earlier was anchored nearby. It was empty. "Call the sheriff and tell him what's happened. That guy looks like an Indian."

"He is," said Bill.

Tavita spoke up, "This guy is too."

"Yeah, and I've seen him before." Denton worked his memory, filtering images until he recalled the group of men watching him while he'd stood on the sidewalk in Hayward after Red Owl's bail hearing. Blue-eyes was one of them.

Were these Red Owl's guys? Had he just fought a second round with the Spirit Warriors? If so, this one was back in Spirit Land.

52

A sullen quiet ruled Bill's cabin. Then it was broken by a mechanical gurgling Denton recognized as the coffee maker finishing its task. Footfalls and ceramic clicks told him Bill was filling coffee mugs. The noises lured Denton's mind away from the man he'd killed, another life he'd extinguished. He watched Bill approach with three steaming mugs, carried on an old tin tray that bore a Jim Beam whiskey advertisement.

Bill set a mug on the side table next to Tavita, whose shoulder was swathed in white gauze. Tavita's bandaged hand moved in a lazy arc and lifted the mug. He winced. "I didn't realize I'd grabbed the knife blade."

Denton took his coffee and gazed at Tavita's wounded hand. "Thanks, Bill. Well, Tavita, better a sliced hand than a cut jugular vein."

"Not necessarily, when it's your only hand."

Subdued chuckles nudged the heavy air of late afternoon, doing little to alleviate the somber mood.

Tavita sipped his beer. "Sheriff Nils wasn't happy with us."

Denton looked at the Jim Beam ad on Bill's tin tray. He'd rather have had the whiskey. "No shit. At least we gave him one *live* prisoner. And we towed the empty boat in, preventing a navigation hazard."

Uncle Bill shrugged. "I don't think he's too worried about navigation hazards, nephew. Besides, that's just Joe's way. Don't worry about it. Those two Indians weren't from here. He's trying to find out who they are. He said they could be from the Ghost Lake Band."

Denton replied, "Red Owl's from the Ghost Lake Band, right?"

Bill said, "Yes."

Denton remembered Red Owl's eyes boring into him during the bail hearing. "That's the first connection I made. These two guys looked like some who were watching me in Hayward. Right after Red Owl's bail hearing. They could have been the so-called Spirit Warriors who attacked me."

The three men mused private thoughts, silence again claiming the afternoon. Denton gazed through the front window at nearby trees, noticing red and yellow hues had claimed more leaves. *What were the odds against us even finding the hotel?* But it was always that way. The odds against most things were long—until they occurred, that is. Besides, they'd had William's GPS marks to guide them.

Tavita shifted in his chair, grimacing from his wounds, drawing Denton's attention to the white bandages. Denton looked back at the trees and their newly colored leaves. A lovely scene, but the colors presaged the death of the leaves. Soon they would fall, their days in the sun fluttering away.

Denton sensed Bill's eyes. He looked up into the old man's intense stare. Bill said, "It's a hard thing to kill someone, nephew."

Denton felt the dead Cuban woman struggle against the door of his locked memory vault. He pulled himself into the present, trying to think only of the now. But the now rushed away like pressured water from a hose. He knew he couldn't run from memory, just as he couldn't escape from fate. You had to let yourself float, let yourself be there as life's instants passed into memory.

Be here, deal with it. He nodded to Bill. "Not so hard to kill someone, Uncle Bill. Not so hard at all. It only takes a little pressure against a trigger."

"I've been through it myself, Lee. Back in 'Nam. Even war, even self defense can get to you if you let it. You did what you had to do, Lee."

"Yeah. That's always what I do. Always the reason." Denton felt the hidden door weakening to the Cuban woman's screams. He needed to change the subject. He took a swig of his now tepid coffee and turned to Tavita. "Tavita, exactly what did you do to piss those two guys off?"

"They just jumped me out of nowhere. I was looking in an old closet in the corner of… I guess it was the basement. Anyway, the door looked like it had been busted open. And recently too, because the broken part of the wood was lighter than the rest. It looked like somebody took something out of the closet."

"Out of it?"

"Yeh, there was a kind of rectangular mark on a shelf that looked cleaner than the rest of the wood. You know, like if you take a box off a dirty shelf. You leave a clean spot in the shape of the box. That's what this was like. I was looking through the rest of the closet when those guys came at me."

Tavita's cut hand went to his bandaged shoulder. His brown eyes shone. "Thanks again, boss. I was in trouble. They cut off my air."

Denton looked into Tavita's grateful eyes. Denton wanted to talk to him about blabbing to Charlotte about Denton's sleeplessness. But now wasn't the right time. "No problem," Denton said and drained his mug. He stood, empty mug in hand. "Look, guys, I need to go talk to Lilly."

Bill leaned forward, and Denton saw he was about to speak. "Hold it, Bill. Don't start. Besides, you better get out there and clean up your girlfriend's boat."

Denton started for his bedroom, but stopped. "Hey. If William Norton took that box, then where is it? It wasn't with the things at the sheriff's office."

53

The urge to see Lilly had overpowered Denton's fatigue, forcing him to find John Batiste's small, whitewashed house near the site of the original French trading post established in the late 1700s. Denton parked in the driveway and scanned the well-groomed lawn, the flower beds with multi-colored wildflowers. A white curtain parted, then closed. Lilly emerged from the front door, her posture urgent, leaning toward Denton as he exited his car. She stopped herself and stood on the porch, delicate hands on slim hips, one knee bent. Her face, at first glad, had turned somber.

Denton's feet crunched on gravel as he approached her. "Hello, Lilly. I came to ask your Uncle John how to find you."

Her hands spread as she smiled. "Here I am."

"Yes. You drove off pretty fast the other day."

"You were mean. Made me cry."

John Batiste appeared on the wooden porch behind Lilly. "Mr. Denton, let's take a walk. I'd like to speak to you."

Denton followed Batiste. He felt Lilly's eyes on him as he and Batiste approached a dome-shaped, birchbark structure near the lakeshore. "This is a prayer lodge," he said, pulling back a blanket covering the entrance. Batiste pointed a thick-knuckled finger to the darkness within.

Denton wasn't going to be trapped in a confining hut with a guy named Dark Panther that Walks in the Woods. "You'll understand if I don't go in there with you, Mr. Batiste. After all, I've had an unpleasant experience with so-called Spirit Warriors."

"That was Red Owl, not me. I want to help you. You are for Lilly. Lilly is for you."

Eerie tingles streamed through Denton. *The willies. These people are scary.* Denton suddenly wondered if Spirit Warriors existed and whether John Batiste could summon them. *No.* He believed in luck, even fate, but not ghosts. *I don't have time for this mumbo jumbo.* But living men could dress like ghosts and swing real tomahawks.

"Mr. Batiste, that's between Lilly and me. Besides I've explained to her that I have a girlfriend."

Batiste pulled a beaded leather pouch from his pocket. His long fingers unknotted leather ties, slid inside, and emerged holding strands of tobacco. The man chanted a few Ojibwe words and let the tobacco fly away on the wind until it landed in the nearby lake.

Denton assumed his tae kwon do stance, his hands up, ready.

"Don't worry, Mr. Denton, I was just praying for you, making an offering to the Spirit Warriors."

Denton gave it a heartbeat, knowing that relaxing could invite a cunning assault. Another heartbeat. Denton eased his fighting stance. "Thanks, I suppose. But you know I don't believe in that stuff."

Dark Panther smiled, revealing stained but strong teeth. "You don't need to believe. What is, is. I cannot entirely protect you from Red Owl or from his clan. I would try to help you, not just for Lilly, but for your Uncle Bill, who is a friend of the tribe."

"I appreciate your concern, but I can take care of myself."

"Can you?" Dark Panther put away his leather pouch and shook his head. "It will be very difficult. Red Owl's medicine is very strong."

Denton sensed soft footsteps behind him and spun around. Lilly approached carrying a small wreath of wildflowers. The flowers drew his eyes to bright reflections from beads of water on soft-colored petals. "These are for you, as I am for you. These will protect you, as I will protect you."

Her eyes peered into Denton's, looking for something she wasn't finding. She extended the wreath. Denton felt compelled to take it. The flowers were light in his hands, and their enveloping fragrance was sweet. He felt drawn into Lilly's glittering black eyes. He leaned toward her, wanting to touch her smooth wet lips, to kiss…

No! Not again! He pulled himself away. "I have to go, Lilly." He glanced back as he strode to his car. She stood on the lawn, proud, erect. But he saw tears, like flower dew, on her cheeks. He climbed into his white car and drove away.

54

Mid-September. Northern Wisconsin.

Allen Sanger horsed his Crown Vic along Highway 27/20, fretting about the "blackmailer." Finally, he spotted the brown Honda parked outside a small café in the village of Radisson. The man was in no hurry. Like most old guys, he probably had to stop for pie and coffee every few hours. Sanger parked down the street and waited, his mind now at ease. It would be simple to take this guy out. *Sorry, pal, but you gotta go.* It wouldn't do to have Governor-to-be Elkin question the man and discover he'd never gotten a dime of payoff money.

The man emerged from the diner, wiping his mouth with the back of a pale hand. He looked thinner than he had at the depot when he'd dropped off the package. Sanger grew impatient as the man fumbled through his pockets for his car keys, unlocked the car, and farted around with something inside before driving off.

Sanger tailed the Honda until it turned off Highway 27/70 onto County Road F and wound its way to a lake cabin. The slanting rays of the setting sun speared Sanger's eyes as he pulled to a stop, five hundred yards from the Honda that was pulling into the cabin's gravel driveway. Sanger watched the thin driver emerge and knock on the cabin door.

He'd had enough of this old guy's shit. As soon as it was dark, he'd take care of business and get back to Madison. Sanger opened his car door and put a piece of duct tape over the button that activated his interior lights. He drank from a bottle of Pepsi he'd bought along the way and ate some peanut butter crackers.

He then popped opened his glove compartment and extracted his Kimber SIS Custom/RL automatic pistol. He dropped out the clip to check his .45 ACP loads, then took satisfaction in the metallic click as he reinserted it. He worked the slide, chambering a steel-jacketed round, and switched on his Crimson Trace laser night sight. He let the red laser dot play in the darkness below the glove compartment, then switched it off. He put the gun on safe and sat back in his comfortable seat to await the night.

Soon there'll be one less asshole in the world.

The sun disappeared behind the tree line at the far side of the lake. Blue and red tones smeared the clouds drifting against the darkening sky. A lamp flicked on, lighting the cabin's front room.

Night claimed the thick, forested acres. Sanger removed his black-framed glasses and looked around. *Yeah, I can see well enough to shoot.* He pulled a black ski mask over his face and exited his car. He walked slowly to the cabin, his soft-soled shoes making no sound as he moved across the grass, avoiding the graveled driveway. He reached the cabin and put his back against the hard pine log sides. His heart pounded with the joy of the hunt. He edged to the window and peered inside. The living room was empty, but two old men were in the kitchen sitting at a table, drinking from big mugs. *Two! Shit, they look just alike.* He hadn't expected two. *Which is which? Hell, who cares?*

He switched on his laser sight and ran the red dot over the front door lock. His lock picks were in his pocket, but he tried the door first. The handle turned easily. *Dumb shits. Didn't even lock the door.* He eased inside, but froze at an unexpected squeak as he closed the door behind him. He stood against the wall, listening. He heard conversation from the kitchen, words he couldn't understand.

He moved slowly toward the kitchen. *This is gonna be good.*

When he stepped into the kitchen entrance, the two men were no longer at the table. They were against the back wall. One held a shotgun. A voice behind him said, "Don't move. Drop the gun on the floor."

"*Fuck* you!" Sanger yelled and lifted his gun. The red dot from the laser sight skittered around the room.

Sanger felt a muscular arm hook his neck.

55

Denton abandoned Lilly and her tears in the grass beside John Batiste's home. Even as he drove away, Denton felt an almost overpowering urge to go back, to pull her to him, to... But he pushed the accelerator to the floor and sped away, following County E until he passed a small tavern, the Stumble Inn. Denton needed a drink —more than "a" drink. He hit the brakes, did a U turn on the narrow road, and pulled up to the bar. Two black motorcycles and an older red Chevy pickup stood outside the entrance.

The bar was dimly lit by neon beer signs and the light over a small coin-operated pool table. Two long-haired young men stood beside the table holding pool cues, watching him enter. A middle-aged couple sat drinking at the bar. Their eyes scanned him as he sat down. "Hi," he said into the silence.

The woman touched her yellow hair and smiled. The man with her said, "Evenin'." The guys at the pool table said nothing.

The tall bartender sidled down the bar, his shaved head gleaming orange and green from the neon of a beer sign. "What'll it be?"

"Whiskey, a double," said Denton. Looking around the room, he added, "And another round of whatever these folks are drinking."

Twenty minutes later, Denton was holding a pool cue and sizing up a bank shot with his new friends Frank and Jellybean. He sipped his third whiskey, then bent over the green felt of the table, sighting along his cue stick and lining the white cue ball with the black eight ball.

"Right corner," Denton said.

"No way," replied Jellybean.

"Way," said Denton. A butter-smooth stroke, and the cue ball struck the eight with a sharp click. The eight rolled across the table, caromed off the edge, and eased its way towards the right corner pocket. The eight ball slowed as it reached the pocket. It almost stopped. Then it fell in with a final "thunk."

"Shit," said Frank as he passed a dollar bill to Denton, who took it with a grin.

56

Mid-September. Northern Wisconsin.

Allen Sanger held a blood-soaked handkerchief tight against his chest as he struggled to pilot his Crown Vic along night-shrouded country roads. Three Percodans had dulled the agonizing pain of the gunshot wound.

It was all a blur. He'd raised his gun and shot at the two old men, but that huge guy behind him had put a massive arm around his neck and spoiled his aim. The guy then threw him back into the living room, where he hit a table. He fired at the monster, but the old guy with the shotgun appeared in the doorway and shot Sanger in the chest. He'd felt pellets rip into him. The big guy staggered back against the wall, then came at him. Sanger began spraying shots around the room, but the big guy grabbed Sanger's shirt with one hand and threw Sanger through the front window.

Sanger staggered to his car and drove away, a commotion of lights and sounds in his rearview mirror. He withstood the pain for ten minutes, then stopped at a crossroads and dug the Percodans out of his bag. He swallowed them with a gulp from the bottle of Pepsi. The taste of blood from his hands mingled with the cola.

He pulled away his mask and found his glasses on the passenger seat. He sat still until the pain dulled, then checked his wounds.

He bled from several cuts he'd received when he went through the window. These he'd patched with bandages from the first aid kit he kept in his trunk. But the hole in his chest was big and ragged. His fingertip had slipped inside when he'd tried to feel the contours of the wound. Despite the drugs, the sudden finger stab felt like he'd been shot again.

He writhed in agony until he swallowed two more Percodans. Then he stuffed the wound with gauze and drove on through the night. He needed help. No, he wanted to shoot someone.

57

Mid-September. Northern Wisconsin.

Denton felt the three drinks buzz within him. *Gotta drive carefully. Not too slow, not too fast.* He scanned the winding road for deer and cops as he made his way to Uncle Bill's cabin. Images of Lilly and Sandy churned in his mind. He couldn't separate the women's faces. Couldn't concentrate on how he felt, what he wanted.

When he made the last turn before the cabin, he saw spinning red and blue lights. Police cars and an ambulance were parked in Uncle Bill's drive. Someone was being wheeled out on a gurney. Policemen were all around—in the house, in the yard, searching the woods. Denton felt his three-drink buzz evaporate.

He parked and ran to the gurney. It was Uncle Bill. No, it was Clyde Norton's dark-rimmed eyes that stared up at Denton. "What happened?" Denton called out.

"He's shot. We're taking him to emergency in Hayward," said the EMT as the ambulance doors slammed.

Denton rushed inside the cabin, where he found Uncle Bill watching another EMT bandaging Tavita's left arm and the right side of Tavita's chest.

"What happened?"

Uncle Bill's shaking hands made a helpless gesture. "A guy followed Clyde up from Ladysmith. We saw him watching the house from his car. We tried to waylay him when he came to the house."

"Waylay?"

"Yeah. When we saw him leave his car, we called the police, but it takes forever for them to get out this far. He was carrying a gun. So I got my shotgun. Clyde got a baseball bat."

"Terrific, just what a couple of geezers need to do."

Uncle Bill smiled. "We had Tavita. Besides, I'm the one that shot the fucker, Lee. Tavita only threw him through the window."

Only.

Tavita walked into the kitchen, his truncated left arm now bandaged. "He nicked me. No big deal."

Denton shook his head. "I'm just glad you guys are okay. Who was he?"

Uncle Bill said, "We're not sure, but Clyde and I have a good idea."

"So?"

"Well, let's go to the hospital and see how Clyde is. We'll tell you the whole story."

Thirty minutes later they were talking to the emergency room doctor, who explained that Clyde had been shot in the thigh, the bullet having passed through his leg, but missing the arteries. He'd lost quite a bit of tissue and blood.

"Can we see him?"

"Tomorrow. I gave him an injection."

As the three left the hospital, Uncle Bill said, "We'll come back tomorrow when Clyde's awake. Then we'll talk."

58

Mid-September. Madison, Wisconsin.

When Richard Elkin entered his private office the next morning, he found Allen Sanger sitting behind his desk. The copper smell of blood hung in the air. Sanger didn't move as Elkin approached. Elkin leaned over to see if the man breathed. He heard short, gurgling breaths. The man's black jacket was soaked with coagulating blood. Blood oozed from multiple cuts. A gash on his forehead dripped blood onto his closed eyelids.

Elkin poked Sanger with a shaking finger, and the man moaned. Something had gone terribly wrong. Elkin leaned closer, looking at the ragged wound, and he caught the odor of Sanger's blood. He smelled like a gutted deer. *Why did he come here? What shall I do?*

Elkin turned away, taking a deep breath, wiping his hands on a white silk handkerchief. *Keep calm. Keep your head. There could be a hundred explanations for this. I'll just call security. But first...*

Elkin put his hands around Sanger's throat and squeezed. Sanger's nostrils flared. His blood-rimmed eyes flew open. He gaped at Elkin. Sanger fought for air, but his frantic struggles were feeble. Elkin choked Sanger's airways for five full minutes, then stepped away. Elkin stared down at the dead man. *Now I'm a murderer.*

Elkin felt tears flowing along his cheeks as he dialed building security. He wiped them away with the back of a steady hand. *Really, it was self-defense.*

When security arrived, he told them his special version of the facts. He'd found Sanger there in his chair. The man was dead when Elkin arrived. He must have gotten into some kind of scrape with criminals, but managed to fight his way to report to Elkin. It was all in the line of duty. After all, Sanger was the chief criminal investigator for the Wisconsin attorney general's office. The man was so dedicated that, despite horrible wounds, Sanger had tried to report to his superior. But he died. It was so sad.

59

Mid-September. Northern Wisconsin

The day after Clyde was shot, the sun rose hot in a cloudless sky. Bill rebuffed all Denton's questions about Clyde's presence at the shooting, saying, "Be patient. I want to let Clyde tell his own story."

Denton sat next to Tavita and Bill at the Rusty Ax Café in Hayward. Tavita was taking the last bite of his second cheeseburger. Denton and Bill were drinking coffee and watching Tavita eat.

Denton closed his eyes, recalling how he'd confronted Tavita in the kitchen that morning. He'd pointed his finger at Tavita and said, "Charlotte got on my case about not sleeping well."

Tavita had fiddled with the toaster, dropping in two slices of rye bread. He shoved down the toaster bar and looked into Denton's eyes. "Not my fault, boss. I know I ratted you out, but it wasn't my fault."

"And whose fault was it?"

"Nobody's. Every time we talk, Char asks me how you are. Are you eating right? Are you sleeping right? How's your mood?"

"So?"

236

"So I always say you're fine, even when you aren't. But she caught something in my tone. You know how she is. She cornered me. Said, 'Don't make me come up there.' "

"And you ratted me out?"

"Exactly."

Denton had shaken his head. "Ahh, forget it."

Now, Denton opened his eyes. Tavita was still chewing his cheeseburger, his eyes on Denton.

Denton said, "Whenever you're done, Tavita. I told them around noon."

Tavita wiped his mouth, grinned, and said, "What are we waiting for?"

They found Clyde sitting in bed, surrounded by wires and tubes. An IV dripped clear liquid through a long needle stuck into the back of his hand. Green blips chased themselves across a monitor behind him. Clyde looked shrunken, like a mummy, his thin body a scant hump under white hospital linens.

A tall, hefty nurse entered. She had brown frizzy hair and a name tag that said she was "Wright, R.N." She told them to take it easy, not overdo the visit. Clyde needed his sleep, didn't need excitement or agitation. "You look like the kind that could agitate him," she pronounced, her pale brown eyes peering, in turn, into each of theirs. Denton noticed her man-like hands.

The men promised to be good and were admitted on a probationary basis. They greeted Clyde, their voices somber.

"Hi guys," said Clyde.

Denton asked, "How's it going?"

Clyde's voice was quiet. "I'll live to fight another day. Thanks for coming to see me. I'm afraid I'm feeling woozy from the medication. Pain killers. Could you come back? Couple days?"

They all nodded, said he was looking good, wished him well, and turned to leave.

"I'd like... Bill to stay... I want to tell him... something."

Denton and Tavita loitered in the hall outside Clyde's room, speaking in undertones.

"He doesn't look so good, boss."

"It *was* a .45 slug."

Nurse Wright's head popped over the counter at the nurses' station, followed by her oversized thumb jerking in the direction of the waiting room. They obeyed.

The two sofas were occupied, so they sat in chrome-colored metal chairs with black and gray checked cloth backs and seats. Tavita jammed himself into one of the chairs and Denton sat across from him, wondering if Tavita's chair would collapse.

Still sore at Tavita for squealing on him to Charlotte, Denton found himself hoping Tavita's chair *would* dump him. Then he saw Tavita grimace, his bandaged hand going to his shoulder. The guy now had a bullet graze to go along with his scuba fight wounds. *Ahh, forget it.*

Ten minutes later Uncle Bill appeared in the waiting area. He'd lost his usual erect posture and now stood with sad eyes and slumped shoulders. "Let's go home. We have to talk."

60

The drive home was silent. Denton watched the forest speed by, a chaos of fall-color-flecked greenery. Speed kills detail. What would be killed by the details his Uncle Bill was about to divulge?

At home, Uncle Bill stacked wood into the fireplace and lit it. "Let's get a drink and talk here in the living room."

"What'll you have, Tavita?" asked Denton as he dropped ice cubes into his glass and poured Jack Daniel's over them.

"A beer, please."

"Uncle Bill?"

"I'll have some of your whiskey."

They assembled in the dimly lit living room. The cardboard taped over the window projected impermanence, a sense of dislocation. The light from the flames licked at the new wood, but did little to ease the dour atmosphere.

"This is going to be difficult, Lee, but it's what Clyde wants. He'll tell you more when he's feeling better. But for now, take a good gulp of that drink."

An hour later, Denton fixed himself another drink as he tried to get his mind around Uncle Bill's story. *Christ! Nothing's as it seems.* He glanced at Bobcat Bill, a hero of his childhood who had kept family secrets.

Bill stood and pulled his car keys from his pocket. The metallic sound was jarring. He patted Denton on the shoulder. "I'll take a drive while you think things over."

Tavita rose from the big green chair, and rubbing the stump of his left arm, said, "I'll take a walk, boss."

Denton watched them go, his mind still reeling. *Just think it through. Sort it out.* He thought best when he worked things through on paper. He pulled his steno pad from his briefcase, feeling the weight of the pistol now back in its compartment.

Denton wrote down a large 1, then put a circle around it. He wrote, "Clyde not Clyde." Denton put down a 2, but that was as far as he got before Uncle Bill's story replayed itself in his mind.

The upshot of Uncle Bill's story was that Clyde wasn't Clyde. He was George Norton Schneider. George had assumed Clyde's identity over sixty years earlier when Clyde was killed by members of the Capone gang. Uncle Bill had known about it. He had even helped George hide Clyde's body.

"George was only fourteen when his Uncle Isaac got him a job on the railroad. They'd lied about his age."

Bill explained how the Soo Line Railroad ran from Capone's home turf in Chicago and through the Hayward, Wisconsin area, where he had his secret hideout in the woods.

"This was 1944. Capone had been paroled in 1939. His syphilis was beating him down, but he was working with Ralph to hide any remaining money trails. One of Capone's guys came to George with a package of ledger books and cash. Told him to carry them to the depot in Couderay, Wisconsin, and hand them off to guys who would be waiting in a black Packard."

Denton had kept quiet, sipping whiskey from time to time, listening to Bill's story while questions buzzed like wasps in his thoughts.

"The guy gave George seven hundred dollars in cash, then said he'd kill George and hurt his family if he didn't do what he was told to do. When George handed off the package, Capone himself was in the car. He told George to get in and go with them. They took him to Capone's hideout, just outside Couderay. They gave him a beer and told him he was going to be their courier from then on. Said if George didn't do it, they'd kill his whole family."

Denton had interrupted. "Wait, Uncle Bill. What was your part in all this?"

"I'm getting to that, but okay, let's skip ahead. So George did what he was told for a couple of months. But then one night he came to see me. We were already friends then; we used to run together during the summers when George spent his vacations at a place near here. George was just a year younger."

Tavita spoke up. "You lived up here even then?"

"Yes. My mother was a distant cousin of Isaac Norton's. Like you and I discussed before, I'm some kinda multiple-removed cousin, too."

Trying to lighten the mood, Denton said, "And they say Appalachia has inbreeding."

Uncle Bill grinned and raised his whiskey glass. "It's a big family, but none of us married our sisters."

They shared a weak laugh, then Bill went on with the story.

George had come to Bill's home one night, carrying a cardboard box. He'd told Bill that Capone had gotten a local girl pregnant. "Lottie Perkins was her name. We both knew her. Anyway, back before he went to prison, she was working as a maid at Capone's hideout. He'd gotten her pregnant... ah, musta been around 1929, just before Capone got busted and ended up in prison. But Capone dumped her. He gave her a few hundred bucks and told her to get lost. Capone had taken the birth certificate and some other records about the child from her."

Denton had gone for a refill. "Another drink? Bill? Tavita?" Both said yes, and as Denton passed them the drinks he said, "So Capone took all the evidence linking him to the baby. What was it?"

"A girl. Lottie named her Mildred."

Denton sat back down with his newly filled glass. "So what happened next?"

"Well, like I said, George knew Lottie—knew her better than I did." Bill's voice had trailed off as he looked out the window and took a gulp of his drink. "To tell the truth, I've always wondered how well he really knew her. He was maybe sixteen then. Shortly after Mildred was born, Lottie married a local farmer. He was a widower, never had any kids—a guy named Ivan Skonsky, who adopted Mildred. Lottie never fessed up to Skonsky that Mildred was Big Al's kid. Anyway, by 1944, Lottie's working the night desk at this hotel in Post called the Thayer Hotel. George stayed at that hotel between railroad runs and jobs for the Capone mob."

Denton asked, "So you think they were getting it on?"

"He always denied it. But he took a lot of interest in her. Stranger things have happened."

"No kidding. Think about all those schoolteachers doing it with teenagers."

Bill smiled, "Believe me, I do. Just sorry I didn't get molested like that."

"Me too," said Tavita, lifting his drink in a mock toast.

Bill paused again, putting down his glass and rubbing his hands. "I don't know why my hands hurt. Must be the weather. Anyway, I figure George knew her pretty damn well because one night at some bar, she spilled out the whole story about her kid being Capone's and how Capone stole the records. George got pissed. Since he's doing work for Capone, he's at the Hideout a lot. He sneaks into Capone's office. Capone's got several boxes stacked in a closet, like he's getting ready to take them somewhere. George digs around and finds the package he delivered. It's now opened and, lo and behold, it contains some documents. Some accounting records *and* the damn birth records. He also takes some kind of birchbark scroll that was in the same closet with the records."

"What kind of birchbark scroll?"

"I don't know. It was something really old. Capone musta taken it away from an Indian. He grabbed whatever he wanted. George didn't know what it was, but since it was in the same box, he figured he'd snag it, too. Oh, and he also took four packets of money. Hundred dollar bills."

Tavita asked, "How much was that total?"

"About ten thousand dollars."

Tavita whistled. "That's a lot of money for those days."

Denton realized the seriousness of George's betrayal. "Yeah, a lot of money. Capone would have wanted to drink blood when he discovered these things were gone."

Bill's whiskey-improved mood took a nose dive. Tears shone in the old man's eyes. His voice trembled. "Yeah. But it took Capone a while to miss the stuff. In the meantime, George gives the stuff to me and I put it in a steel ammunition box and bury it out behind my dad's barn. Then George goes back to Chicago, where he gets sick and can't make his next run with the railroad. Well, Clyde and George were close in age, just a year or so apart. Clyde finds out George is sick and he decides to make George's runs for him because George gets paid by the trip and Clyde knows they need the money. The two boys looked like twins, and Clyde must have figured nobody would know the difference. Besides, it was just the kind of lark Clyde liked. He was always pulling stunts."

Denton had thought he saw what was coming next. "The plot is getting pretty thick, Uncle Bill. I hope I don't know what happened next."

Bill hung his head. "Yeah, actually the *plot* got pretty fucked up. Clyde's mom tells George's mom what Clyde's up to, and she tells George. George freaks out and, though he's sick, he catches the next train to Wisconsin. He rides all night in the caboose wrapped in blankets and drinking cough syrup. When he gets off in Couderay, the stationmaster just about faints when he sees George because he'd seen Clyde, masquerading as George, come through earlier carrying a package. The stationmaster thinks he's having visions. George claims he's *Clyde*, George's cousin. And the stationmaster says he hasn't seen *George*—who was actually Clyde—since he took off in a black Packard."

"Oh, oh," said Tavita.

"Right. Well, George phones me to pick him up with my car. He explains the whole thing to me when I get there, and we take off for Capone's place. But we get a few miles up County Road CC, just past the resort at Ashegon Lake, and we see a body in the road. It's Clyde, shot full of holes and run over. He's dead."

Uncle Bill's eyes misted. He fell silent, and Denton sensed the old man was reliving the bloody scene. A quick flicker of the Cuban woman's screaming mouth reminded Denton he had his own bad visions.

Denton shook his glass, clinking the ice cubes. "Want another, Uncle Bill?"

"Nah, I'm almost finished. George and I figure they've killed Clyde thinking he was George. We know they'll come after George if they find out he's still alive. We take Clyde's body and put it in my car trunk. We drive until we find dense forest out in the middle of nowhere. We bury Clyde in the woods."

Bill's eyes gazed down the years. "I know Clyde was dead, but I still have dreams about him lying out there in the dirt."

Denton nodded. "Yeah, dreams can stay with you a long time."

Tavita's hand covered his stump. "Yeh."

Denton thought it through. "What happened to the documents George took from Capone?"

"As I said, he gave them to me and I put them in that ammunition box. You know, those metal olive drab ones that seal up real tight to protect the ammo?"

"Yeah. What happened to it?"

"I buried it in the woods near Couderay."

61

Two days later, they returned to the hospital to see George Norton Schneider, aka Clyde Norton. The gray-haired man lay quiet in his hospital bed. He looked weak, but his color had improved. At least he had a tinge of red in his thin lips and sunken cheeks.

George confirmed Uncle Bill's story. "We didn't know what else to do. Nothing would bring Clyde back. There didn't seem much point in getting killed, too."

Denton said, "We understand. It couldn't have been easy to pull this off."

Tavita chimed in, "Yeh, what about your parents? And Clyde's?"

George nodded. "I took off and joined the Army. The war was still going on and they weren't too picky. Besides, I looked older than I was. I sent Clyde's folks a telegram from boot camp, telling them he'd signed up. When the war ended, I was with the occupation troops in Japan. When I got out of the Army, I settled in California. I didn't go back to Chicago for ten years. By then Clyde's parents had passed away, and my father had, too. My mom was in a rest home and didn't really remember me."

"What happened to the stuff you took from Capone?"

"I gave most of the money to Lottie—mailed it to her anonymously with a note telling her to keep quiet about it. I kept three hundred dollars for getaway funds. I kept tabs on Lottie. I even called her about ten or fifteen years ago. She seemed reluctant to talk to me. I guess she wanted to let the past stay the past. She did tell me her daughter Mildred had had some medical problems as a kid—Lottie didn't say what—but Mildred got over them and grew up nice. Mildred eventually married a guy named Elkin and had a couple of kids, a boy and girl. Lottie didn't want to tell me the kids' names. Said the past should stay in the past. But she did say she was worried about her granddaughter, worried she'd contracted something down through Mildred from Lottie and Capone."

The name Elkin struck a memory with Denton, but he couldn't place it. He asked, "What about the documents and scroll?"

Uncle Bill and George exchanged glances.

Bill said, "I told them about the ammunition box."

"Yeah," said George. "Two days after we found Clyde's body, Bill and I dug the ammunition box up. I was staying at the hotel in Post at the time, but the lake was getting close to flooding out the village. I stored my things, including the box in a closet in the hotel basement while I figured out how to become Clyde. But I was driving my car down County Road E when I passed Capone's black Packard. The driver stared at me as we passed, and I saw the car stop and begin a U-turn. I floored it and ducked into a side road over by the St. Francis Indian Mission."

George stopped, breathing hard.

"Are you in pain?" asked Bill.

"No. I'm okay. Anyway, they lost me. I got on E and drove the other way as fast as I could. I cut over to Highway 70 and drove to Chicago and joined the Army."

Denton's mouth had turned to cotton. He noticed an orange plastic water pitcher beside George's bed. "Could you spare a glass of water?"

"Help yourself."

Denton poured half a glass and drank it down. "Thanks. What happened to the scroll and the other stuff in the ammunition case?"

"Well, that's the weird thing. William Norton got into genealogy and became interested in his Uncle George, who had vanished. He starts asking around and runs into the lady that used to work at the hotel in Post, back before the lake covered it. Her name was Kaitlin Massey. She was related to the owners and worked the day desk. She'd been a lovely young woman back in 1944, and she remembered me. I'd, ah, taken her out once or twice. Anyway, she told William about the stuff I'd left. She'd forgotten about it when the rising water forced them to move out of the hotel. She told William it was probably still there. Isn't that weird? I mean... well, weird?"

"Yeah. So William went diving for it."

"Exactly. And he found it. And believe it or not, that damn sealed box stayed tight for all those years. There were a few drops of water that got inside, but nothing to worry about. They knew how to make seals in those days."

Denton recalled his dive at Truk Lagoon, where he'd turned the water-logged pages of songbooks submerged over sixty years. "Yeah. They made those ammunition boxes well. Wanted them to survive war trauma."

"Anyway, William gave the scroll to his Aunt Sylvia, my cousin, because she was interested in Indian lore. William also showed her the birth certificates. Sylvia had known both Lottie and her daughter Mildred and was stunned at the Capone connection. She told William Mildred had married Jack Elkin. William does his genealogy thing and figures out Mildred's son is Attorney General Elkin, who's now running for governor."

Denton said, "I knew I'd heard the name Elkin before."

A tall blond nurse in a blinding white uniform opened the door. She asked, "Are you doing all right, Mr. Norton?"

"Yes, fine."

"The doctor said you needed rest. Your visitors shouldn't stay much longer."

"We'll only be a few more minutes."

The nurse nodded and left.

Denton watched her go, listening to the starchy friction. He shifted back to George. "But how do you know all this?"

"William told Sylvia all about it, and she told me. She was worried because William sent Attorney General Elkin an anonymous note saying he had Elkin's mom's original birth certificate. Sylvia was worried about the situation, but William told her he'd given Elkin the phone number of one of those TracFones you can get at Wal-Mart. That way he couldn't be traced."

Denton asked, "Why anonymous?"

"He didn't know how Elkin would react. He felt an obligation to let Elkin know this stuff was still around, but he didn't want to have to explain how he got it."

Denton shifted in his chair, setting down his empty glass. "If he'd already found the documents, why was he diving again on the day he was killed?"

"Sylvia said after he'd recovered the documents, he'd heard a rumor someone had left a bag of gold coins in another part of the hotel basement."

"Christ! How could he fall for that?"

George shook his head. "Well, I suppose he figured it was possible. The way stuff gets strewn around the world, anything can be anywhere."

Denton shook his head. *What a goofball William was.* But goofiness seemed to run in the family. *All these cockamamie schemes.*

"I suppose. What happened to the birth records?"

"After William's death, I went to his house and took them. I was afraid they could have been the reason for his death. I took the TracFone he'd used for Elkin to contact him. I was surprised when Elkin's guy called one day, but I decided to play out William's hand. I thought it might be kinda fun." George's thumb pushed the black button that delivered his morphine. He glanced down at the bandages that swathed his torso. "Some fun," he said.

The blond nurse re-entered and chased them out. George waved the hand without the IV as they left. "Come back tomorrow?"

"Sure," said Bill.

62

That afternoon Denton and Tavita were back at the cabin. Denton sat at the kitchen table finishing a drawing while Tavita lounged on the wooden deck outside the kitchen door.

"Hey Tavita, come and look at this. I'm trying to chart the Elkin/Capone connection."

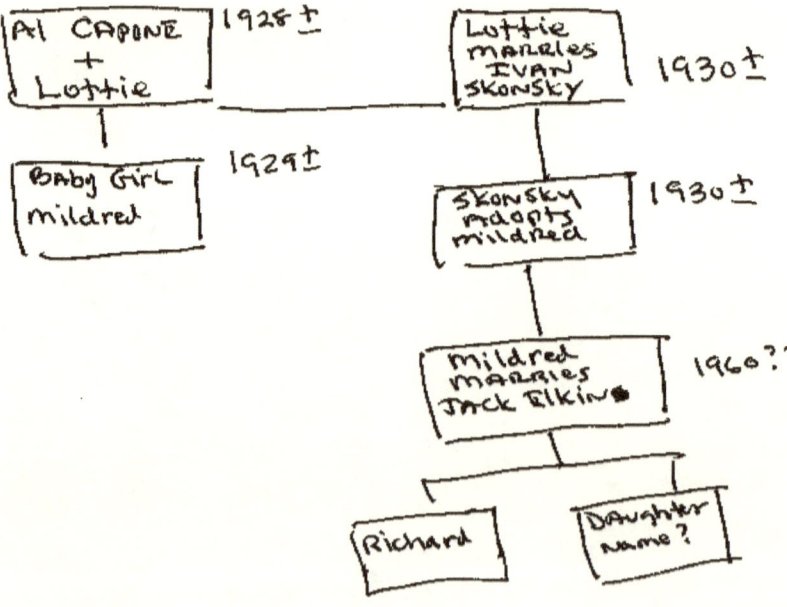

Tavita ambled in, clutching a book titled *Indian Nations of Wisconsin,* letting the screen door slam behind him with a bang that startled Denton.

"Jesus, try not to slam the door."

"Sorry, boss. Just one hand, you know."

Denton eyed him and started to respond, but instead pointed at the chart he'd drawn. "Is this the way it works as you understand it?"

Denton leaned out of the way as Tavita gingerly moved his stump over the boxes he had drawn. Tavita's eyes glanced up dolefully, then looked back at the chart. Denton almost laughed. *Ham it up, Tavita. Ham it up.*

"Yeh. It looks like what Bill and Clyde, er, George explained. You don't know Mildred's daughter's name, I guess."

"Right, that's why—"

Uncle Bill shouted, "Red Owl's escaped! It's on the radio."

Denton's mind shifted into fight mode. He pulled his Hi-Power from his briefcase and searched his suitcase for his box of bullets.

Someone knocked at the cabin door. Tavita's eyes caught Denton's. Uncle Bill emerged from the back room carrying his shotgun. Denton signaled Tavita to open the door.

Creaking hinges pierced the silence of held breaths.

John Batiste stood at the entrance. Lilly was beside him. They froze in place, looking at the armed group confronting them.

"I guess you've heard Red Owl escaped," Batiste said.

Despite the tension, Denton laughed. "Yes. Bill just heard it on the radio. Come on in."

Lilly rushed to Denton, hugging him. "We came to tell you. To protect you." She stepped back and held out a hand holding another wreath of wildflowers.

"Lilly, I appreciate the gesture, but I think we'll need more than flowers to defend ourselves."

John Batiste opened his jacket, exposing a holstered, matte steel revolver. "It's a .357 Magnum. We brought more than flowers."

"I'm not here for trouble," said a deep voice from the porch.

All eyes snapped to the door. There stood Red Owl with his hands raised, his black eyes feverish. "I don't have a gun. I don't want trouble."

Denton eyed the large knife stuck in Red Owl's belt. "What *do* you want?"

"I didn't kill Sylvia Norton Smith. I have nothing against you, Mr. Denton. I'm not the one you should worry about."

"Who is?"

Red Owl pointed his thin finger at John Batiste. "Where's the magic scroll, Dark Panther?"

"What scroll?"

"The one you took from Sylvia Norton Smith."

Denton signaled Tavita to close the door. He snuck his hand into the concealed weapon pouch in his briefcase and withdrew his Hi-Power. Then Denton moved against the wall, holding his pistol low at his waist. He caught Uncle Bill's eye and motioned him back toward the bedroom door. Denton wanted fighting space, but didn't know who the enemy was. Until he did, he wanted the wall against his back.

John Batiste's eyes flicked around the room, then at the back door. His hand moved to his holstered pistol as he sidled towards the door. "I'll be leaving now."

Denton leveled the Hi-Power. "No, I think you should stay while we get the sheriff. Then we can all have a chat."

Lilly stared at Denton, her eyes frightened. Her body leaned. Denton realized she was about to do something abrupt. Something that would set things off. "Please stay still, Lilly."

John Batiste used the distraction to pull his pistol and level it at Denton. Lilly screamed, "Don't, Uncle John," and rushed between Batiste and Denton.

John Batiste's finger squeezed his trigger. Red Owl's knife flew across the room. Gunshots shook the cabin.

Denton dropped his gun and held Lilly in his arms. Blood spurted from a hole in her chest. Her panicked eyes stared into his, begging for help he could not give. "Tavita. Call 911. Get an ambulance."

As Denton held his palm tight against the red flow, he spotted John Batiste dead on the floor with Red Owl's knife in his throat. Blood pooled under Lilly's gasping body. Denton felt her heart beat. Flutter. Then stop.

Her black eyes gazed into his, her lush red lips slightly open.

Lilly's face dissolved into the screaming face of the Cuban woman. Denton's vision grew dim, then blossomed into a collage of red lips, screaming mouths, spurting blood. Where was he? What was happening?

Denton squeezed his eyes shut, straining to seal his eyelids. But the visions continued, playing against the back of his eyelids. He strained to stop thinking, but his thoughts came ever faster. He panicked, wanting to scream. Then blackness sucked him down, extinguishing his agony.

63

Denton swam in black. No dreams. No thoughts. No pictures. Sometimes he heard faint voices. Other times, the sting of needles or gentle caresses.

One morning he heard a soft voice calling his name. He smelled a delicious aroma. It was familiar, yet not. What was it? He released his eyelids, letting them flutter open. But his eyesight was blurred.

A woman's voice said, "Look, his eyes are open."

He recognized the voice. Then he recognized the smell. His voice croaked. "Don't tell me that's *chicken soup*, Charlotte."

A long pause. "So what else?"

The blurriness popped like soap bubbles, and he saw Charlotte. She wore a practical yellow dress. In her hands was an open Thermos of warm chicken soup. Tavita hovered behind, his smooth face smiling.

Fifteen minutes later, Denton was sitting up in bed finishing his soup. "Mmmm. That was good. What happened?"

"You had a little mental thing, Lee," said Charlotte, her blue eyes full of concern. "But the doctor said you'd be all right when you came out of it—if you came out of it."

"Yeh, boss. You went nuts. Been whacked out almost a week. You're in the Hayward Hospital."

"Hush, Afa," hissed Charlotte.

Denton ran a hand over the smooth white sheet, feeling its texture. Lilly's face appeared. His mind shifted. His identity fled into the sheet's whiteness. He wanted to go there, inside the weave, tucked away from his thoughts.

Sandy Jones' voice cut into his white nothingness. "Oh… Lee … Lee."

Denton felt her arms enfold him and her urgent whisper calling him back. His mind cleared and he saw her face. "I'm fine, Sandy. I'm fine."

Charlotte's face came close, her eyes peering into his. "Lee, you were looking weird. Are you really all right?"

"Yeah. Fine."

Sandy dried her wet eyes with a tissue from the box next to Denton's bed. "I wanted to be here when you woke up. I just went down to the cafeteria for some coffee."

Denton reached for her hand. "You're here *now*, baby."

"Mutt wants to say hello," she said and placed the little dog on the bed.

Mutt was licking Denton's face when a stern-faced nurse arrived with Denton's meds. "Get that dog out of here," she said.

Charlotte gestured to Tavita. "We were just leaving, miss." She patted Denton's arm. "We'll leave you two alone. If you're sure you're okay, we'll go back to San Diego tomorrow. The office needs attention. You've got that Komatsu case hearing coming up."

Denton waived a hand in goodbye. His mind still yearned to meld with the white sheet. He forced himself to focus. *Yeah, the Komatsu case. What a pisser that's going to be.*

64

Late September. Hayward, Wisconsin.

A short and stocky, gray-haired woman entered Denton's hospital room. Her friendly eyes smiled at Denton and Sandy. "Hello, Mr. Denton, I'm Dr. Rosenberg. I've been studying your charts."

"Hi, doc. This is Sandy Jones."

They shook hands all around, and Dr. Rosenberg said, "I understand you'll be leaving the hospital later today, and I wanted to spend a few minutes with you before you go."

"Sure, what's up, doc?"

She smiled, her hand fiddling with a pair of brown plastic reading glasses on a cord around her neck. "They said you had a sense of humor, Mr. Denton. You must enjoy being with him, Sandy."

Sandy grinned, her eyes dancing. "Yes, I do."

"I'm a shrink, Mr. Denton. And you need to listen to me."

Denton squirmed, knowing he wasn't going to like what he was about to hear. "Call me Lee. Have a seat, doc."

The doctor glanced at Sandy. "She can listen."

The chair squeaked against the linoleum floor as Dr. Rosenberg scooted it to Denton's bedside. "Here's the deal. You've had a serious episode of post-traumatic stress disorder. You entered some odd kind of fugue state. And it could happen again."

"Don't you have some kind of pill?"

"No, and it doesn't make me feel comfortable that you've taken at least three gunshots and have an assortment of other scars on your body. I don't like your sleeping pill habit either. You know pills don't always solve things; often they just smear them over. I thought you were a lawyer."

"I am."

"You present like a war veteran."

"Well, a couple of cases have gotten out of hand, I guess."

Sandy reached for Denton's hand. "He'll take a vacation."

Dr. Rosenberg rose to her feet. "Sandy, you two make a lovely couple. I hope you can convince him that a *vacation* isn't going to solve this. Lee, when you get back to San Diego, you need to spend some time with a psychiatrist or psychologist. Your condition could become very, very serious. You might not come out of another episode like this one."

Denton glanced into Sandy's pleading eyes. "Yeah. Okay, doc."

The doctor patted Denton's shoulder. "You need to change your case load, choose different kinds of cases."

Sandy tightened her grip on Denton's hand as they watched the doctor leave. Her wet eyes probed Denton's. "You didn't mention the Komatsu case."

"What, you think I'm crazy?"

65

Late September. Hayward, Wisconsin.

As Uncle Bill eased the car into a space in front of the Sawyer County sheriff's office, he said, "Relax, nephew, the sheriff just wants to go over the report he got from Attorney General Elkin."

"I know, but he sounded pissed when he called."

"That's just Joe's way sometimes. If he was mad at *you* he'd have shown up at the cabin with a squad car."

Ten minutes later, they were sitting on Sheriff Nil's brown leather couch sipping coffee while the sheriff summarized Attorney General Elkin's report. "Bottom line, Alan Sanger was a nutcase. Elkin got the blackmail note and..."

Bill raised his hand. "It wasn't blackmail."

"Well, yeah, as it turned out, but the note could have been taken that way." Sheriff Nils reached into a manila folder, extracting a slip of paper. "Here's what it says: *I realize this is very sensitive information because it might indicate your sister's mental institutionalization is connected with Mr. Capone's syphilis. Further, the press might suggest the disease affects you. I prefer to remain anonymous, but will turn these documents over to you if you will contact me as indicated.* It doesn't mention money, but it sure could be read that way."

Denton leaned back, his eyes meeting the staring orbs of stag heads adorning the wall. "Yes, I agree. I still think Elkin's involvement is fishy. It's hard for me to believe Sanger was operating on his own."

Bill added, "Yeah, seems fishy to me, too."

The sheriff slid the paper back into the file. He shook his head. "You two know as well as I do that you can't take legal action because something seems *fishy*. Shit, I see weird situations all the time. But you gotta have hard evidence."

Denton sighed. "I realize that. What happens next?"

"I'm not going to spread these details around. I think Elkin is entitled to the benefit of the doubt and we need to respect his privacy. Besides, the election is just around the corner. I expect Elkin will be our next governor."

Denton's stomach turned, and a sense of lost justice overcame him. He'd studied equitable principles in law school and fervently believed the idea that *for every wrong, there's a remedy*. But if Elkin had committed a wrong—and Denton believed he had—there wasn't going to be any remedy. "What have you found out about Sylvia Norton Schneider and William Norton?"

"We found a hair stuck in the pool of blood at Sylvia's. It matched John Batiste. Of course, with Batiste dead, he isn't talkin'; not to me at least."

The sheriff watched their reactions, then waved a hand towards Bill. "And the guy Bill here bonked with the fire extinguisher has confessed he and the other guys were hired by Batiste. He doesn't know if Batiste was getting orders from someone else. His trial will come up in five months or so. I expect he'll spend a lot of time in prison."

Denton crossed his arms over his chest. "So much for Spirit Warriors. But what about the fact that Lilly told me there was a guy in Madison telling them what to do?"

The sheriff's staghorn-handled knife was suddenly working at his fingernails. "If that was true, and we don't know it was, I figure it was Sanger. But I expect Batiste wanted that old scroll. He would have thought it was holy and been pissed that she had it."

Bill said, "Elkin could have been behind it all."

The sheriff shrugged his heavy shoulders. "*Could* don't fly."

66

Late September. Northern Wisconsin.

Long, inconstant shadows washed over tombstones. Mindless clouds coiled overhead. Thick air lay inept against encroaching night. Chirps from a circumstantial bird stabbed the silence as Denton knelt beside a grave. He watched his shaking hand as it scattered tobacco into a strangely rising wind.

He closed his eyes, then opened them to an image of Lilly approaching from the edge of the woods. Her arms reached for him. He felt himself oozing away, going to meet her, leaving behind the false reality of all the tomorrows to come. He turned his face to watch the last strand of tobacco fall upon her grave. When he looked back, there was only the forest.

67

One Week Later. San Diego.

Denton stood outside the entrance of his law office and con-templated the doorknob. The double walnut doors mocked him with their frosted glass and gold letters: *Leland E. Denton, Attorney and Counselor.* The golden letters shimmered their proclamation of identity. All he had to do was turn the knob and walk through the entrance. Then he'd wear that identity like the somber, charcoal-colored suit he'd worn for his homecoming. It was all he had to do. But could he?

He placed a hand on the door handle. His legs felt weak, and vertigo took his mind. He shut his eyes and saw Lilly handing him a wreath of wildflowers, her sweet voice promising, "This will protect you, as I will protect you." But nobody had protected Lilly. Least of all him.

He opened his eyes and willed his hand to turn the brass han-dle. *Showtime.*

Charlotte's face lit as he entered. She called out, "Afa, he's here."

Tavita appeared from the kitchen, dressed in a gray suit with a white shirt and a well-knotted mauve tie.

Charlotte rushed to hug Denton, her orange dress shining.

Tenderness suffused Denton's being. He *could* do this. He could return to his law practice.

"Nice dress, Char."

"Thanks, boss. It's new. Welcome home. Do you feel like bringing us up to date?"

He didn't feel like talking about it. But they seemed so happy to see him, so eager to know the facts. *They deserve to hear the end of the story.* "Sure. Let's assume the usual positions in the conference room."

They gathered around one end of the long oak table. "You guys know most of the story. George, aka Clyde Norton, is recovering from his wounds, though it's taking time because of his age. They matched a hair left at Sylvia Norton Smith's murder scene to Batiste. So we know he was the killer."

Charlotte asked, "Why did he do it?"

"That's not entirely clear. I suspect Richard Elkin had something to do with the whole situation. Still, she had that birchbark scroll. It was old, from the late 1700s. Batiste considered it holy and wanted it back. Sylvia had refused to turn it over. I guess that's why he killed her. They found the scroll at his house."

Tavita shook his head. "Kind of an overreaction, if you ask me. We have a lot of sacred stuff in Samoa, but I wouldn't kill someone over it. Probably not, anyway."

Denton smiled at Tavita. A good man who deserved Charlotte. He decided to lighten the mood, as his doctors had told him to do. "That's comforting, Tavita. Please let me know if you ever want your lucky owl back."

Their eyes turned glad and they smiled at one another, feeling good, happy to be a team. Charlotte brushed a stray blond hair from her forehead. "What about what's-his-name—that Red Owl guy?"

"Jack Mathers is his name. He's out of jail now that he's cleared. I suppose he's back shaking his conch rattles, curing hives, and giving people the Burning Bagel Curse or whatever."

Denton was enjoying the levity, happy to finally know the answers.

Charlotte removed her granny glasses and held them to the light. A soft cloth appeared in her hand as she said, "How do these things get so dirty?" As she cleaned the lenses, she glanced at her legal pad. "The autopsy came back on Peter Norton. His heart attack was real. No poison or any other evidence of foul play." She worked the cloth. "Oh, and the police investigators say there's not a shred of evidence Jim's death was other than accidental." She replaced her glasses, her eyes shining. "So what's the rest of the story from Wisconsin?"

Denton smiled. "Nice to see clearly, eh, Char? Those two Indians that attacked us at the lake worked for John Batiste. They killed William because they thought he was going to take more artifacts. At least that's the survivor's current story, though he claims he was sitting in his own boat when the other guy hit William and shoved him into the water. He also admits several of them dressed up and attacked me."

The room lapsed into silence. Denton suspected Charlotte and Tavita were pondering the unpredictability of life, fate's capriciousness. So was he. The notion of fate engendered a forlorn sense of helplessness. He shook it away by returning to the story.

Charlotte smiled. "By the way, you received a wedding invitation. Mary Norton's marrying a guy named Gustav Cutler. A June wedding." Her amused eyes looked into his. Denton pasted on his poker face. *I guess Mary decided Gustav wasn't such an asshole after all.* "How nice," he said.

Charlotte smiled. "Yep. And her mom, Alice, called to make sure you got the invitation." Her lips made a small smacking sound as she said, "Well, I'm gonna get a cup of coffee. Want some?"

Denton and Tavita declined. Denton stood and stretched while Charlotte fetched her coffee. He turned to the window. Puffy white clouds graced the distant horizon. *Bruja Loca* waited in her slip at Shelter Island, just a few minutes away.

Charlotte returned, holding a purple mug with the yellow logo *Hayward—Heart of the Muskie Country*. "How's Sandy?"

"Great. You know, she came up to Wisconsin to be with me. I was worried she'd stay at her mother's, what with the new job and all. She helped me a lot."

Charlotte cleared her throat, her eyes now serious. "Lee, I'm very sorry about that young woman, Lilly."

Denton lowered his eyes. "Yeah," he said.

After a few seconds, Charlotte broke the silence. "I suppose we'll have to get back to work on the Norton case."

Denton shook his head. "No. It's over. That's the latest news. John Norton Jr. and Clyde, I mean George, had a long talk over tall drinks. They decided that it was unfair for guys their age to keep their claws on all that money."

Tavita said, "Yeh, no kidding."

"Well, they married younger women and had kids quite late in life, just like their father and grandfather did. But now they've seen the light. They agreed to a judgment that will grant termination of the trust, but distribute the funds to everybody equally, including Asa II, Mary, and John III."

Tavita's hand smacked his knee. "Ha! So, boss, I guess we can say: for the fucking Norton case, finally it's...The End."

When the meeting ended, Denton returned to his office. Queeg and his ready fists were again guarding the corner of his desk. He patted the small wooden figure, careful not to knock him over. He thought of Richard Elkin and how justice isn't always served. He shook his head and winked at Queeg. "You oughta get a tomahawk, pal."

He heard Charlotte and Tavita out in the lobby, talking. He couldn't make out the words, but they sounded happy.

Behind Denton, the sound of rain pattered against the windows. He turned and was confronted by sharp rain lines slanting from dark clouds, obscuring his view of the open sea.

Epilogue

Early November. Madison, Wisconsin.

As predicted by the polls, Attorney General Elkin won the election. His gala victory party was held at the Madison Concourse Hotel in the heart of downtown Madison. The brightly lit Wisconsin State Capitol building was nearby.

Elkin had booked a room for himself and his wife, Sally, and they celebrated the occasion with missionary-position sex in the king-sized bed. Then they joined their hundreds of deliriously happy guests, most of them looking forward to jobs in the Elkin administration. Being on the winning side was so fun. Elkin wore a tuxedo, and Sally was dazzling in the organdy gown she had bought specially for the occasion. They danced divinely. Everyone thought they were such a beautiful couple—and so much in love.

Everyone except Elkin's secretary, Marge Hawkins.

As Elkin danced with Sally, he spotted Marge watching him with angry eyes. He knew he needed to do something about her. But what?

I'd better get her up into the room. Give her a quick screw. He kissed Sally's neck and whispered, "I have to make a few phone calls, sweetheart. Why don't you mingle with the guests? I'll be back soon."

"Sure, darling."

Five minutes later, Marge's fingernails dug into his back as he shoved himself into her. She was wet and warm, hungry for him. Afterwards, they lay still, breathing heavily, relaxing in the post-coital glow.

Marge asked, "When will you get the divorce?"

"What?"

"The divorce that will let you marry me."

He got off the bed and zipped up his tuxedo pants. "I can't do that."

She sat up, pulling a sheet between her legs, wiping herself off. "Yes you can. Remember your little story about Mr. Capone?"

Oh shit. I fucked up big.

Marge sidled to the dresser and ran her hands over the things Sally had left there. Elkin moved to her and put his arms around her. "Listen, Marge. You know I can't get a divorce. I'd be out on my ass in no time."

"You said you loved me."

"I do. Of course, I do. But I can't marry you. We'll keep doing it. We'll get together as much as possible. I'll get a new secretary so it'll be more discreet."

Her eyes grew hot. "A *new* secretary?"

"Sure. That's the smart thing to do."

Her lips grew pale, her face immobile. She twisted out of his embrace for a moment, then turned back.

He was confident as he pulled her to him and kissed her. Then he felt a horrible pain in his solar plexus. He coughed, couldn't catch his breath. He stepped back and looked down. Blood soaked his ruffled tuxedo shirt. Was that Sally's gold letter opener? That thing sticking out of him. A letter opener?

Then the real pain hit, the unbearable pain. He tried to scream, but what emerged was "Wha—"

ALSO BY JACKSON BASS:

Hard Numbers
Durban House Press, Inc.
ISBN: 978-0-9818496-5-5

Attorney Leland Denton is hired to advise James McKenzie, an insurance examiner probing the possibly cooked books of a Los Angeles insurance company. McKenzie is brutally murdered—the cops say by a hooker— but Denton discovers the dead man may have been involved in a conspiracy between the insurance company and a large New York bank to embezzle $300,000,000 of policyholder funds.

The hooker could have been an assassin hired by Alejandro Silver, the president of the insurance company. Or was it John Rainier, president of the bank? On the other hand, McKenzie's young wife, who is having a lesbian affair, could have had him killed for his $700,000 life insurance policy.

Aided by his ex-Marine paralegal, Charlotte Logan, and one-armed Tavita, a Samoan ex-wrestler, Denton must untangle the web of financial fraud and discover who was behind the murder and embezzlement. His efforts are resisted by hard-nosed businessmen and beautiful women who, in the face of Denton's unrelenting investigation, decide Denton must die.

Praise from the Midwest Book Review for *Hard Numbers* by Jackson Bass:

When financial times get tough, some take it as a sign to play dirtier. *Hard Numbers* is a thriller following attorney Leland Denton and his client James McKenzie as they dive deep into the sour side of economics, turning to the world of crime to make their fortune when the economy crashes around them. But when you play dirty, everyone around you plays dirty as well and you may find yourself turning up dead. *Hard Numbers* is an entertaining read that can't be beat.

—Wisconsin Bookwatch, January 2010